To Catch a Bad Guy
Book 1 of the Janet Maple Series

The Janet Maple Series

Book 1: To Catch a Bad Guy

Book 2: Catching the Bad Guy

Book 3: Bad Guys Get Caught

Sign up for the mailing list at www.MarieAstor.com to be notified as soon as a new book comes out.

GW00730375

To Catch a Bad Guy

Book 1 of the Janet Maple Series

By Marie Astor
Copyright © 2013 Marie Astor
All rights reserved.
ISBN-13: 978-1493645930

Author Contact
Website: www.MarieAstor.com
Facebook: Author Marie Astor
Twitter: @MarieAstor

Chapter One

Janet Maple took a deep breath while she waited for her train to arrive. She was twenty-nine years old, but this morning she felt like a first-grader. The same sickening feeling churned her stomach that she remembered when she first entered a room full of strangers as a five-year-old. She was much older now – a professional with a law degree to boot, and, until recently, with a successful career at the District Attorney's office, but today none of these things gave her comfort or confidence.

It was not merely the prospect of starting a new job that gave Janet the heebie-jeebies, but it was the fact that she would be working for Lisa Foley. Talk about stirring up old insecurities… Lisa Foley had been the queen bee in high school. Come to think of it, Lisa was still the queen bee. Every time Janet talked to her best friend from high school, Lisa never failed to bring back 'the old glory days' as she called them. With friends like Lisa, who needed a time machine? One could always count on Lisa's sharp memory to recall every embarrassing incident of adolescence.

Well, the past is the past, Janet thought. I should be thankful to Lisa for giving me a job. When your former boss also happens to be your ex-boyfriend, the subject of references becomes dicey to say the least. Regardless of how stellar one's background looks on paper, employers always want references, but Lisa had hired Janet without any references. In fact, Lisa's phone call had come with unsettlingly perfect timing. Just as Janet was about to give up all hope of white-collar employment, her old friend had come to the rescue. That was another one of Lisa's remarkable qualities: for as long as Janet had known her, her friend seemed to have a radar for people's misfortunes. In high school, Lisa was always the first to know who got dumped, who didn't make the cut on the football team, and whose parents got laid off. So it was not surprising that Lisa knew about Janet's being "downsized" by the District Attorney's office, and when she offered her a job as Assistant General Counsel at Bostoff Securities, Janet literally jumped at the chance.

"Janie! Come in, come in!" Lisa rose from behind her long mahogany desk and opened her arms in an offer of a hug.

"Hi, Lisa." Janet stooped for an air kiss. At five seven, Janet was no giant, and her weight was smack in the middle of the healthy range for her height. But at five two and ninety five pounds, Lisa made everyone feel as though they were towering over her.

"Sit, sit." Lisa waved her hand at the leather chair opposite her desk. "I'm so excited that we'll be working together – it's going to be just like old times."

"I'm really glad to be here, Lisa, and thank you again for giving me the job."

"That's what friends are for, right? To help each other out when you're down in the dumps," Lisa answered her own question. "So, how was your orientation?"

When Janet started her employment at the DA's office, there had been a rigorous four-week orientation to initiate her and fellow law school recruits into the intricacies of the Assistant District Attorneys' job responsibilities. But here, at the Bostoff Securities, the orientation only resembled the process by its title– the entire affair had taken scarcely thirty minutes, as Janet was shoved into a tiny room for her photo ID picture and given a thick binder with the company forms to sign. Janet supposed she was an experienced attorney now, and it was time she started acting like one around Lisa.

"It went well; I got all this paperwork to complete." Janet raised the thick folder she'd been given at the orientation.

"Don't worry about that; it's just your generic HR stuff. What time is it now?" Lisa fumbled with her Cartier watch. "Perfect timing; we're going to lunch. But first, let me show you to your office." Lisa slid from behind her desk. As usual, she looked spectacular: her navy pinstriped suit seemed to have been made for her miniature body (and it probably had been), her four-inch Louboutin stilettos elongated her slender legs, and her pixie cut emphasized the perfect features of her face. She looked like a corporate version of Winona Ryder.

As Janet followed Lisa down the hall, she made a conscious effort to resist her urge to stoop; let Lisa stand on the balls of her feet instead.

"Our offices are on the same floor as the trading floor," Lisa explained over her shoulder as she wove her way down the mahogany-lined hallway. "But there's a shortcut through here, so that you don't have to enter the trading floor unless you need to. And I'll be honest with you, I try to avoid it as much as I can. It's a veritable zoo out there." Lisa paused, indicating that they had arrived. "Ta-daa!" Lisa flung the door open and ushered Janet into the spacious room.

Janet bit her lip with remorse. If her office was any indication of her employment at Bostoff Securities, she owed Lisa an eternal debt of gratitude. The size of the room was about twice the size of Janet's digs when she worked for the DA, and it even had a window! Having an office with a window had been a sign of great recognition in the DA's elaborate hierarchy. Granted, Janet had been only a few steps away from getting to this high honor before Alex snatched everything she had worked for four years of her life, but all that was history now, as were the long hours she'd put into her investigation, the credit Alex took for her work, and Alex himself.

"You like?" Lisa asked.

Janet snapped out of her reverie. Being caught daydreaming was not a good way to start her first day. "I love it, Lisa. Thank you."

"I bet it beats that DA dump you've been slaving away at. I still can't understand what possessed you to go there. You were always such an idealist."

Lisa did have a point there: Janet was an idealist. Correction, Janet had been an idealist. For four years, she had toiled away as Assistant District Attorney at the New York Office for a minimum salary, but as ridiculous as it sounded, money was not the reason why she had pursued a career in law. She had wanted to help the wronged and go after the bad guys, like the guys who had stripped her retired grandfather of every penny he had ever earned, sending him into fatal cardiac arrest. But when the results of your investigation are handed over to your boss to take credit for, and you're sent packing, it becomes hard to remain an idealist; and so far, employment at Bostoff Securities was proving to be a very comfortable reality.

"So, you're ready for lunch? I must say you're looking very dapper in this suit of yours."

"Thanks." Janet blushed, aware that her boxy brown suit was nowhere near as elegant as Lisa's. But, on a positive note, with her salary bump at Bostoff Securities, she would finally be able to move past the one hundred dollar suit racks she'd made a habit of frequenting at J.C. Penney.

"You might want to let your hair down, though."

"What's wrong with my hair?" Janet clasped her French twist protectively. She had spent nearly forty minutes this morning putting up her hair.

"Oh, it's perfectly fine if you're going for that tough prosecutor look, but if you're looking to get a guy interested…" Her hand reached for Janet's hair. Lisa's four-inch heels made them almost equal in height.

"I wasn't aware I was being set up on a date." Janet lips knitted into a prim line – a lifelong involuntary reaction to irritation. Sure, Lisa was the boss, but that did not give her the right to control her employees' looks and personal lives.

"Oh, come off it." With a swoop of her hand, Lisa plucked a handful of pins from Janet's hair, undoing her tightly knotted French twist. "There." Lisa stood back and eyed Janet appraisingly. "Much better."

Janet ran her hand over her hair. It was full of kinky waves from being wound up in a twist.

"Do you mind telling me what's going on?" Janet struggled to keep her voice level for the sake of job security.

"I got you a date, you silly! Well, it's not exactly a date…" Lisa retracted.

Janet made a mental effort to shut her mouth, as her jaw was having a hard time taking this much obnoxiousness without dropping.

"Calm down, will ya?" Lisa continued. "It's a business lunch: we're meeting Tom Wyman at Aquavit. Tom is a really nice guy, and he's not too shabby in the bringing home the bacon department either, if you know what I mean. He's a partner at Ridley Simpson."

"Look, Lisa, I really appreciate your thinking of me, but I'm not looking to date anyone at the moment. I just got out of a relationship, and I want to take it easy for a while…"

"Please. It's me you're talking to – your best friend since forever."

And now my boss. Janet forced a smile.

"The last thing you want after," Lisa paused, making a quotation sign with her fingers, "'getting out of a relationship' is to take it easy. Just because you're working for me does not mean that things have to change; I always got you dates in high school, didn't I?"

Yes, you did, Janet thought, even when I didn't ask you to.

Lisa glanced at her watch. "We'd better get a move on. A man like Tom Wyman should not be kept waiting. Put some makeup on, and let's go."

Janet raked through her handbag for her makeup case. She obediently ran a powder puff over her face and applied a quick coat of lipstick to her lips. Then she ran her comb through her hair in an attempt to tame it – a futile effort, since she still looked like she had just ridden a motorcycle without a helmet. Oh, well. At least her wild hair would compensate for her overly conservative outfit.

∞∞∞

Bostoff Securities was located on Park Avenue and Fifty Third Street, and Aquavit, the restaurant for the rendezvous with Tom Wyman, was on Fifty Fifth Street, between Madison and Park. Despite her monstrous heels, Lisa nimbly maneuvered her way down the street, while Janet struggled to keep up in her kitten pumps. After four years of working downtown, midtown felt like a foreign country: she'd forgotten how touristy and crowded the streets there could get.

"Ah, here we are." Lisa motioned at the screened restaurant entrance.

Just as they were about to go inside, a man smoking nearby hurried to open the door for Lisa – a concrete demonstration of the power Lisa had been wielding over men ever since she had entered her teens.

Inside, the décor was Nordic minimalism, with wooden paneling accompanied by slender white fixtures hanging low from the ceiling. It was Monday afternoon, and the atmosphere was all business: financial and advertising types sporting expensive suits loitered by the bar, waiting for their clients.

"There is a reservation for three under Tom Wyman," Lisa addressed the hostess.

"Oh, yes." A rail-thin blonde smiled at them. "Mr. Wyman is already here."

"Lisa!" A velvety baritone called from across the room. A man rose from his seat by the bar and walked toward them.

"Tom, so wonderful to see you!" Lisa leaned in for an air kiss exchange. "So sorry we are late."

"Nonsense, good company is worth waiting for." Tom grinned.

"You're such a charmer." Lisa batted her eyelashes.

She's flirting with him, Janet felt a sting of irritation. She was not even interested in this Tom Wyman character, but, in spite of herself, she was hot with resentment. Lisa's behavior was reminiscent of all those teenage double dates Janet had endured, with Lisa flirting away with the very guys Lisa had supposedly invited as Janet's dates. Sure, Janet was much older now, but when it came to her friendship with Lisa, other than the number of candles on her last birthday cake, not much had changed.

"Tom, Tom Wyman." Tom's eyes locked in on Janet's as he extended his hand. Coiffed was the word to describe him. Everything about this man was polished: his manner of speech, his silky dark eyes, his curly black hair, which was carefully slicked back, and his tailored outfit of Brooks Brothers suit and pink shirt with onyx cufflinks.

"Janet Maple." Janet blinked, sensing Tom's smooth, manicured fingers wrap around her hand.

"Janie just started working for me today," Lisa cut in.

Janet nodded good-naturedly. She hated it when Lisa called her Janie – the diminutive was reserved for family only, but somehow, years ago, when Lisa had overheard Janet's mother call her Janie, she had picked it right up and Janet never had the heart to tell her to stop.

"Some would say never hire your best friend, but I'm of a different opinion. Janie and I are the best of friends, and I know that we'll get along splendidly at the office."

Tom let go of Janet's hand and looked at Lisa, bemused. "Well, Lisa, from what you've told me about Janet, she is going to be a great asset to the firm."

Janet beamed him a smile. She did not know much about this Tom Wyman character, but she could have kissed him on the spot for putting Lisa back in her place.

As if reading Janet's mind, or more likely her facial expression, Tom said, "Columbia Law School graduates rarely come clamoring for employment, especially those who graduated magna cum laude."

"I see that Lisa has been talking about me." Janet returned Tom's wink with a smile. She might not like the idea of Lisa meddling in her personal life, but that did not mean that she would let Lisa steal the limelight from her date – not anymore.

"Yes, she has." Every word uttered in Tom's silky voice sounded like a caress. "And I for one am glad to know that I'll be working with an alumna."

"You went to Columbia also?"

"I did: class of two thousand."

He is seven years older than me, Janet's mind did an involuntary calculation. "It's always a pleasure to meet fellow Columbia alum."

"Indeed. And I hope that we'll be seeing quite a bit of each other." Tom's eyes lingered on Janet a second too long for a casual glance, and she was not quite sure how to respond.

"Well, should we get seated?" Lisa tapped her foot. "I'm starving."

"Forgive me, I seem to be forgetting myself." Tom nodded at the restaurant hostess who had been lurking in the background, careful not to interrupt their conversation.

"Please follow me." With gazelle-like grace, the hostess glided across the floor.

Her head cocked, Lisa sashayed after the hostess. Tom stepped aside, letting Janet go in front of him, and she could not help a warm, giddy feeling spreading in her chest. She certainly did not intend to get involved with Tom Wyman, but it sure felt nice to be the center of his attention.

"So, Janet, tell me more about yourself," said Tom after they had ordered lunch.

"I'm not sure where to begin. I'm afraid I'm not that interesting." Janet lowered her eyes, breaking away from Tom's gaze. His eyes were like two black olives: dark, glistening, and unsettlingly sharp.

"Why, Janie, as usual, your modesty is getting the best of you!" Lisa pursed her lips. "Tom, do you know that Janie has spent the last four years at the DA's office?"

"Oh?" Tom's eyebrows shot up high. "What an interesting career choice. And may I ask what division you were in?"

"I was in the Investigation Division." When Janet spoke of her former occupation as Assistant District Attorney, most people were either impressed or terrified – the latter were usually employed in the financial industry. There was one memorable occasion when Janet had mentioned her employment while being flirted with by a handsome financial type during happy hour, which resulted in the guy's falling off his bar stool and promptly vacating the bar premises. But then there were plenty of occasions when her choice of occupation elicited accolades and admiration – those were mostly from members of senior citizen communities who were frequent victims of financial rogues whom Janet so diligently tried to catch. In either case, most people never went as far as inquiring about the specifics of her job, which made Tom's pointed question surprising.

"Very impressive. I hear it requires a special transfer to get into Investigation, correct?"

"Yes." Janet nodded. "I started with the DA right after law school. My first assignment was with the Trial Division, but I asked to be moved into Investigations, and my supervisor agreed to recommend me."

"No doubt for exceptional performance."

Janet blushed, unaccustomed to such keen interest in her work. "Well, I did contribute to several important cases."

Tom's pointed gaze traveled from Janet to Lisa. "Well, Lisa, it sounds like you hired a first-rate sleuth: a qualification that is bound to be an asset for employment with Bostoff Securities."

Just as Tom finished his convoluted compliment, a waiter approached the table, carrying a bottle of wine.

"I believe this calls for a toast. Here's to the latest addition to Bostoff Securities." Tom raised his glass.

"I'm so glad you're here, Janie." Lisa raised her glass.

Janet eyed the wine hesitantly. Alcohol during lunch would most certainly be frowned upon at the DA's office, but she was no longer at the DA's office, and it was time to put her former employer behind her.

"Relax," Lisa jeered, "it's all right to have a sip with your boss."

Janet picked up her glass.

"Welcome to the family, Janet." Tom's glass clinked against Janet's and Lisa's. "Forgive me if I sound too forward, Janet, but I do so much work for Bostoff Securities that I feel a part of the team."

"Thank you, Tom." Janet smiled. Perhaps she was being too guarded after all. This Tom Wyman was bound to be a decent fellow if he called his employer 'family.'

The rest of the lunch was spent in gastronomical exploration as the waiter brought out one intricate dish after another. By the end of the two-hour meal, Janet felt the waistline of her skirt pinching. There was one good thing to be said about having a limited budget: it prevented one from overindulging, and if four-course lunches were de rigueur at Bostoff Securities, she would have to acquire formidable self-restraint.

"Ah, I'm stuffed." Lisa leaned back in her chair, and Janet noticed that Lisa's plate looked like it had been barely touched, while Janet's was swept clean.

Tom checked his watch. "Wow, it's after two o'clock. I hate to break up the party, ladies, but I've got to get back to the office. I am, after all, working on billable hours." Tom grinned.

"Please, Tom." Lisa waved her hand. "With the bill you sent me last month, I think you've fulfilled your quota for the rest of the year."

"In the words of Hank Bostoff, there's no such thing as too much money."

"Yes." Lisa nodded. "I'm constantly reminded of it by Jon. Hank Bostoff is the founder of the firm – he is the CEO," Lisa explained for Janet's benefit. "You haven't met him because he only interviews the most senior people. I might as well tell you about all the big wigs. Jonathan Bostoff is Hank's elder son. He is the company president."

"Paul Bostoff is Hank's younger son and the company's COO, and Lisa's soon-to-be fiancé," Tom explained.

"Please, Tom, don't jinx it!" Lisa smiled coyly. "But, getting back to business, Tom, it would be great if you could give Janet an overview of Bostoff Securities' business. Do you think you could do that?"

"Certainly," Tom replied. "It will be my pleasure. Shall we say eleven o'clock tomorrow?"

Lisa reached for her purse and leaned over to whisper into Janet's ear, "See, he likes you."

"Eleven is fine." Janet nodded. If Lisa wanted to play matchmaker, Janet had no choice but to play along. She needed this job.

Chapter Two

Dennis Walker surveyed the contents of his closet and reluctantly pushed away his tailored suits. His current persona as Dean Snider, Chief IT Analyst at Bostoff Securities, did not allow for dapper attire. Instead, Dennis reached for a brown Men's Wearhouse suit in size forty two regular, while he normally wore forty long. Next followed a shirt of swamp green Dennis had also acquired at Men's Wearhouse and a mousy gray tie of fabric so stiff that it virtually would stand if one were to lay the tie down on the side. The one thing Dennis refused to give up was his shoes. His feet, after all, were important – he only had one pair for his entire lifetime, so he reached for a discreet pair of Johnston and Murphy's. Last came a pair of glasses. The lenses were plain plastic, but their purpose was not to correct Dennis's twenty-twenty vision, but to obscure the blue-gray of his eyes. It was a known fact that people rarely noted eye color behind corrective lenses. For the finishing touch Dennis slouched his shoulders and stuck out his neck. When he looked in the mirror, the transformation was complete: the suave charmer Dennis Walker had been replaced by a nerdy computer geek.

When Dennis had proposed his candidacy for the assignment at Bostoff Securities, his boss had shrugged him off as too good-looking and too suave. In the past, Dennis had impersonated traders, lawyers, company executives, and even aspiring political candidates. Any time an assignment required balls and charisma, Dennis was the 'go to' man. Without a doubt, those had been Dennis's preferred roles, but the Bostoff investigation promised to be a career-making case, and Dennis was a careerist. Sure, he liked catching the bad guys, but he liked being recognized for his achievements even more. His boss was dead set on assigning the job to Peter Laskin. At thirty-five, Laskin was already balding, and the frames he wore had thick corrective lenses in them. Laskin, a forensic accountant by training, was a genius behind the desk, but his last assignment in the field had been over five years ago, and all it took was one hiccup – one slip – for a case to go down the drain. So Dennis took it upon himself to save the day. Not without much struggle, he abandoned his bi-weekly visits to his favorite hair stylist, opting for a local barbershop instead. He purchased the most horrible suit he could find on the sale rack at Men's Wearhouse, ordered a pair of glasses with fake lenses in them, and worked on slouching and sticking out his neck. When, two weeks later, Dennis showed up in all his geek glory on the doorstep of his boss's office, the Bostoff case was his and so was the office pool – to Laskin's relief, Dennis had won the bet. Now he had to prove that he deserved the assignment.

ߓߓ

The next morning, Janet left for work in much better spirits than the day before. All in all, Bostoff Securities was shaping up to be a far better gig than she had expected. Lisa Foley was still Lisa Foley, but yesterday's lunch with Tom Wyman proved that now Janet was much better equipped to handle her high school friend than when she was a teenager. Despite Lisa's efforts to steal the limelight, Tom's attention did not stray from Janet throughout the meal, and while Janet intended keeping her interactions with Tom Wyman on a strictly professional level, she would be a liar to deny that her scheduled meeting with Tom this morning did not contribute to her uplifted spirits.

At a quarter to nine, Janet was approaching the Bostoff Securities building. Midtown was mayhem compared to downtown, but her commute from Second Avenue and Ninetieth Street had been shortened by twenty minutes. Tempted by the sight of pastries in the nearby coffee shop window, Janet made a quick stop to grab breakfast to go. After all, she had skipped dinner last night, which, considering the huge lunch she had indulged in, was no great sacrifice, but it was still better than nothing. This morning she would allow herself to indulge in hazelnut coffee with extra half and half and a croissant, but tomorrow it would be yogurt or oatmeal.

Janet entered the marble lobby of Bostoff Securities and pressed her floor button. The elevator doors opened, and she gingerly stepped out, straining to recall the shortcut to her office Lisa had shown her the day before. The details were fuzzy now. After a moment's hesitation, she walked through one of the doors. As Janet made her way through the double doors, she heard a loud buzz of human, mostly male, voices. A few moments later, she found herself smack in the middle of the trading floor. Seemingly endless rows of desks with stacked-up computer monitors stretched the entire length of the room, which had to be the size of ten basketball courts – or maybe it was five basketball courts – she could not tell exactly. Everywhere there were men dressed in slacks and collared shirts with their sleeves rolled up. Some wore ties and had their suit jackets flung over the backs of their chairs. The average age had to be between twenty-five to thirty, and the atmosphere was that of startling chaos: jokes and yells flying across the room, feet being put up on desks, and paper being thrown on the floor. Janet straightened her back, doing her best to look as though she belonged. "Must not show fear," a line she had heard a wild animal trainer utter on the Discovery channel popped into her mind. The advice seemed applicable now, as the floor of

Bostoff Securities was very much a jungle. Janet kept making her way down the trading floor aisle for several more agonizing minutes when she finally saw another set of doors. Fighting the urge to lunge for the door handle, she steadily opened the door and found herself in the corridor that Lisa had shown her the day before. A few steps to the right was the door to Janet's office.

The corridor was empty, and abandoning all restraint, Janet rushed inside her office and shut the door behind her. The offices at Bostoff Securities were sturdy: there was none of the see-through flimsiness of glass, but the reassuring impenetrability of solid wood. Glad of the privacy, Janet pressed her back against the door and took deep breaths. Calm down, she thought, you're going to be working with these people and you can't run for cover every time you need to get something done.

"Oh, I'm sorry, I'm almost done here," a male voice made Janet drop her purse on the floor. At least it was not her breakfast, which she was still clutching in her hand. Janet picked up her purse and touched her pinned up hair for reassurance. Whenever she was in distress, her neat hairdo was always a source of comfort.

"I was running late," she blurted out, immediately regretting her words. This was, after all, her office.

"First day, huh?" The bespectacled man sitting behind Janet's desk smiled at her, and she could not help noticing that he had really lovely blue-gray eyes.

"Second day, actually," Janet replied curtly, wondering how best to broach the subject of the unknown stranger taking over her office.

"Oh, I'm sorry, this is very clumsy of me. I'm Dean, Dean Snider, IT." The man jumped to his feet, sticking out his hand for a handshake. "I was just sent in to set up your computer, so I assumed that today is your first day."

Janet placed her purse on her desk and shook Dean's hand, sneaking a better look at him. He was wearing clothes that were too short for his height and slouching when he should be standing up tall, but this goofiness rendered him an unlikely kind of charm.

"Yesterday was more of an orientation than hands-on work," Janet improvised a description of her work, which, honestly speaking, had not involved any work at all.

"Well, that's no skin off anyone's nose." Dean grinned. "One thing I found in this place is that work will always be here for you the next day. Sometimes it helps to take a breather and reassess things."

Sensing Dean's glance lingering on her, Janet looked up. She was not used to IT specialists giving work advice to lawyers.

Dean squinted at the computer monitor. "I'm all done here. Your email is up and running, and so is the rest of your computer. Have a good one – don't work too hard."

Once the door behind the IT support guy closed, Janet settled in her chair. This had certainly been an eventful morning. She reached for her by now lukewarm coffee and took a sip. Then she took a bite of her croissant, but could take no pleasure in either one. For reasons unknown to her, the IT guy's remark was humming in her head. What was his name? Dean, Dean Snider, that's right. "Sometimes it helps to take a breather and reassess things." No doubt Dean was simply making small talk, but something in his tone made Janet uneasy.

Janet dumped the rest of her croissant into the garbage bin and opened the orientation package she had received the day before. She had meant to look at it yesterday, but had been too woozy from the wine-laced lunch with Lisa and Tom. At the top of the pile were five different non-disclosure agreements. According to the terms and conditions of her employment at Bostoff Securities, she was virtually prohibited from mentioning anything other than her title and the fact that she worked at Bostoff. This was odd to say the least. At the DA's office she had worked on confidential investigations, but she never had to sign such elaborate disclosures before. Perplexed, Janet put the forms aside. She would have a word with Lisa about them later.

Remembering her appointment with Tom Wyman, Janet checked her watch. It was ten thirty a.m., and she was due to see Tom at eleven. She grabbed her handbag and headed for the ladies' room. Yes, it was silly, but she wanted to touch up her makeup for Tom. Not that she was interested in him: he was a colleague, but that did not mean that she couldn't enjoy Tom's attention.

Janet examined her reflection in the ladies' room mirror. Today she had opted for a less conservative outfit of a navy pencil skirt and silk blouse with a bow-tie detail. The 1980's inspired combination was very much in style at the moment. Janet had to admit that she was pleased with what she saw: the skirt ended just at the knee, exposing her favorite part of her legs: her calves, which were elongated by her three-inch heels. The pointy-toed black patent leather Mary Janes were not the most comfortable shoes in her closet, but they were by far the most flattering. The blue-green pattern of the blouse brought out her green eyes, and the bow-tie detail accentuated the slightly lower than average neckline, while her neatly put up chestnut hair provided the necessary counterweight to make her outfit office-appropriate. She looked like a sexy librarian, minus the glasses. If Janet knew anything about men, she was certain that Tom Wyman would be intrigued. She quickly reapplied her lipstick and dusted a light coat of powder over her face. She did not need any blush since her cheeks were already pink with anticipation.

At a quarter to eleven, Janet was back at her desk. For reasons beyond the powers of her common sense, her heart was palpitating with expectation. Her reaction was absurd, and she was the first to admit it. But right now her mind had the rationale and the clarity of that of an oversexed teenager, and she was powerless to control it. Yet again Lisa had prevailed –

thanks to her meddling, a business meeting had acquired romantic connotations, fraught with nerve-wracking anticipations of a date. But then it was dishonest to put the blame entirely on Lisa, for Janet knew full well the underlying cause of her flustered state. After being backstabbed and dumped by her boyfriend of almost five years, her confidence was not what it used to be. Say what she might about keeping her relationship with Tom Wyman purely professional, she could not deny that the attention of this handsome and successful man would be a welcome poultice for her bruised ego.

A knock on her office door made Janet jump up in her seat. She looked at her watch. It was eleven o'clock on the dot. "Janet?"

"Hi, Tom." Janet slowly looked up from her computer screen. She might have spent the last hour agonizing over her meeting with Tom, but he did not need to know that: to him, she was a busy lawyer in a leading securities firm. So what if her computer monitor merely had her email screen? Thankfully, even a man as suave as Tom Wyman did not possess x-ray vision.

"So nice to see you again, Janet." Wyman beamed her a smile that could put a Colgate commercial to shame. "So how do you find your second day at the firm?"

Janet sensed Tom's eyes gliding from her face to the neckline of her blouse. "Great, thank you. I've just been going through some paperwork."

"Ah, yes, the infamous non-disclosure paperwork, which I'm proud to say I personally drafted."

Janet shot Tom a curious glance, unsure whether to voice her concerns.

"It's nothing to be alarmed about," Tom addressed her silent question. "For someone like yourself, the paperwork is a mere formality. We legal folks are more than aware of the importance of confidentiality, but some of the traders we've got working here may not be as sensitive… The biggest risk comes with disgruntled employees who are out to take their revenge on the firm by spreading false rumors. The purpose of the non-disclosure paperwork is to stop them from doing just that."

"I see." Janet nodded. "I'll have it completed shortly."

"So, are you ready for an overview of Bostoff Securities' business model?" Tom grabbed a chair and placed it next to Janet's. Suddenly, her office seemed incredibly small.

Janet could feel Wyman's breath touch her skin where it was exposed by the low cut of her blouse. Perhaps she should have opted for a different outfit after all. "We could go into a conference room."

"Why bother? It's nice and cozy in here."

Tom's knee brushed against Janet's thigh. She froze like a rabbit hypnotized by a python. Her earlier plans to flirt with Tom Wyman seemed juvenile now. She was no match for her overpowering opponent. Tom Wyman was not the kind of man to be toyed around with: he expected a woman to either go all in or stay out of his way. And Janet certainly was not ready to go all in.

Janet's thoughts must have been plastered all over her face because a moment later, Tom pushed his chair away from hers.

"Right, so here's a quick overview of Bostoff's structure." Tom opened his briefcase, laying a thick manila folder on the desk. "This is a chart of all the entities that Bostoff Securities owns."

"I see." Janet hoped that her bewilderment was not apparent on her face as she examined the chart of Bostoff entities. She had never seen a corporate chart so convoluted, but she did not yet know enough about Bostoff's business to ask intelligent questions, so she decided to listen to Wyman for fear of appearing a novice. After all, Tom was a partner at Ridley Simpson, which was a top-ten national law firm, and corporate structure he approved had to be legitimate.

"Bostoff strives to keep as much of its business offshore as possible. As long as it is within the permitted legal and regulatory framework, of course," Wyman added quickly. "As far as the actual creation of offshore entities is concerned, the process has pretty much been streamlined, so you won't have to be concerned about anything there. I'll take care of that." Tom smiled. "Your judgment will be needed when new business ventures come up—that's when you are to notify me to devise a game plan."

Janet felt her face grow warm. She might not have Tom Wyman's expertise, but she was not going to sit on her butt, deferring all decisions to him. At least she hoped that was not the 'job' that Lisa had hired her for.

"I thought Lisa had explained the structure to you already. Bostoff keeps a very lean internal legal staff, with the bulk of the work outsourced to yours truly," said Wyman.

"Lisa gave me a cursory overview," Janet lied. Other than her title, Lisa had hardly explained the details of Janet's employment at Bostoff Securities at all, but when faced with a choice between being a department store clerk and an assistant general counsel at Bostoff Securities, the latter seemed like a much more attractive option, at least at the time. "I look forward to working with you, Tom." Janet conjured up her most guileless smile. "These structures seem so complicated. I will need all the help I can get to get up to speed."

"Not to worry, Janet. That's what I'm here for. Now, let's go over some of the recently created entities…"

An hour later, Janet found her head spinning from all the information that Tom Wyman had imparted on her. He had assured her that Bostoff Securities' structure was perfectly legitimate, but while Wyman's flowery assurances were spoken with much confidence, Janet felt a steady sense of unease growing inside her.

Chapter Three

Dennis Walker was giving himself a mental browbeating for nearly blowing his cover. What on earth had possessed him to get all mushy with that stand-offish girl whose computer he had been fixing or, to be more specific, bugging? Well, actually, Dennis knew perfectly well what had possessed him. The girl was damn good-looking, and if he had to admit to having any weaknesses, it was to not being able to pass by a pretty skirt without looking and, preferably, much more than just looking. Still, this was work – not play, and if he wanted to get that promotion he had set his eyes on since he had started his career in the Department of Treasury Investigations Unit, he'd better get his mind out of the gutter and get focused on the game.

Still, even with today's minor lapse, Dennis could afford to pat himself on the back: he had already tapped into the most critical employees' computers, and the data that he needed to substantiate the case was flowing in. The most difficult part of his assignment would be to remain undiscovered, which, as the morning had shown, was going to be much trickier than Dennis had anticipated. Playing the role of Dean Snider was proving to be more challenging than he had expected. Dennis was a naturally social creature who was keenly aware of his masculine charms, which he enjoyed exercising on members of the female sex with great success. Dean Snider, on the other hand, was a mousy and shabbily pathetic excuse of a man who was afraid of his own shadow – a role that Dennis detested playing, but was determined to excel at, lest his boss prove to be correct in his initial intention to give the assignment to Laskin. Dennis scratched his neck, which was beginning to chafe from the rigid collar of his cheap shirt, and focused his attention on his computer monitor.

As a senior member of the IT department at Bostoff Securities, Dennis had the administrative rights to computers of the firm's employees, which allowed him to install data gathering software. The software was transferring the data from Bostoff's computers over a web-based connection to the Treasury analysts. Dennis had the option of viewing real-time data, but the fact that his desk was smack in the middle of the trading floor made matters difficult. With a title like Chief IT Analyst, Dennis had expected to be allotted an office or at least a cubicle, but apparently Bostoff Securities was short on real estate. Thankfully, initial data sorting was conducted by junior analysts at the Treasury. In the evenings, after having spent the day behind his desk at Bostoff, Dennis would catch up on the reports in the privacy of his home office. A work schedule that intense would pretty much eliminate any presence of social life for the duration of the assignment, but Dennis was used to making sacrifices when they were warranted.

The mere opportunity of infiltrating Bostoff was a huge stroke of luck. Who would have thought that Bostoff would post an opening for an IT specialist just as the Treasury Investigations department was looking for a way to gather additional evidence to build their case? The chances were zero to none, and yet, an opening had come up. Some would call it happenstance, some divine providence, and some pure dumb luck. But if anyone had asked Dennis for an explanation of this fortuitous timing, he would have replied simply: the bad guys always got caught because, sooner or later, they always got sloppy.

Dennis Walker had a multitude of talents to his name, but superior knowledge of IT was not one of them. He had picked up plenty of tricks during his employment with the Treasury – enough to make him seem like a computer pro to a person possessing average prowess in computers. But Head of IT at Bostoff would not be someone with average prowess, or so Dennis had thought when he had begun his prep work for the interview, which had involved spending five hours a day with the top analysts of Treasury IT department. Even so, Dennis was nervous when the interview day came. Once he met his boss-to-be, Warren Merchant, Dennis knew he was safe. After a fifteen minute conversation, it became apparent that Warren Merchant knew about as much about IT infrastructure as Dennis knew about classical ballet, which was not much. Apparently, Bostoff Securities was not all that discerning when it came to hiring staff for the support functions – a factor that played to Dennis's advantage. Not only did Warren Merchant give him the job, he would be unable to detect the spyware Dennis had installed on the company computers if his life depended on it.

All in all, Dennis had every right to be pleased with his progress so far, and yet, he could not help the uneasiness in his chest. Everything that he had learned about Bostoff Securities so far indicated that the firm was knee-deep in financial violations. Dennis had no compunction about putting away the top brass who were the organizers and the leaders of the corrupt scheme, but, invariably, the rest of the employees would get caught in the mix. People who worked simple jobs without having an inkling about the corruptness of their employer would end up unemployed, with blemished resumés to boot. Such thoughts had rarely troubled Dennis during his previous investigations, but then this was going to be his biggest case to date.

Still, Dennis had not been bothered with such scrupulous considerations when he had set out to bug Bostoff Securities' newly hired lawyer's computer. But after meeting Janet Maple face to face, he wished he had left her off the radar. After all, she was only a junior lawyer, and Dennis already knew that all the important legal work was being farmed out to Ridley Simpson law firm, specifically to the slickster, Tom Wyman. Now, Wyman's computer would be worth bugging, but during his visits to Bostoff, Tom Wyman always used his personal laptop, which made it virtually impossible for Dennis to gain access to it. It would take time to gather evidence for the case, and Dennis hoped that for her sake, Janet Maple would find other employment in the meantime. An employment record with a corrupt firm would not be a plus on any lawyer's resumé, and Dennis certainly did not want to be the one responsible for a pretty woman's loss of her ability to earn a living.

ℰ𝒪𝒞ℛ

On her way home from work, Janet picked up a pack of Pedigree for Baxter – her one-year-old Jack Russell Terrier. No doubt Baxter would be hungry and antsy by now. Janet felt guilty about leaving him alone for the entire day. Before she lost her job, before Alex had told her that he just wanted to be friends, Janet used to hire a dog walker to take Baxter for his daily hour at the dog playground. But then Janet and Alex broke up – no – the idea of being friends had not fared well, and Janet had lost her job. She no longer had the income to hire a dog walker, so she became Baxter's own walker. In fact, it was those early morning and late night walks with Baxter that helped her keep her sanity as she brooded over the sudden change in her relationship with Alex and the circumstances of her being downsized from the DA's office.

It was Alex's idea to get a dog in the first place. He thought of it as a prelude to their moving in together. It seemed silly to maintain separate apartments when Alex was practically spending all his time in Janet's apartment. It was silly, except for one thing – at the office they had kept their relationship a secret. This secrecy was the result of Alex's insistence. He maintained that announcing that he and Janet were involved could harm them professionally – at least that was the reason that he voiced, and if there were other reasons that Alex had kept unsaid, Janet tried not to think about them. 'Soon' was the word that Alex liked to use a lot: soon we will tell people at work about us, soon we will move in together, soon. As it turned out, getting a dog was the only part of Alex's promised plan that had materialized. One night Alex showed up at Janet's apartment with Baxter in tow, and Janet was instantly smitten. It did not matter that Baxter became Janet's sole responsibility – she did not mind taking him for his morning walks and carrying him to routine doctor appointments. She was used to making things work behind the scenes. In fact, looking back, she suspected that her prowess in seamlessly taking care of things had been the glue that kept her and Alex's relationship together.

They had started dating in their last year of law school. Their paths had crossed frequently during Janet's first two years at Columbia Law, but even though she had been keenly aware of Alex's intense dark brown eyes and his closely cropped hair, which so becomingly framed his chiseled features, Alex was hardly aware of Janet. At least he had never let on about it until the last year. Then, in the beginning of the fall semester, she had found herself in the same class with Alex Kingsley, and things were never the same. At first she had thought that Alex was only interested in her studious class notes, which she let him copy, but when he asked her to a movie, Janet began to have an inkling of hope. Alex's invitation had been casual, but the movie turned out to be a French film with subtitles; afterwards they enjoyed a stroll around the Lincoln Center, concluding their outing with dinner and drinks at one of the cafés across from the Metropolitan Opera. Sometime after coffee, Alex had leaned in to kiss her, making Janet the happiest girl on earth. Alex was perfect – he was handsome, charismatic, and best of all, Alex made Janet feel like she was part of something incredibly exciting by sheer virtue of being his girlfriend.

Janet turned the front door key and heard the tapping of Baxter's paws, accompanied by his baritone bark, as he raced to the front door to greet her.

"Baxter!" Janet scooped Baxter up into her arms. "I missed you, boy. Have you been a good dog or have you been naughty?" Janet flashed Baxter an all-seeing look. He was a year old now and mostly well-behaved, but as a puppy he had a penchant for chewing up Janet's shoes (for some reason Alex's shoes had never appealed to Baxter), and every now and then Baxter experienced a relapse.

Janet started to unpack her bag from the pet store. In addition to the Pedigree, she had also bought some doggie treats, and she started to open the package now to give some to Baxter. At the sound of the wrapping being torn, Baxter trotted next to Janet and sat back, eyeing her intently. Baxter's sharp nose must have caught the scent of the food because he started to paw at Janet's legs.

"Here you go." Janet gave him a doggy biscuit. "But please don't ruin my work skirt, okay?"

Baxter sat back on his hind legs, delicately taking the treat from Janet's hand. Then, he quietly chewed the biscuit and looked at Janet in anticipation of more food to come. Janet caved in and gave him one more biscuit.

"But that's it or you'll spoil your appetite for dinner." Although Janet doubted that was likely to happen – given an opportunity, Baxter would eat anything in sight.

Janet headed into the alcove section of her studio, which served as a makeshift bedroom. The alcove just fit a full-size bed, leaving a twenty-inch space from one side to get into the bed. Some would consider the set-up claustrophobic, but Janet had never been bothered by small spaces. In fact, at times, even her tiny apartment seemed too large to her without Alex in it. But then, of course, the space itself was not to blame – it was its emptiness that bothered her. As she took off her work clothes, Janet stole a glance at the caller ID of her phone. No messages. It had been six months, but she still harbored a secret hope that one day Alex Kingsley would call. After more than four years together, he owed her an explanation, and at times, Janet still hoped that the much-fantasized phone call from Alex would bring about reconciliation.

"Come on, Bax." Dressed in slacks and a windbreaker, Janet grabbed Baxter's leash. "It's time for your evening walk."

Clutching the handle of Baxter's leash, Janet walked through the lobby of her building and headed in the direction of Carl Schurz Park.

It was the end of September, and the muggy heat of the New York summer had finally retreated for good, surrendering to the glorious autumn coolness. A night like this made one wistful for companionship. When she and Alex were together, they would often take a stroll along the park's promenade at night with Baxter in tow.

Janet felt Baxter tugging on his leash impatiently and sent him a mental thank you for the distraction. Slowly but surely, she was getting used to being on her own.

Chapter Four

When Janet exited the elevator of Bostoff Securities the next morning, she chose the correct set of doors, expertly making her way through a network of corridors and thereby avoiding the trading floor entirely.

Once inside her office, she looked at her watch – it was eight thirty, and Lisa had mentioned that she did not get into the office before nine thirty. Janet opened her bag and took out a pack of instant oatmeal she had brought from home to avoid the temptation of pastries in nearby bake shops.

She found the kitchen easily enough and set out to prepare the oatmeal. It was hardly an exciting breakfast to look forward to, but it was the right one – one could not continue eating pastries every day and expect to stay a size six – yes, a size six, not four, but given Janet's height, she thought she was all right. Janet placed the contents of the oatmeal package into a paper cup and debated between water and skim milk. In the end, her determination relented and she caved in to the skim milk option, but she decided to skip the sugar. Janet put her concoction into the microwave and focused her attention on the microwave's timer. If one were not looking, the oatmeal would overcook and spill over, leaving an embarrassing mess.

"Hello there."

Janet turned around at the unexpected sound of a male voice.

"Hi." Janet remembered the IT guy she had found in her office the day before. It was impossible to forget him. She had never seen anyone who was so incongruously good-looking and clumsy at the same time.

"It's Janet, right?" The IT guy focused his blue-gray eyes on her. "I'm Dean."

"Yes, I remember," Janet lied, making a mental note to commit Dean's name to memory. "Do you work on this floor?"

"Yep." Dean nodded. "My desk is on the trading floor – this way if any of the traders need help, I can be summoned to their rescue."

"Sounds terribly important."

"It is." Dean puffed out his chest. "Not really." He shook his head. "The other day I had to explain to a guy that his monitor was black because he forgot to turn his computer on."

"Oh…" Janet laughed a bit louder than she intended. "I'm sorry."

"Is that your oatmeal?"

"Yes. I'm sort of on a diet," Janet blurted out.

"I think it's about to run over." Dean reached for the microwave and popped it open just as the oatmeal was about to topple over the rim of the cup. "Here you are." Dean set the oatmeal on the kitchen counter. "And if I may add, you don't need to be on a diet, Janet."

"Thanks." Janet blushed. Was Dean flirting with her? If he was, she could not say that she minded it, except for the fact that she seemed to have forgotten what it was like to flirt with a cute guy. I'm sort of on a diet. Nicely done. And Dean was not even that good-looking; he was just mildly cute. What was going to happen to her if she were up against a real stunner? Would she unravel completely and blabber uncontrollably?

"Well, Janet, have a good one. I've got to get back to my charges. Who knows, while I was away, all kinds of disasters could have struck: knocked-out power cords or coffee spilled on keyboards."

"Sounds serious. Good luck." Janet grinned. "And thanks for rescuing my oatmeal."

"You're welcome, Janet." The corners of Dean's mouth lifted in a smile as his eyes met Janet's for a moment. "I'll see you later."

"Bye," Janet mouthed. Thanks for rescuing my oatmeal. She just brimmed with charm and mystique this morning. Enough with this nonsense, Janet snapped at herself. Her third day on the job, and instead of focusing on her work, she was flirting – correction, miserably failing at flirting – with idle IT guys, and, how could she forget, lascivious attorneys. Her awkward encounter with Tom Wyman still made her cringe. Well, it takes practice to get better at things, Janet reasoned, so perhaps she should practice on Dean Snider for now.

Back in her office, Janet looked over the chart of Bostoff Securities' corporate structure that Tom Wyman had given her. There were about ten different entities. The structure seemed odd to say the least, but Tom had cited a specific business purpose for each entity. His reasoning had made perfect sense when Tom had been explaining the set-up to Janet, but the moment he departed from her office, leaving a trail of masculine cologne, questions began to stir in her mind.

Janet's last investigation at the DA's office had been on a money laundering scheme, which was operating through a use of off-shore entities. Well, that had been the crux of Janet's theory, and she thought she had gathered powerful evidence to support it. She had not actually unraveled the scheme, because Alex had taken the details of her investigation to the Head of the Department and was appointed to be the lead on the case. Shortly afterwards, the case was closed without any findings, Alex was promoted, and Janet was let go, or to be more specific, downsized with a month's salary as recompense. She had spent months replaying the details of the case in her mind. She had thought she had gathered solid evidence, but apparently her manager thought otherwise. Apparently, Janet had been wrong, and perhaps she was getting overly alarmed now. After all, Lisa was a Harvard Law graduate: she would not be working in a disreputable firm, would she?

When Janet approached Lisa's office, she saw that the door was half-closed. She hesitated for a moment between knocking and coming back later. Her indecision was ended by the sound of Lisa's voice coming through the door.

"Janie, is that you? Come on in!"

"Hi, Lisa." Janet ran her hand over her hair and smoothed her skirt as she made her way through the door. Somehow, one always felt a few bars below par next to Lisa.

Lisa, on the other hand, looked as splendid as ever. Today she was sporting an ensemble of a tweed sheath dress and a matching box tweed jacket – very Jackie Kennedy-like.

"Sit, sit!" Lisa motioned at the chair across from her desk. "Oh, and close the door," Lisa added, just as Janet was about to lower herself onto the seat.

"So how was your day yesterday?" Lisa inquired once Janet had finally sat down. "No, wait, let me rephrase myself – how was your meeting with Tom?" Lisa's eyes lit up with curiosity.

"Informative." Janet pretended to ignore the subtext of Lisa's question. "Actually, I had a few questions..." Janet reached for her notes. "Tom had explained the corporate structure to me, but there are still some things that are unclear..."

"Janie!" Lisa pursed her lips. "Do you really think that's why I organized the meeting between you and Tom?"

Janet stared at Lisa. "Yes."

"Seriously, you never cease to amaze me. You haven't changed since high school when you could never tell if a guy was interested in you." Lisa shook her head. "Tom's firm does all the legal work for us. He is more than capable of handling everything himself. I wanted you to meet with him because I could see that he liked you. Janie, Tom is a real catch: snatch him, and you'll never have to work a day in your life."

"But don't you need me to get involved workwise?"

"Janie, how do I explain this... Things are taken care of. There's no real need for us to do much. The firm keeps a general counsel for appearances' sake, but Tom does the actual work."

"Then why did you hire me? Why are you here?"

"Because you needed a job, and I'm your friend – your best friend. And what do friends do? They help each other in times of need. Your mom called my mom, you know." Lisa smiled benevolently.

Janet clasped her forehead in mortification. The Maples and the Foleys had been neighbors for years. As young wives who had recently moved out to the suburbs, Mrs. Foley and Mrs. Maple had become close friends and had continued to remain such. It had been expected that their daughters would continue the tradition, and they had, for a while. At least Janet had done her part, but there was no denying that Lisa was no longer her best friend – had not been for a while. Yet, apparently, Janet's mother had a difficult time reconciling herself to this fact.

"Are you still wondering why I'm working here?" Lisa mimicked Janet.

"Yes. Why? You graduated from Harvard Law; Berman Erling snatched you up right after graduation. It's a top law firm. You could have had a stellar career there. Why did you leave and come here?"

"Why did I leave?" Lisa smirked. "Have you ever worked in a private law firm? The hours are hell, and you get treated as though you're gunk stuck to the soles of partners' shoes. I had to stay until ten o'clock at night, every night, and work on weekends. Thank you, but no, thank you." Lisa flung up her hands for emphasis. "But then I met Paul...." Lisa smiled like a cat that had just swallowed a canary. "And he got me a job here. When I found out that I could leave at five o'clock, I couldn't believe my luck. And once Paul finally proposes, I'm out of here." Lisa stretched out her arms. "If you'd like, I'll put in a good word for you for them to give you my job."

"Thanks, Lisa. I really appreciate everything you've done for me." Janet told herself to keep calm. After all, she did need the job, and it was not as though she was being overworked. If Bostoff Securities was prepared to hand her a paycheck for doing nothing, she'd take it, at least for now.

Lisa nodded approvingly. "That's better; you almost scared me. Now tell me about how it went with Tom."

Before Janet could answer, there was a knock on the door.

"Lisa?" A young, handsome man's head poked through the door.

"Paul!" Lisa jumped off her chair, rushing toward the visitor. She was about to fling her arms around his neck, but checked herself upon remembering Janet's presence in the room. "Paul, I'd like you to meet Janet, our new Assistant General Counsel. Janet, this is Paul Bostoff, our COO."

By the possessive tone of Lisa's voice it was clear that Paul Bostoff was much more than 'our COO': he was Lisa's boyfriend and soon to be fiancé, and although Lisa had refrained from a physical demonstration of her relationship with him, her body language made the nature of their relationship crystal clear.

Same old Lisa, Janet thought, remembering how quick Lisa was to abandon friendship over male attention. In their senior year of high school, Lisa did not speak to Janet for a month after Justin Trenner had asked Janet to the prom. The invitation had come as a surprise to Janet, and as an insult to Lisa, who had expected Justin to ask her. Not that Lisa particularly liked Justin, but she expected all the good-looking boys in the class to ask her first. Justin was the fastest on the swimming team: his torso was like a triangle turned upside down, with his wide shoulders in striking contrast to his cinched waist. He had blue eyes and strawberry blond hair. He was also good at drawing and did all the art for the school newspaper, of which Janet was the editor. When they were pressed against a deadline, they'd stay late to finish up. Janet still remembered the stirring

33

sensation she got in her chest when Justin Trenner was sitting at the table across from her: his face a picture of concentration as the pencil moved quickly in his hand over the paper. After one such night, Justin leaned across the table, took Janet's face into his hands and kissed her. It was her first kiss, but she had been too embarrassed to tell him – after all, eighteen was way too old to have never been kissed by a boy before. Lisa had boasted of her first kiss at twelve. Well, now, Janet finally knew what it was like to kiss a boy, and her head felt like it was about to inflate and float up into the ceiling like a balloon. The evening went on, as Justin continued his work, and Janet sat by, watching him secretly. She was too distracted to do any of her own work on the newspaper. She would just have to come in early the next morning and finish up.

"Well, we're all done here," Justin had said, as he looked at Janet and smiled. "Will you go to the prom with me, Janet?" That night everything seemed possible and Janet nodded a breathless yes. But in the morning, doubts began to creep in, partly out of loyalty to Lisa and partly out of fear that no good could come out of it: Justin would be going to Duke in the fall on a full scholarship. Janet reverted on her decision and refused Justin's invitation. So Justin asked Lisa, who said yes, only to stand him up a week before the prom. In the end, Lisa went with Brick Riley – the captain of the football team. All the girls wanted him, but Lisa was the one who got him. As always, Lisa had thought of Janet and got her a date with Brick's buddy, Ted Hunter. Ted was going to Rutgers on a football scholarship. He could bench-press two hundred fifty pounds and drink a keg of beer without taking a breath – or at least that was what he claimed. Janet had not bothered to stick around to find out. She left the prom just as Ted and Brick began to exchange meaningful glances and talk about having rented a "suite" at the Marriot. As for Justin Trenner, he spent the prom with Valerie Meehan – the class valedictorian. The two of them danced all night, and, as Janet was dismayed to find out during last year's class reunion, had gotten married two years ago.

"It's a pleasure to meet you, Janet. Lisa has told me so much about you. I'm sure you'll be a wonderful addition to our team." Paul's voice brought Janet back to reality. Now was no time to reminisce about high school crushes.

"Thank you, Paul. I'm very excited to be here." Janet lowered her eyes and made sure to add just the right amount of corporate pep to her voice, lest Lisa suspect flirtation in her demeanor.

Paul's baby-blue eyes shone brightly as he smiled. He was about six two, athletically built, and his beach-blond hair was neatly trimmed. Janet thought that he looked like the spitting image of a Ken doll.

"Well, baby, I've got to run." Paul leaned in and kissed Lisa on the cheek. "I'm meeting with Jon – he's schooling me in the ways of being COO. We're organizing our annual charity ball, and Jon wants me to plan the entire event."

"Sounds wonderful," Lisa gushed. "I'll see you later, honey. Isn't he just adorable?" Lisa beamed with self-satisfaction after Paul left.

"Yes," Janet obliged. "Paul is very nice."

"Now, do you see why I want you to give Tom a chance? He's the perfect match for you – just like Paul is for me."

That night, back in her apartment, Janet sank into the couch with a groan. Working for Lisa was mentally exhausting, and the worst part was that she could not even call her time at the office work. It was not as though Janet had a list of assigned tasks or responsibilities. It seemed that Lisa had hired her simply out of pity. No matter, Janet was determined to learn as much as she could. As much as she had loved her job at the DA's office, Janet had to admit that her world had been one-sided. She had gotten used to thinking as an investigator, but now she had to learn to think as a defender of Bostoff's interests. Sure, Bostoff Securities was not running a Boy Scout operation, but everyone knew that there were loops in the law, and as long as you used the loops to your advantage without breaking the actual law, you were okay. In fact, that was exactly what being an attorney entailed – enabling people to do things that were within the bounds of the law.

ଛୁଓଙ

Dennis Walker turned off his computer and poured himself a scotch. It was eleven o'clock at night and he was dead tired. Irritated was more like it. His eyes were beginning to hurt from his having sifted through tons of meaningless information. Wiring the computers of Bostoff's employees had seemed like a brilliant move in the beginning, but so far the feedback that Dennis had received from the analysts at the Treasury had not produced any meaningful information. At first Dennis blamed the ineptness of the analysts and chose to bore through the data himself, but he too came up empty-handed. There were hundreds of emails, but none of them had any meat in them: it was as though employees of Bostoff Securities labored under the delusion that they were working for a truly legitimate business, which, of course, could very well be the truth when it came to the worker bees. But Dennis was convinced that the top brass had to know what was going on. He had wired computers of senior executives and those of the Bostoffs. He had expected their emails to be goldmines, but both Bostoffs were surprisingly laconic in their conversations, which left Dennis with two possibilities: either both Bostoffs were extremely cautious, or they had begun to suspect that their computers had been wired. Dennis certainly hoped that the latter was not the case.

In all of his investigations, he had never blown his cover, and he certainly did not want to start now, especially given the fact that his candidacy had been a long shot for the case in the first place. Which reminded him: he needed to stop chatting up Bostoff's female employees. This morning's kitchen chat with that recently hired cute lawyer, Janet Maple, had been a glaring lapse in judgment, and yet Dennis could not help smiling at the memory. The girl definitely liked him. She nearly let her oatmeal run over while talking with him, and Dennis, ever the hero, saved Janet from embarrassment by popping the microwave open just in time – well, he saved her from further embarrassment, as the girl was already as red as a beet.

A grin of self-satisfaction glinted on Dennis's face. Sure, he could be vain when it came to female attention, but it felt good to be admired, and, in his defense, one never knew when a casual acquaintance could turn into a useful ally. Given the results that Dennis had gotten from his surveillance of the Bostoffs so far, he just might need a friendly inside source.

Chapter Five

At ten o'clock the next morning, Janet was seated behind her desk when Lisa swung open her office door.

"Hey," Lisa panted, almost out of breath. "Got a sec? I need you to come with me."

"What's up?" Janet promptly rose from her chair and grabbed a notepad and a pen.

"An impromptu meeting request from Jon Bostoff." Lisa grimaced. "Don't know what that busybody wants now. You'd think he was the owner of the company."

"Jon Bostoff is the president, right?"

"Right," Lisa confirmed. "And Hank Bostoff's elder son. Paul is his younger brother and COO. You met him yesterday." Lisa grinned.

Janet nodded, suspecting that dating the company owner's son was more complicated than Lisa let on. "Do you know what's on the meeting agenda?"

"No idea. I guess Mr. Know It All wants to meet you. Between you and me, Jon acts like he is the boss, and I think that's partly because the old man is planning to retire. I think he's going to choose his heir successor soon, and Jon is doing all he can to ensure that it will be him."

"I'm ready to go when you are." Janet thought it best to steer clear of a discussion about the boss's family politics.

Lisa took a loud breath. "Follow me. We'll have to go through the trading floor."

Janet's second encounter with the trading floor of Bostoff's Securities was not much different from her previous experience. It was like walking into the boys' high school locker room: the atmosphere reeked of testosterone and horny jokes. She did her best to keep her walk in check as she kept close to Lisa, who had her lips firmly pressed together as she powered on, seemingly oblivious to frank stares and occasional whistles that were coming from men seated in endless lines of long, narrow desks.

"We're almost there," Lisa muttered under her breath. "Jon's office is at the other end of the floor." Lisa motioned to an aquarium-like office that loomed smack in the middle of the far wall. Unlike the rest of the offices at Bostoff Securities, Jon Bostoff's office had walls made of glass. "Jon had his office remodeled when his father made him president," Lisa explained. "I suppose this way he feels that he's got an eye on everybody."

Through the glass office walls, Janet could see that Jon Bostoff was not alone – or at least she assumed that the man behind the long, steel-framed desk was Jon Bostoff. The physical resemblance to his younger brother, Paul, was apparent, but so was the age difference. Jon's blond hair was beginning to thin at the temples, and his eyes, although as blue as Paul's, had a sharp and inquiring quality about them. Paul Bostoff was also in the office, standing irresolutely by his brother's desk, and Janet could only assume that the older man seated in one of the angular modernistic chairs that surrounded the conference table was Hank Bostoff.

"Here we are." Lisa conjured up a smile.

Before Lisa could say another word, Jon Bostoff motioned for them to come inside.

"Lisa, come in, come in!" Jon Bostoff half-rose from his chair.

"Good morning, Jon." Lisa flashed her trademark smile. "Allow me to introduce Janet Maple. She recently joined our legal department as assistant general counsel."

"Hello, Janet, it's a pleasure to meet you. I'm Jon Bostoff, and this is my brother, Paul." Jon motioned at his younger brother who was still lingering by his desk.

"We have already met." Paul smiled briefly at Janet.

"And the distinguished-looking gentleman over there is my father and the founder of this company, Hank Bostoff," Jon concluded.

"Well, I don't know about the first part, but the second part is certainly true." Hank Bostoff replied from his chair. "You must forgive me, Janet. I'd stand up to shake your hand, but I seem to be having trouble getting up from this contraption." Hank Bostoff motioned at the uncomfortable-looking chair he was sitting in. He had the same blue eyes as his sons, and his direct, frank gaze made him instantly likeable. His hair was mostly white, but its fullness more than made up for its loss in color. With his lean physique and expertly tailored clothes, Hank Bostoff looked dashing despite his age, which had to be somewhere in the vicinity of sixty, given the fact that he had two grown sons.

"My father has a delightful sense of humor." Jon Bostoff chuckled. "Please, have a seat." Jon motioned at the empty chairs adjacent to the one occupied by Hank Bostoff. "It will be much more comfortable if we're all gathered behind a table."

"Oh, I don't know about the 'comfortable' part." Hank Bostoff chuckled. "Where was it you ordered this furniture from, son, Italy?"

"My father and I have our differences in taste." Jon Bostoff smiled thinly. "Please," he said curtly, as he motioned for Janet, Lisa, and Paul to take their seats.

Janet perched at the edge of a chair. Hank Bostoff had been right: the rigid seat was far from comfortable.

"Well," said Jon Bostoff after everyone had taken their seat, "the reason I called this meeting today is to get better acquainted with the recent addition to our legal team." Jon's glance lingered on Janet. "Janet, I understand that you have already met some members of our executive management team..." Jon's eyes shifted to his brother. "But neither my father nor I have had the pleasure of meeting you, so we thought it would be a good to have a quick introduction. Why don't you tell us about yourself, Janet?"

Lisa cut in before Janet could answer, "Well, Jon, I just would like to add that Janet has very impressive credentials: she's a Columbia Law School graduate and she'd spent four years at the DA's office."

Jon Bostoff's eyebrows rose in surprise. "Thank you, Lisa, but I'm sure that Janet is more than capable of introducing herself. So, Janet, you worked for the DA's office?"

Janet sensed Jon Bostoff's intent glance. "Yes, I did. I spent four years there, the last three in the Investigations division, and as Lisa mentioned, I did graduate from Columbia Law."

"Wonderful. And what made you want to switch your career path?"

"I was downsized," Janet answered frankly. There was no other way to explain the gap on her resumé, and in any case, she had always been of the opinion that honesty was the best policy.

"I see." Jon Bostoff seemed to be pleased with the answer he received.

"These government budget cuts are really most regrettable." Hank Bostoff shook his head. "But it all works out for the best in the end, I suppose. Bostoff Securities could most certainly use a bright, remarkable lady like yourself."

"Thank you, sir." Janet blushed in spite of herself.

"Welcome aboard, Janet," Paul said.

"Yes, indeed, we're most glad to have you here," Jon Bostoff conceded.

"Thank you." Janet felt her face grow warm again. Jon Bostoff's curt tone did not exactly match his words.

"Well, Janet and Lisa, thank you for stopping by."

"The pleasure is all ours." Lisa flashed one of her dazzling smiles and rose from her chair, motioning for Janet to follow suit.

"Thank you, gentlemen." Janet followed Lisa. To say that she was perplexed would have been an understatement. She had expected the meeting to at least have some substance, not a mere hello, how are you? But what was she to do – question Jon Bostoff? Lisa certainly did not find anything perplexing with the current set-up of things, and at least for now, Janet was not going to disagree.

༄༅

After the door closed behind Lisa and Janet, Jon Bostoff threw an irate glance at his brother. "Paul, do you mind explaining why no one bothered to consult with me before hiring that broad?"

"Now, Jon." Hank Bostoff interjected. "There's no need for this kind of language. I'm sure there's a reasonable explanation."

"I'm sorry, Dad." Jon Bostoff shook his head. "Paul, do you mind telling me why was I not consulted about the decision to hire that remarkable young lady?"

"I didn't think it would be an issue, Jon," Paul replied with an obnoxiousness that made Jon seethe. "As the COO of this company, Dad has given me the authority to hire staff within certain salary limits. Janet Maple's hire was within that bracket. Furthermore, the hire is within the legal department, which falls under the COO's office, so I did not see how it would concern you."

Dad has given me the authority. Jon fumed. How many times had he told his brother not to use the word "Dad" at the office? Hank Bostoff was the owner of the company, and even if he was losing his grip on reality, Hank was still their boss, and at work he was to be addressed as such. "Would you listen to this, Hank! Why do we need two people in Legal when Tom Wyman is doing a perfectly good job? First, Paul hires his girlfriend, so I let that one slide, but then she brings over her friend. What are we – a charity factory?"

"Now, Jon, you can call me 'Dad' when it's just the three of us, and I do think that Paul's idea is a pretty good one. Fred Rossingram and the junior fella who worked for him used to do all the work for us for a fraction of what Wyman is charging us. Perhaps we should reconsider our approach."

Reconsider our approach. Jon Bostoff loved his father, but he could not help wishing that the old man would retire already. Fred Rossingram had been Bostoff's general counsel before Jon became president. Old Rossingram had the risk tolerance of a turtle, and Jon Bostoff did not need a lawyer telling him what he could not do; he needed a lawyer who would tell him what he could do within the bounds of the law. If he just so happened to tread on the border now and then, occasionally stepping over, that was no biggie either, as long as matters were kept under wraps, and Tom Wyman was just the man for the job.

"Rossingram was too conservative," Jon chose his words carefully. "His views put Bostoff at a disadvantage compared to our more aggressive competitors."

"I hope you're right, son, but sometimes, the turtle wins the race," Hank Bostoff chuckled.

Jon restrained himself from sighing at his father's penchant for Aesop's fables. This time he had a comeback that would be a real kicker. "Personally, I prefer Lord Dunsany's take on the famous fable: after the tortoise had been hailed the victor, a fire took place in the forest, but very few of the animals survived." Jon paused for impact. "It turned out that several of the animals, including the tortoise, saw the fire starting while standing atop of a hill. They called a meeting to decide whom to select as the messenger to alert the other animals and they chose to send the turtle."

Hank Bostoff shook his head. For a moment, Jon Bostoff worried that he might have overdone it, but when he heard his father's laughter, he knew he was all right.

"Well done, son, well done. I sure hope you're right."

"I am right, Dad. Tom Wyman is a partner at Ridley Simpson, which is a leading law firm that handles affairs for New York's top financial institutions and has excellent contacts with regulators and politicians. Tom knows which way is up, and if he costs a bit more than Rossingram did, well, that's the price of doing business. And besides, Rossingram had been with the company for years, which brought his salary below market levels. If we were to hire someone of Tom Wyman's caliber in-house, we'd have to pay a pretty high salary."

"But do we really need someone of Tom Wyman's caliber, Jon?" In uncharacteristic defiance of Jon's authority, Paul interrupted his brother. "Lisa is a Harvard Law graduate. Surely, she could handle our affairs, and now she has Janet to help her…"

"That's exactly my point, Paul," Jon Bostoff snapped. "You should have talked to me first before hiring that Janet Maple character. I can understand hiring your girlfriend, but what do we know about her friend? She used to work for the DA, for Christ's sake! For all we know, she could turn out to be a whistleblower."

"Now, son, we've got nothing to hide," Hank cut in, "Bostoff is an honest name."

Honesty never filled anyone's bank account, Jon thought, but out loud he said, "Yes, Dad, but as you know, in the hands of a malicious person even the most innocent circumstances could be twisted. And in today's environment, where regulators are paying people for snitching on their employers, you can't be too careful. Do you know that most of the cases brought by the SEC resulted from whistleblowing?"

"Lisa wouldn't bring in a snitch!" Paul's face was red with indignation.

"I'm sure she wouldn't do that deliberately, but it is always better to be safe than sorry. I for one wouldn't hire anyone who spent four years at the DA's office."

"So what do you suggest? That we fire her?" Paul glowered at his brother.

"No, I didn't say that; we wouldn't want to get hit with an employment lawsuit either, but let's keep a close eye on her, okay? And next time you want to hire someone in Legal, talk to me first, Paul, all right?"

"Fair enough." Hank Bostoff rose from his seat. "Now I hope that you gentlemen will agree with me that we've sufficiently beaten this dead horse. Unless there are any other items to discuss, I'd like to call this meeting adjourned."

Jon nodded in curt acquiescence as he watched Paul rise from his seat, wishing his Vassar-educated brother would keep his nose out of the business affairs altogether. Left to his own devices, Jon might actually be able to squeeze some much-needed revenue out of Bostoff Securities after all. Of course, his father had no idea about any of this. The old man was under the impression that you could still run the business as though it were the eighties and nineties. Well, things had changed since then. Bostoff Securities was generating a fraction of the revenues that it used to bring in. Other firms had adjusted to the changing landscape, but Hank Bostoff liked doing things the sure way, which made Bostoff Securities a dinosaur among its competitors. The firm desperately needed new clients. Now that Hank was finally ready to retire, Jon was determined to make up for all the missed opportunities.

Chapter Six

It was six forty-five p.m. on the dot when Jonathan Bostoff pulled into the driveway of his house. At the Bostoff household, dinner was served at seven, and his wife did not take kindly to tardiness. But then it was not as though Jon minded: he was all for working hard, but he preferred to let his subordinates burn the midnight oil. Jon was at his desk at eight a.m. every morning, and he usually left work no later than six p.m. to spend the evening with his family. His wife, his three children, and his sizeable house were the sources of his pride.

As he often did upon arriving home from work, Jon paused on the front stairs of his seven-bedroom house to survey his domain. He had signed the deed for the house two years ago, but the reality of it was still pleasantly new to him. The prestigious Westbury, Long Island location filled him with warming pride every time he came home. His children were enrolled in the best schools in the state, and his wife presided over some of the most prestigious social committees in the country. But then Candace Bostoff, nee Covington, did not need Jonathan Bostoff to give these things to her. They were hers by birthright, and the fact that she chose to become Candace Bostoff, allowing Jon to be the one to give them to her, was an honor in itself.

"Hello, darling!" Candace's voice carried through the hallway, as she rushed to greet him. As usual, she looked stunning. Her honey-blond, shoulder-length hair fell loosely down her back, and her serene, oval-shaped face was immaculately made up. Jon never understood his friends' drooling over twenty-year-old nymphets. Candace was Jon's age. Actually, she was six months his senior, and he thought she looked more stunning than any twenty-year-old.

"Hello, baby." Jon leaned in for a kiss. God, he loved his wife's smell – had loved it ever since he had stolen a kiss from her in college. It was the smell of old money, class and success: everything that Jon had yearned for for years, and everything that was finally within his grasp.

"Honey, the kids are home!" Candace disengaged herself from Jon's embrace when his hand began to wander past her waist.

"Yes, well, their daddy missed his wife," Jon whispered into Candace's ear.

"Dad!" Jon's youngest son ran down the corridor toward him.

"Oliver!" Jon hugged his son. When Oliver was younger, Jon used to lift him up and twirl him around, but he was eleven now and too grown-up to be lifted up.

"Hi, Daddy." Jon's daughter, Amber, greeted him from afar, and he respected her newly reserved demeanor. She would be thirteen in a few months, and already the awkwardness of adolescence was beginning to manifest itself in her. Not physically, of course - Jon's beautiful daughter was the replica of her gorgeous mother - but emotionally.

At seven o'clock sharp, Jon Bostoff sat at the head of the vast oblong table in his dining room with Oliver and Amber seated on either side of him. His eldest son, Tyler, was eighteen and had just started his first year at Princeton. The kid was a bona fide brainiac. Having taken college level classes in high school, Tyler was already a fully-fledged sophomore in his freshman year. Jon was proud of his eldest son, but he was also worried. He did not want the kid to spend his college years with his nose buried in books. Sure, knowledge was important, but it was never what you knew; it was whom you knew. There was a reason why Jon had sent his son to Princeton. He wanted Tyler to develop connections that would set him up for life, and Jon was more than prepared to foot the steep tuition bill for that.

Candace smiled at Jon from the other end of the table. The table itself had cost somewhere in the vicinity of twenty grand; it was hand-made from solid oak by an exclusive furniture designer. The price tag was obscene in Jon's opinion, but he wanted to make sure that Candace had everything she deserved. God knew it had taken him long enough to procure it, so when he signed the deed on the house, he told Candace that she had carte blanche to furnish the place.

"Daddy!" Oliver brought Jon back to reality.

"Yes, Ollie?"

"Can we go to the beach house this weekend?"

Jon shot a questioning glance at Candace. When it came to child rearing matters, he left all the decisions to his wife. After noticing a barely perceptible nod from his wife, Jon nodded.

"Sure, buddy. I don't see why not. It will be too cold to go into the ocean, but we could still have a picnic on the beach. What do you say, Amber?" Jon shot a hopeful glance at his daughter.

"Can I bring one of my friends along?"

"Sure, pumpkin, by all means," Jon conceded. Lately, it seemed that his daughter had become incapable of doing anything on her own. Everywhere she went, she had to be accompanied by a clique of shrieking, gum-chewing, constantly text-messaging teenage girls. Well, the house in the Hamptons had nine bedrooms. The beachfront property had become Jon's in the beginning of the year, and the past summer had been the family's first season at the property. For Jon Bostoff, that summer would forever retain a magical quality. Sure, they had owned a summer house before, but their old summerhouse was a mere shack in Connecticut with a whopping fifteen minute drive to the beach to boot. Jon was no fool; he realized that many people would give their right arm to have his old, perfectly cozy, three-bedroom beach house in Connecticut that had since been sold to its new owner, but, in Jon's opinion, the shack in Connecticut was not good enough for Candace, and by extension it was not good enough for him.

"And, Dad?"

"Yes, buddy?"

"For the winter break we'll go skiing just like last year, right?"

"Slow down, Ollie. It's only September." Jon grinned. "But yes, we will go skiing just like last year." Jon's mind started doing the calculations, as he tousled his son's hair. If the business panned out the way he hoped (and he could think of no reason why it should not) he just might swing that ski lodge he had been eyeing in Vail, Colorado. It was bound to be a nice Christmas surprise for Candace and the kids.

"Ah, Dad, I might have some Christmas break plans," Amber ventured.

"Oh?" All at once Jon awoke from his musings.

"We'll talk about it, Amber," Candace shot a warning glance at her daughter. "You know how important family time is to us. Your daddy works very hard to make all of this possible." Candace made a sweeping motion with her graceful arm through the air.

"But I want to go somewhere warm." Amber pouted. "I was going to stay with Christy. Her family's got a house in the Caymans."

Jon gulped. There was a downside to having your kid attend one of the most prestigious schools in the state. You were bound to be outdone by the parents of the other kids, and there was just no way Jon could swing a tropical mansion this year. Maybe next year. Definitely next year, Jon resolved.

Later that night when Jon waited for his wife to join him in bed, his mind returned to its usual activity: tallying things up, as

Jon called it, or keeping score. He was thirty-nine years old. In a year, he would be forty. Things were finally starting to get on track. At times, he wondered at Candace's patience. In all their years together, ever since he first had kissed her at a party at Duke, she had remained faithfully by his side. Throughout their marriage, she had never once complained about their starter three-bedroom house in Connecticut, their kids attending public schools, or her driving a five-year-old Audi instead of last year's Mercedes or BMW. Not that her family had been of the same opinion.

The Covingtons came of old money made in oil and real estate, and they expected their only daughter to be married to a man of solid stock. Granted, Jonathan Bostoff had two pennies to rub to his name, but Bostoff was not the name that Mr. and Mrs. Covington expected their daughter to carry. At Duke, Candace had many suitors vying for her attention: wealthy, handsome undergraduates with seven-figure futures all lined up for them, courtesy of their fathers. And then there was Jonathan Bostoff, the first generation in his family to go to college, and with a pedigree that was nothing to speak of. While the Covingtons had accepted Candace's choice of a husband, they had made it clear that they were not going to help the young couple. Candace had a small inheritance left to her by grandparents. When her parents passed on, she would receive her share of their wealth, but while they were alive, in no way would the Covingtons aid Jon Bostoff, either with their capital or with their connections. Not that Jon wanted his in-laws' help. He wanted to give Candace the life she was meant to have all on his own.

During his years at Duke, Jonathan Bostoff fervently had wished he could alter his family history. The idea was not all that far-fetched, as many who rose to money and wealth from obscure origins often replaced their less than stellar beginnings with glamorous pasts, but in Jon's case, it was utterly impossible. Hank Bostoff was fond of reminiscing about his "humble beginnings" in interviews and speeches. A son of a construction worker and a homemaker, Hank Bostoff went to the University of Life, as he liked to put it, and did not have any formal education beyond a high school degree. Even that he had finished at night. While he went to school at night, Hank got a job as a shoeshine boy on Wall Street. That was his first exposure to the world of finance, and even though at the time he had no idea how to accomplish it, Hank vowed to one day join the ranks of the expensively suited men who tipped him generously for polishing their fine leather shoes. While he thought of a way to materialize his aspirations, Hank bided his time by polishing his clients' shoes vigorously enough to see his own reflection in them and reading left-over copies of the Wall Street Journal he found on the train and took home to his parents' multi-family house in Brooklyn.

As luck would have it, Hank did not have to wait long. After about a year on the job, an old floor broker noticed how quick Hank was on his feet and offered him a job as a floor runner on the trading floor of the New York Stock Exchange. The job was exactly what it sounded like: it involved running orders up and down the trading floor. Sometimes the order entrusted to Hank could be as large as several hundred thousand dollars, but that never worried Hank Bostoff: his feet were fast and nimble, and he had a stellar memory aided by a mind that could tally up numbers quicker than a calculator. Within two years, Hank was promoted to a broker. From that point on, Hank Bostoff's life was on the upswing. Within the next three years, he paid off the mortgage on his parents' house and bought a three-bedroom house for himself in an adjacent neighborhood in Brooklyn. A year later, Hank married his high school sweetheart, and nine months later his first son, Jonathan, was born.

Jonathan remembered vividly the gradual transformations of his family's house in Brooklyn: the addition of extra bedrooms and bathrooms, the expansion of the kitchen, and then, one very exciting spring, the sight of sweaty men in work clothes digging up the ground in the backyard for the pool. The pool was only fifteen feet long, but to Jon it had seemed huge. He relished picking and choosing among his friends, who suddenly almost doubled in numbers, the lucky ones who would get to enjoy the cool water reprieve from the stifling summer heat. Jon had heard it many times that money could not buy happiness, but he knew firsthand that money could most certainly buy popularity and respect, and if that was not happiness, he did not know what was.

Several summers later came another big change: the Bostoffs' move to Connecticut. By then Hank Bostoff owned his own firm: Bostoff Securities. His wife had convinced Hank that it was time for them to upgrade their living quarters. After all, Hank often entertained at home, and he could not very well bring business associates to Brooklyn. Jon had been fourteen at the time, and he became keenly aware that while money was important, it was not enough in itself. It might have been enough in Brooklyn, but in Connecticut people wanted to know where you came from and what school degrees your father had. At neighbors' barbecues, Jon flushed red when he heard whispers behind his father's back, ridiculing his Brooklyn accent and saw Connecticut housewives raising eyebrows at his mother's choice of makeup and dress.

Thankfully, his mother was as perceptive as Jon. Within a matter of weeks, she had reinvented herself, shunning loud prints for subdued pastels and toning down her makeup to the natural shades the neighborhood housewives favored. Even her diction had changed, becoming softer. Within a matter of months, Mrs. Bostoff became the neighborhood's favorite, helping with the committee at the country club, active on the local school board – you name it, Jon's mother was on it. His father, on the other hand, was not nearly as perceptive. He refused to alter himself for anyone; moreover, he was ridiculously proud of his beginnings – something that Jon wished his father would obliterate. There was nothing wrong with reinventing one's past to match one's station in life; people did it all the time. During a confidence Jon had shared with one of his dates, Stephanie Douben – a pretty blonde with an upturned nose and sky-blue eyes – Jon learned that her real name was Dobrowski, which her father, a manufacturing magnate, had changed to Douben. The fact that his own father could not be as enterprising vexed Jon to no end. Still, Jon had managed to make a good enough career in high school. Contrary to his father's advice to go for football, Jon joined the lacrosse team and made captain. Thanks to his handsome looks, he dated some of the most popular girls in his school, and his quick wit as well as the generous allowance granted by his father made Jon well-liked by all his classmates. In his senior year of high school, Jon received an acceptance letter from Duke University. Jon still remembered his parents seeing him off to college: his father full of pride and his mother teary-eyed.

Duke University turned out to be very different from Connecticut. The anticipation of the great and wonderful things that were bound to take place during his college years was desecrated by the cool reception that Jon received upon his arrival on campus. His roommate, Connor Hale, made it clear that he did not socialize with anyone whose daddy had not gone to Duke. The white Ferrari that Connor drove made Jon's red Mustang look plebeian, and when Jon tried to ingratiate himself with Connor by letting him copy his homework assignments, Connor cut off any possibility of social ties by putting a crisp fifty-dollar bill on Jon's desk. Still, Jon did not despair. After rigorous tryouts, he made the lacrosse team, and his prowess with the sport gradually began to win him the respect of his classmates and even got him into a fraternity. Yet, despite these tokens of acceptance, Jon was keenly aware that he was never really one of the team. His social background doomed him to remain an outsider.

All of that changed when Jon kissed Candace Covington at his fraternity's party. Unlike his classmates, most of whom were heavily drunk halfway into the night, Jon had kept his wits about him. Even back then he knew how to handle his liquor, and that night he stayed away from alcohol entirely. He had already been inebriated by Candace's beauty. So, after chatting her up most of the night, he had decided to go all in and kiss her. Even after almost twenty years of marriage, Jon had not stopped wondering just why Candace did not slap him when he leaned into the velvety smoothness of her lips that night. Instead, she had answered him, openly and fervently, ushering a whole new era of his existence.

Finally, the bedroom door opened and Candace entered the bedroom, bringing Jon back to the present. "Sorry I took so long," Candace whispered. "I was putting Ollie to bed."

Jon's eyes lit up at the sight of his wife. He lifted himself up on his elbow to take in the view. And what a view it was: clad in a black lace corset from Agent Provocateur, with black stockings, garter belt, and black stiletto heels that Jon had gotten her last week, his wife looked hotter than a Playboy model. "Some things are worth waiting for." Jon kicked the comforter to the floor. "Come here, you."

Giggling, Candace jumped into the bed next to him. As Jon undid the laces on the back of his wife's corset, he got as hard as if he were a buck of twenty, ready to go on for hours. Candace never failed to illicit this reaction from him, and for that alone he loved her to no end.

Chapter Seven

At a quarter to five on a Friday afternoon Janet was staring at the clock on the wall of her office. She was beginning to have serious doubts about her qualifications as an attorney. She had been on the job for a week, and she had yet to claim one completed task to her name. What kind of firm hired a lawyer to sit around and do nothing all day? She wanted to think that next week things would be different, but all of her experiences at Bostoff Securities spoke to the contrary. Take the recent meeting with the Bostoffs: Hank, Jon, and Paul. Jon Bostoff's demeanor had seemed to stiffen when Janet mentioned her past experience at the DA's office. And the whole set up with Tom Wyman just seemed strange to begin with.

The way Janet saw it there were two options: either Bostoff Securities was a clean shop, and she simply had failed to understand its intricate operations, or her employer was a crook. Sooner or later all crooks got caught. Granted, she had only been on the job a week. Her experience working for the DA did not exactly make her the most trusting of people, but she figured that if it looked like a duck, swam like a duck, and quacked like a duck, then it probably was a duck.

Short of quitting, which due to the mounting pile of bills she had accumulated while unemployed was not an option, there was nothing Janet could do at the moment to change her situation. What she needed now was a drink—a vodka martini would get her mind off things. Thankfully, she would not have to wait long. She was meeting her law school friends, Katie Addison and Joe O'Connor, at Smith and Wollensky for drinks at six.

"You're still here?" Lisa appeared in the doorway of Janet's office.

"Yeah, I'm waiting to meet Katie and Joe for drinks." Janet immediately regretted her lapse, lest Lisa invite herself to join them.

"Oh, that sounds like fun." Lisa yawned. "But I've got a date with Paul. I think he is going to pop the question this weekend."

"You think so?" Janet tried to force excitement into her voice. She had no doubts that Lisa actually possessed an ability to physically bend men to her will. If she wanted Paul to propose marriage to her this weekend, the poor man would no doubt oblige.

"Yes, I think so. We've been dating for a year; this weekend is our anniversary, and Paul is taking me to a secret getaway."

"That sounds like fun."

"Now, if you would just give Tom Wyman a chance, you too could be wearing a diamond on your finger in the near future."

"I don't think I'm his type," Janet lied. From what she had seen of Tom Wyman, every woman was his type, at least for one night, but Janet was not looking to be somebody's disposable fun.

"Well, maybe if you weren't so prim all the time. Are you going out like that?" Lisa eyed Janet critically.

"Yes," Janet mumbled, already anticipating what was about to follow. Since her unsuccessful flirtation with Tom Wyman, she had reverted to her conservative business attire.

"Nothing. You look perfectly swell to take someone's statement, but I doubt any guy is going to ask you for a date with your hair tied up in that bun of yours and your blouse buttoned up all the way to your ears."

"Good." Janet pressed her lips together. If Lisa refused to observe boss-employee boundaries, she would do the same. "That's precisely the effect I'm going for."

"Well, have fun." Lisa lingered, no doubt waiting for an apology, but Janet sat back in her chair with her eyes fixed on her desk.

And then the impossible happened. Lisa smiled wanly and shifted on her high-heeled shoes.

"Look, Janie, I'm sorry. I didn't mean to tick you off. I know it's the end of the week, and you're probably tired and all. I just want you to be happy, that's all." Lisa halted. "And, truth be told, I'm a bit nervous about Paul. What if he doesn't propose? I don't think his brother likes me..."

Janet blinked. "I know you mean well. I'm sorry." And just like that, Janet was back, apologizing to Lisa the way she had done countless times before during all the years of their friendship. "And don't worry about Paul. The two of you are great together, and he doesn't look like the kind of man who would let anyone sway his mind," Janet counseled with the confidence of a relationship expert, trying not to think about the fact that her latest relationship had ended with heartbreak instead of an engagement.

At six o'clock on the dot, Janet was seated at the bar of Smith and Wollensky. A dirty vodka martini with three olives was in front of her. Janet bit into an olive and washed it down with a sizeable gulp of the martini, wishing that Katie and Joe would get there already. Ever since she had turned old enough to enter the establishment, she had hated sitting alone by the bar. Tonight was no exception, as Janet worried about her outfit, courtesy of Lisa's comments, and wondered whether any of the noisy suit types crowding the place were checking her out. Not that she was interested, but at the moment, male attention would be a welcome boost to her ego.

"Janet!"

Janet turned around at the sound of the familiar voices.

"Joe! Katie!"

"Congratulations on the new job! Come here, you!" Katie held out her arms for a hug. "I feel like I haven't seen you in ages. You look great."

"Thanks, you look great too." Katie was dressed in a gray sheath with a matching jacket and conservative two-inch pumps, instantly making Janet feel better about her own outfit.

"It's good to see you, Janet." Joe beamed at her, his hazel eyes twinkling.

"You too, Joe." Janet felt warm from the compliment. She liked Joe; he was a good friend. There had been one late study night, just as Janet had started seeing Alex seriously, when Joe had hinted that he hoped they could be more than friends, but at the time Janet had been too enamored with Alex's charms to consider Joe. She had always thought of him as a safe, cuddly teddy bear. After graduation, Janet and Katie saw each other regularly, but even though Joe and Katie worked for the same law firm, Joe always seemed to have an excuse not to come when they invited him to join them for drinks. Tonight, Joe looked very much the part of legal counsel in his dark navy pinstriped suit that was expertly cut to fit his muscular physique.

"I see a table opening up." Katie headed in the direction of the emptying table close to the bar.

"After you." Joe waited for Janet to pass.

"So, tell us everything about your new job," said Katie after they had ordered drinks.

Janet decided to omit her misgivings about Bostoff Securities for the time being. "Oh, it's only been a week – I'm still learning the ropes. How are things with you guys?"

"What can I tell you?" Katie shrugged. "If I have to proofread another contract, I'm going to hang myself."

"I told you that you should have gone for litigation." Joe chuckled. "The hours are crazy, but the work is so much more interesting."

"Yes, it may be interesting, but it's way too intense for my taste." Katie shivered. "I can't imagine myself being up before the judge and the jury."

Joe shook his head. "That's the best part. Not that I've gotten to do much of it yet. I'm mostly doing research for the senior lawyers and helping with witness prep, but lately the senior partners have been letting me come along to court with them. Already, I've learned so much. I can't wait to actually be up there, defending my own case someday."

"You will." Janet smiled. Joe's passion reminded her of the way she had felt when she started her job at the DA's office. Only she had wanted to bring wrongdoers to justice instead of defending them, and now she was in a different boat entirely. Her employment with Bostoff Securities had not been a long one yet, but Janet doubted she would ever be as passionate about her current occupation as Joe was.

"It's a good thing you switched jobs, Janet. Otherwise, we might have faced each other from the opposite sides of the defense," said Joe.

"Well, if you put it that way." Janet managed a smile. "But to tell you the truth, I miss the DA's office. I guess I was a better sleuth than I am an attorney." She shrugged.

"You don't sound very excited about your new job. Is everything okay?" Katie cut in. "Or is it because of Lisa?"

"Partially," Janet answered evasively. She knew that Katie had no special place in her heart for Lisa, but old loyalty prevented her from agreeing. Besides, Lisa did get her the job, and for that she deserved credit, even if the job did not turn out to be anything like Lisa had promised it would be. "I'm still learning about their business model, but some of their practices seem a little unorthodox…"

"Welcome to the real world, honey!" Katie smirked. "In addition to drafting contracts, I've had the pleasure of helping some of the financial firms with their regulatory battles. I'm talking major names, which, of course, I can't name, but you'd be surprised to hear what goes on inside some of these so called reputable firms. Some of the stuff they do for their clients is bordering on tax evasion and insider trading."

"And no one is doing anything about this?"

"I didn't say that. The regulators slap them on the wrist now and then; they pay a fine and go on their merry way, doing the same thing all over again. Are you going to tell me that every investigation you were on at the DA's office resulted in a successful finding?"

Janet shook her head. She knew only too well that it did not. At least not her most recent and most intricate case – the one that she had been sure was going to get her a promotion, but instead got her fired. Correction: downsized.

"You listen to me, Janet." Katie leaned across the table. "If you want to succeed at your new job, you've got to change your mentality. You aren't catching the bad guys anymore. You're covering their butts. And if they happen to cut a few corners here and there, you've got to come up with a way to make them look like they've crossed all the T's and dotted all the I's."

Joe nodded. "Katie is right. Let's face it. An innocent client rarely needs a lawyer, and when you're an in-house counsel, the client expects you tell them what they can do, not what they can't do."

"I know." Janet nodded. Suddenly she felt completely out of touch. She had thought she had gained substantial experience during her time with the DA, but now it seemed to her that she had only gleaned the surface of things.

"Sorry to burst your bubble, Janet." Katie smiled guiltily. "But I couldn't be this frank with you when you were in prosecution. Take my advice. If you want to make it in the private sector, you've got to become more lenient."

Janet nodded. "You may be right. Like I said, I'm not jumping to any conclusions. I just need more time to learn the ropes."

The conversation was interrupted by a petite blonde appearing by Joe's chair. "Hi, baby, I'm so sorry I'm late!"

"Daphne... I didn't think you were coming." Joe pushed back his chair. "Janet, this is my fiancée, Daphne," he added awkwardly. "Daphne, this is Janet. We went to law school together, and you've already met Katie."

"It's a pleasure to meet you, Daphne." Janet hoped that her smile looked genuine. She did not have anything against Daphne per se. She did not even know the girl, but something inside her had constricted when Joe had called the pretty blonde his fiancée.

Daphne settled into the chair next to Joe, prominently displaying her left hand on the table. Her ring finger was adorned with a sizeable diamond. "Isn't it lovely? We just got engaged last week. I'm still getting used to the feeling of it."

"It's beautiful. How long have the two of you been seeing each other?" Janet's curiosity was getting the better of her.

"Oh, we've been dating on and off..." Joe started.

"For two years," Daphne cut him off. "I finally had to put my foot down and say, 'You either propose, mister, or else!'"

Janet sipped her drink. For a future litigator, Joe was certainly very easily bulldozed when it came to his personal life. But then maybe that was exactly what he needed – someone to take charge when he got home after a long day in the courtroom. In any case, Janet would never find out for sure. She had missed that boat. Not that she had wanted to be on it – not really. If she had, she would have given Joe a chance when he had asked her to.

Later in the evening Janet and Katie were waiting for a cab together. They had let Joe and Daphne take the first cab, not so much out of generosity, but rather to get rid of Daphne, who had grown overly chatty after her second Cosmopolitan. Joe seemed embarrassed as he climbed into the cab after Daphne, bidding them a hasty goodnight.

Katie shook her head. "Joe didn't tell me he got engaged to that nutcase. It just proves that he's working too much. He's got no time to date. That's one of the hazards of being a lawyer in a private firm. You either end up single, like me, or hitched with a nutcase, like poor Joe." Katie sighed. "You should have given Joe a chance while he was still available," she added pointedly.

"I was too head over heels with Alex to notice anyone else."

"That dirt bag." Katie ground her heel on the pavement. "I never liked him, and I told you as much. Something about him just didn't feel right. Too suave, too…"

"You can let it go now, Katie – it's been long enough." Janet shrugged. She was only too familiar with the direction in which the conversation was heading, but contrary to what she had just said, she found it hard to let go of Alex just yet.

"So how did Lisa land the general counsel job at Bostoff?" Katie took the cue and switched the conversation.

"Lisa went to Harvard Law. She's smart."

"Wahoo! And you and I went to Columbia. I don't get anyone knocking on my door offering me general counsel jobs and neither do you. So, how did she swing it?"

"Well, she's dating the owner's son. They are about to get engaged…"

"That figures. Leave it to Lisa to sleep her way to the top. Darn it, I should start wearing sexier clothes to the office. Did I tell you that one of the senior partners propositioned me?"

"No way." Janet's eyes flew wide open.

"One night I was there working late on an assignment for him when the old bugger cruised over to my office and asked me if I wanted to get something to eat. I was starving, so I said yes. We went to a Chinese place close to the office, and he ordered a bottle of wine. I didn't think anything of it – two coworkers unwinding after a long day at the office. But then, after the second glass, he reached for my hand and told me that he wanted to take our working relationship to the next level. And you should see this guy. He looks like a benevolent grandpa, all proper and dignified, with a handkerchief in his suit jacket. The jerk is in his late sixties, married with two kids who are in their thirties, and, as I found out later, he is also sleeping with his paralegal. I told him that I didn't date coworkers. I had to be polite – he is a senior partner. The next day, the bugger had the nerve to ask me for the assignment as though nothing had happened. Come to think of it, I should have said yes, taped the whole thing and sued his ass for sexual harassment."

"Well, maybe it's not too late." Janet literally felt her sides splitting from trying not to laugh. She would not want to be in Katie's shoes, but the story was hilarious.

"Sure, go ahead, laugh," Katie snapped. "But I'm not telling you this just for laughs: life's no picnic at any job. So you're working for Lisa now. At least she's not trying to sleep with you. And who knows, if you play your cards right, she just might promote you."

Janet found herself wondering if getting a promotion at the firm of Bostoff Securities would actually be a good thing.

Chapter Eight

Half-awake, Lisa Foley stretched languidly in bed and looked at Paul sleeping contentedly next to her. The events of the previous night sprang up in her mind, as a contented smile spread over her lips. She surveyed her surroundings through half-closed lids. She knew the furnishings of the room of the prestigious B&B in Southampton where they were staying by heart. It was the same room Paul rented for their summer weekends, but there was something incredibly special about the Hamptons in the fall. The town was devoid of the pesky summer crowds, and the beach was deliciously deserted. But all of that paled in comparison to the events that had transpired last night, making Southampton forever Lisa's favorite destination. Last night, after a quiet dinner at Pierre's followed by dessert, Paul had asked her to be his wife just as Lisa was contemplating a forkful of strawberry shortcake.

Careful not to wake Paul, Lisa extended her left hand in front of her eyes and admired the ring on her finger. It was indeed a gorgeous ring. She had been expecting a diamond, but a five-carat sapphire of perfect clarity would do. The ring had belonged to Paul's mother, and he had made a big deal about it, so Lisa had pretended to be impressed. Personally, she would have preferred Paul to shell out the cash for a new ring. What better way could there be for a man to demonstrate his affection for a woman? But Paul could be sentimental at times – a quality that Lisa adored about him. She had never lacked for male attention, but dating was a far cry from marriage, and Lisa had found that unless a girl had a sizeable trust fund to supplement her good looks, it was not an easy task to snag an eligible bachelor. And while Lisa's family was comfortably middle class, her parents were far from wealthy. She did not have rich grandmothers or aunts bequeathing her unexpected millions, so marrying a capable provider was the only option. In Lisa's definition, an eligible bachelor was handsome, agreeable, and capable of taking care of his future wife. Thankfully, Paul was all of these things.

Lisa's thoughts turned to the time when she and Paul first met. One night, tired from work, Lisa had dragged herself to Mindy Lawlor's – Mindy Frank's – birthday party. Lisa and Mindy had gone to college together, but that's where their similarities ended. Mindy had been fortunate to land herself with a husband who provided for her splendidly: Josh Lawlor was in the investment banking division at JP Morgan. Not that Mindy had to worry about making a living: her parents had provided her with a sizeable trust fund. Lisa figured that the party would likely be a bust, filled with engaged and married couples, but it was still better than brooding alone in her apartment. For the first time in her life, Lisa had not even bothered to check her makeup, neglecting to dab concealer over those horrible dark circles under her eyes. She did not care how she looked; she just wanted a drink after a terrible day at the office. But suddenly, there was Paul Bostoff, Josh's friend from summer camp. Sensing Paul's keen gaze upon her, she rushed to the ladies' room and hastily repaired her makeup. Ten minutes later, she looked as good as new. Well, at least in the dim lighting of the place, she could pass for looking as good as new. Paul's attraction to her was undeniable. Lisa took things slowly, alternating oozing sexuality with demure coyness, building up Paul's anticipation, yet being careful not to overdo it. Men wanted challenge, and yet they did not want to be challenged too much. At the time, she was twenty-seven years old: three years away from thirty, and there was no time to waste. Paul's lineage might not have been as glamorous as that of Lisa's previous boyfriends, but he was the one who put the ring on her finger, and it would have to do.

Lisa heard Paul stir and smiled with the anticipation of many carefree years that stretched before her as Mrs. Paul Bostoff.

"Good morning." Paul smiled at her.

"Hi, baby." Lisa cuddled next to Paul, her foot reaching for his under the covers.

"How did the future Mrs. Bostoff sleep?"

"Perfectly fine, thank you." Lisa smiled, sliding her trim body over Paul's. "And she can't wait to make love to her future husband."

Later that morning, Lisa wiped the remaining drops of the maple syrup from her plate with the last bite of the pancake.

"That good, huh?" Paul smiled as he watched her devouring the last of the pancakes.

"Your lovemaking has made me ravenous." Lisa batted her eyelashes.

"Well, then, we'd better stock up on food."

We'd better not, thought Lisa. Already she felt guilty about this decadent feast, but it was Sunday, and she was simply in too good a mood for the usual gray option of oatmeal and half a grapefruit. Come Monday, she would be back on her strict eating plan. At her height of five two, even an ounce of extra weight would be instantly noticeable.

"So, what do you want to do today?" asked Paul.

"Anything you want." Lisa smiled dreamily. She might have hooked the fish, but she had yet to haul her catch ashore, and until she became Mrs. Bostoff, Lisa's last name was going to be Obedience. "We could take a stroll around town – check out the galleries or walk on the beach."

"I like the galleries idea." Paul decided. "Perhaps we'll find something interesting for our new place."

Lisa's heart jumped. She had planned to delicately broach the subject of moving in together, but Paul had beaten her to it.

"I hope I'm not rushing things." Paul took her hand. "But I'm sure once we tell Dad, he's going to want a big wedding, and I just can't wait a year to wake up to you every morning."

"I can't wait either." Lisa squeezed Paul's hand. She tried not to think about the year-long engagement. If it were up to her, she would board the plane to Vegas tomorrow. That way if things did not work out between them, she could at least get alimony. But family had to be contended with, and if Mr. Bostoff wanted a big wedding for his son, Lisa would sit back and bide her time.

Lisa turned her face to the gentle breeze as she walked next to Paul, her hand entwined with his. They were strolling down the main town street, throwing leisurely glances at the window displays of galleries that peppered the town. To put it mildly, the ratio of galleries and souvenir shops to the local population was disproportionate, but then these ornate displays of overpriced merchandise were intended for the tourists, and now, with the summer crowds gone, this imbalance was palpable. Almost every store was empty, with clerks yawning discreetly behind the counters. A few more weeks and many stores would reduce their hours and some would shut down entirely for the winter.

Lisa felt Paul's grip tighten around her fingers and looked up.

"It's my brother's wife, Candace, over there," Paul muttered. "I had no idea that they would be down here this weekend. I just hope we won't get sucked into coming over to their house. Ever since my brother bought that ostentatious place, he's been showing it off to everyone he knows."

"Let's go over and say hello." Lisa put on a smile: spending the afternoon with Paul's brother's family was not at the top of her list. Still, she knew that Jon Bostoff did not hold a warm place in his heart for her, but maybe, just maybe, she could manage to change his mind by turning Jon's wife into an ally.

"We have to. She's nodding at us; there's no escape," Paul grumbled.

A few moments later, a beautiful blond woman in her late thirties was smiling at them and kissing Paul on the cheek. Lisa thought that Jon's wife looked exactly like Christy Brinkley: the same golden hair, sky-blue eyes, and a million dollar smile. And from what Lisa had heard about Jon's wife, her smile was indeed worth millions. Jon's wife came from sizeable wealth; the kind of wealth that the Bostoffs could only dream about.

"It's so nice to see you again, Lisa," Candace was saying.

"You too, Candace," Lisa chirped. "Paul did not know you were going to be up here this weekend. We would have stopped by and visited."

"Jon didn't tell you, Paul?" Candace began and then caught herself. "Oh, well, he's been so busy lately... But now that I've run into you, you're coming over: Jon is making barbecue, and I don't want to hear any excuses. Paul, your nephews will be so happy to see you."

Paul tightened his grip on Lisa's hand. "I'm looking forward to seeing them too."

"I'm parked right over there." Candace motioned to the parking spot across the street.

"Great. We'll follow you in my car," said Paul. "Let me help you with these." He motioned at Candace's packages.

"Oh, thanks. You're a sweetheart."

As they walked to Candace's car, Lisa wondered why Paul did not mention their engagement. Could it be he was too taken aback to remember, or was it that he simply did not want to break the news to his family? Well, whatever it was, Lisa was not leaving Jon's house without announcing the big news.

ಬಿಲ

Jon Bostoff looked at his watch. Candace would be getting back any minute now. They were supposed to have barbecue for lunch.

At the sound of a car pulling into the driveway, Jon hurried down the stairs. He was surprised to see two cars parked in the driveway. He was even more surprised when he saw that the second car was his brother's.

"Jon!" Candace smiled at him as she got out of the car. "I ran into Paul and Lisa in town, and I thought it would be wonderful to have them over for barbecue."

Of course you did, Jon thought. He loved his wife, but at times her overly good manners drove him mad. God knew he saw plenty of his idiotic brother at work. There was no need to see him over the weekend, not to mention his girlfriend. "Wonderful." Jon kissed Candace on the cheek. "What a splendid idea."

"Hi, Jon." After helping Lisa out of the car, Paul joined his brother and sister-in-law.

"I'm glad Candace ran into you. The kids will be glad to see you," Jon managed. "Lisa, always a pleasure," he added, nodding at his brother's pesky girlfriend.

"Hi, Jon." Lisa ran her hand through her hair.

At first, Jon thought he had imagined it, but as he took another look, he knew that he had been correct. The glint on Lisa's ring finger was unmistakable. It was his mother's sapphire ring.

"Is there something you want to tell us?" Jon eyed his brother.

"Lisa and I got engaged. I proposed to her last night." Paul placed his arm around Lisa. "I was going to tell Father once we got back to the City."

When were you going to tell me? Jon felt like exploding, but managed to squeeze out of himself a polite, "Wonderful, congratulations to both of you."

"Paul, Lisa, congratulations!" Candace exclaimed as she wrapped her arms around Lisa and kissed her on both cheeks.

"We've got to celebrate." Jon slapped Paul on the shoulder. "Well, let's get the barbecue started and give the girls a chance to catch up." As he turned on the grill, Jon made a mental note to talk to his father first thing in the morning.

Chapter Nine

"Did you have a nice weekend?" Lisa stood in the doorway of Janet's office.

"Yes, I did." Janet hoped that Lisa would not ask for details, for Janet would be hard pressed to come up with a convincing story. She had spent the weekend cooped up in her apartment, with the exception of morning and evening walks with Baxter.

"So did I." Lisa grinned, sliding into one of the chairs that stood opposite Janet's desk. "Paul proposed." Lisa produced her left hand as confirmation of her words. On her ring finger shone a gorgeous sapphire set in diamonds.

"Lisa, congratulations!" Janet leaned in to examine the hefty piece of jewelry. One did not have to be a jeweler to see the stones of stunning clarity and the exceptional workmanship. "The ring is beautiful."

"To tell you the truth, I wanted a diamond, but this was Paul's mother's ring, so I kept quiet."

"So, when is the wedding?"

"Oh, I think in a year from now. We'll need time to get the whole thing organized and to give people time to RSVP. There's so much to do. I'll have to start looking at venues, seeing caterers, and then there's the wedding dress..." Lisa clasped her forehead in a gesture of utter exhaustion. "It almost makes me wish we could elope, but then I've always dreamed of a big wedding… Will you be my maid of honor?" Lisa's eyes lit up.

"Yes." Janet nodded. Even though she knew that being Lisa's maid of honor would really mean being Lisa's wedding planner, she was happy to take on the task. Lisa might have her faults, but in moments like these, years of friendship mattered more than petty grudges.

"Oh, goody!" Lisa squealed. "I'll tell my mom; she'll be so excited! She misses you, you know. You should say hello the next time you go to see your folks. Remember all those sleepovers we had in school?"

Janet nodded. Lisa's slumber parties had been impressive. Every girl in the class had hoped to be invited. Lisa's mother, a marketing executive at Estee Lauder, would give out makeup sample kits to all of Lisa's friends – pretty pouches with lip gloss, perfume, and scented soaps inside them. A slumber party at Lisa's house was an event to prepare for. You didn't just dress in any old pajamas. Every party had a theme: Lisa had thought that it would be a wonderful idea for all the girls to wear matching pajamas, and once the invitees were selected, she would reveal the outfit for the party. Then every girl who had been invited would have her parents drive her to the mall to buy the pajamas of Lisa's choice. There was one occasion when Janet's parents were not able to drive her to the mall until the weekend, by which time the pajamas in her size were sold out. Janet's panic was replaced by gratitude when Lisa presented her with a brand new spare pair. Ever the caring friend, Lisa had bought an extra pair specifically for Janet.

They were twelve then, and it seemed that nothing would ever come between them. But already talk of boys was finding ways into their conversation, with some girls, including Lisa, boasting of their first kiss – the having-been-kissed status separating the popular from the nots, and Janet had to admit that even now, seventeen years later, she found herself in the latter crowd. Only now the popularity ranking had been raised from a kiss to an engagement.

"But I digress," Lisa sighed. "Believe it or not, I actually have a work-related question to ask you. I just got this audit notice." Lisa pushed the fax from the SEC across Janet's desk. "Can you believe the nerve of these buggers coming in at a time like this? How am I supposed to plan my wedding with these jerks hovering over my back?" Lisa frowned. "Anyways, I'm sure Tom will help us handle most of it, but we've got to pitch in for appearances' sake. My paralegal, Meredith, will help you. Let's start by reviewing the client forms to see if we need to add any disclaimers. I've been meaning to get to it, but I kept putting it off…"

"Sure." Janet nodded. As luck would have it, she was very familiar with the subject. She had worked on several cases on these matters at the DA's office. "Where are the client files?"

"The form templates are on the shared computer drive."

"But where are the actual files?" Janet inquired. "I might as well take a look to make sure everything is in order."

Lisa perked up. "Oh, sure, that's a good idea. The Operations group handles all of that. My paralegal, Meredith, can show you where they sit."

"Sounds good. I'll get right on it."

"Thank you, Janet. You're a lifesaver. Without you, I'd be in a pickle."

After Lisa left, Janet opened the shared computer drive that Lisa had mentioned. She was relieved to see that the client agreements and disclosures were up to the industry standards. So far, things looked good. Now, if she could also confirm that these forms were diligently completed and maintained, she would be in lawyer's paradise.

Janet noticed several folders with the names of the employees of the legal group, including Lisa's and was interested to see a folder entitled Fred Rossingram. The name did not ring a bell; she clicked on the folder and found a variety of letters and documents with dates predating Lisa, leading her to conclude that Fred Rossingram had been Lisa's predecessor. The last of the documents with his name dated a little less than two years ago, which was shortly before Lisa's start date. Janet thought that it was strange that Lisa had never mentioned Fred Rossingram, but even more peculiar was the caliber of work that Rossingram did for the firm – the work that was now being outsourced to Tom Wyman. But as interesting as this discovery was, Janet had a pressing assignment to attend to.

Janet picked up the phone to call Lisa's paralegal, Meredith.

Half an hour later, Janet was walking down the trading floor accompanied by Meredith.

"So, how do you find working here so far?" Meredith inquired.

"I'm learning a lot." Janet prided herself on being an honest person, but she could not very well answer Meredith's question truthfully. "How about yourself? Do you like it?"

"Can't complain," Meredith chuckled. "I worked for a senior partner at a law firm for fifteen years; the pace is much calmer here, so that's the good part."

"Do you miss your old place?"

"I do," Meredith admitted. "I used to know the entire firm like the back of my hand. It was a small firm with only three partners, and they all retired and sold off the practice." Meredith sighed. "I've been here for a year, and between you and me, I still can't seem to make heads or tails of things. That Tom Wyman fella sure likes to convolute things."

Tell me about it, Janet thought.

"Let me introduce you to the Operations folks," said Meredith after they had reached the far end of the trading floor.

"Rosemarie, I'd like to introduce our new assistant general counsel, Janet Maple. Janet, this is Rosemarie March. She is in charge of the Operations group."

"Hi, Janet, it's a pleasure to meet you." Rosemarie rose from her chair. She looked to be in her mid-forties and was rail-thin, with red hair pinned up haphazardly. "So you're working for Lisa, huh?"

"Yes." Janet nodded. "And I was wondering if you could help me with the audit request we received."

"Sure, love, I'd be glad to. Lisa usually never makes it to our neck of the woods. What do you need?"

"If you could just show me where the customer files are."

"I've got the hard copies right here." Rosemarie motioned at a filing cabinet behind her desk. "How far back do you need to go?"

"Oh, just this year."

"Here you go, honey." Rosemarie pulled out a large stack of manila folders. "This is for the past three months. Once you're done with these, just holler, and I'll give the next three months."

"Great, thank you, Rosemarie. I'll look over these at my desk and will bring them back to you when I'm done."

"No problem."

Janet stuck the files under her arm. As she walked down the floor, she opened one of the folders and skimmed through its contents. The client was a hedge fund called Emperial – a recently opened account. The first thing that caught Janet's eye was the missing address and ownership information, but that did not make any sense. It simply had to be in the folder somewhere. She would just have a closer look once she got back to her desk.

Suddenly, Janet heard running footsteps and felt a rough push. Good thing she was wearing flats; otherwise, it would have been impossible for her to maintain her balance. But while Janet managed to stay on her feet, half of the files dropped out of her hands and fell to the floor.

"Sorry, miss!" The man who had just rammed into Janet called over his shoulder. "I've got to get back to my desk!"

"Are you okay?" Dean Snider had materialized out of thin air and was scooping the files from the floor.

"Hi." Janet blushed. It seemed that every time she ran into Dean, she needed rescuing. "I'm fine, thank you. It was my own fault. I wasn't looking where I was going." She bent down to pick up the rest of the folders.

"That guy is a jerk for running you over like that and not even stopping to make sure you were all right." Dean looked at her. They were both kneeling on the floor. Dean smiled and Janet felt her entire being tingle. It was not an alarming tingle like she got when Tom Wyman's knee brushed past her thigh, but a pleasant one. She did not know much about Dean Snider, but she wanted to get to know him.

"These look important." Dean peeked at the folders, as he handed them to Janet.

"They are." Janet confirmed. "These are customer files; I was taking them back to my office to make sure everything is in order for the upcoming audit."

"And are we in good shape?" Dean grinned.

"I think so," Janet answered. "At least I hope so."

"That doesn't sound very promising," Dean probed.

"I haven't really looked through them yet, as I was interrupted," Janet alluded to the embarrassing incident.

"Well, I hope that you find everything up to your satisfaction."

A yell from one of the desks interrupted them. "Dean, over here, my computer email won't open up!"

"I've got to get back to work." Dean shrugged. "It was nice seeing you again, Janet."

Janet smiled: it was nice seeing Dean as well. "You too. Thanks for your help."

✺

After showing a trader with the attention span of a three-year-old how to reset his email password for the umpteenth time, Dennis Walker settled behind his desk. A smile was playing on his lips. It seemed that circumstance had a way of bringing him and Janet Maple together. He found his encounters with Janet most entertaining, but now Dennis realized that Janet Maple could be a lot more than a flirtation. While Dennis was certain that he could gain access to Bostoff's customer files, navigating Bostoff's systems on his own was a lot like trying to find his way in the dark. Turning on the light would make things so much easier, and Janet Maple could be the light switch he needed. Dennis had spotted a very important detail while helping Janet to gather folders off the floor: one of the customer files was entitled Emperial.

The Treasury Investigations unit had been trying to get its hands on the Emperial hedge fund for a long time. While Bostoff Securities had enough violations to build a solid case, Bostoff's clients were the main reason why Dennis had jumped on the assignment. For the past two years, the Treasury Investigations division had been tracking several notorious hedge funds that were suspected in a number of infractions, including tax evasion and insider trading. Getting access to the hedge funds had proven to be next to impossible: all attempts at turning former or current employees into informants had failed, and getting Treasury investigators inside as undercover employees had proved impossible as well. Bostoff Securities had appeared on the radar because of its client base, which included Emperial and other shady hedge funds. With Janet's help, Dennis could bring the Bostoff investigation to closure much more quickly. His boss's recognition aside, the added bonus of this achievement would be retirement of Dean Snider's persona. For as much as Dennis loved his job, he was getting tired of wearing ill-fitted clothes and being snapped fingers at as though he were a maid.

Now that Dennis had a valid reason to get close to Janet, he had to devise his plan, which would not be too difficult given the fact that Janet and he were located on the same floor. There were a number of places where they could run into each other – the kitchen, the employee cafeteria, or the copy room. Of course, Dennis would have to tread lightly lest he risk compromising his cover. He would become Janet's office buddy, and gradually, he would become her confidant. For any other man, these plans might have sounded overly ambitious, but not for Dennis Walker. He had tested his powers of persuasion on many occasions. Granted, the persona of Dean Snider was not the most advantageous one when it came to the art of female seduction, but Dennis was not planning on seducing Janet Maple – at least not while he was on the assignment. Instead, he planned to become her friend, and Dean Snider was just the sort of man women tended to trust.

Chapter Ten

It was Monday morning, and Jon Bostoff had already breached his irritation quota for the week. He tried to restrain himself from throwing irate glances at his father, who sat opposite from him with an absurdly cheerful expression on his face.

"Well, I think that it's wonderful news about Paul and Lisa getting engaged." Hank Bostoff smiled. "It was about time Paul settled down, and I for one am glad that he's not marrying an actress."

A clueless bimbo would be better than a money hungry schemer, Jon thought, but restrained his impulse to vent. Until Hank Bostoff retired, he was still the boss.

"Between you and me..." Hank leaned across the table, his face growing serious. "I was worried about Paul for a while – that whole acting shtick... The odds of making it in that business are so remote, I feared that Paul might become a perpetual drifter, a shirker... But the kid has turned out real good; you both have." Hank patted Jon's hand. "I am especially proud of you, Jon, for taking Paul under your wing. Paul's got real potential, don't you think?"

Jon just stared blankly at his father as he tried to come up with a diplomatic remark, but he need not have worried: Hank was on a roll.

"Paul really proved himself in marketing, and I think he'll be really good in the COO role once he becomes better-rounded in his knowledge of the company operations. And that's where I need your help, Jon. I need you to train Paul to become your right arm. I built this company to pass it on to my children. Once I know that I can leave the company safely in the hands of my two sons, I will finally be able to retire."

Jon wondered if this was the beginning of Hank's descent into senility. Paul had about as much business acumen as a monkey. He might have been great at fussing with press releases and advertisements, but when it came to running a business operation, Paul hadn't a clue, and no amount of on-the-job training was going to change that.

"That's something your mother would have wanted as well," Hank added. "She always worried that you and your brother were not close enough. She blamed it on the age difference between you when you were growing up, but I always told her that in time it wouldn't matter. Nine years seems like a lot when you're a kid, but as you get older, the difference vanishes."

Jon nodded. If he were to succeed in getting his father to agree with his point of view, candidness was not an option. He'd think of a way to open his father's eyes to Paul's faults as a businessman later, but right now there was another matter he wanted to address.

"Oh, Dad, I meant to ask you: did you know about Mother's ring?" Before Jon finished the sentence Hank cut in.

"I wanted Paul to have it; I think your mother would have agreed."

"But I thought she wanted the ring to remain in the family," Jon retorted.

Hank frowned. "As your brother's future wife, Lisa is now part of this family."

Jon was too rattled up to hold back. "Yes, Dad. I only meant to say that family heirlooms should be passed on to children and grandchildren, but obviously you know best. Suppose Lisa calls off the engagement, then what?" The sapphire ring that now adorned Lisa's ring finger had been a present from Hank to his wife on their twentieth wedding anniversary. It was a custom design, consisting of a flawless sapphire, framed by highest clarity diamonds in a platinum setting. The trouble was that Jon's mother had passed away without a chance to leave a will. At the time, his father had been too overwrought by grief for Jon to approach the sensitive subject, and now it was obvious that he had waited too long.

"When Paul told me about his plans, I was too overjoyed to think about something like that... Look, son, I understand your concern, but I think that Lisa is a decent enough woman to return the engagement ring should she wish to call off the engagement, and I, for one, sincerely hope that it will not come to that. And as for my grandchildren, there will be plenty to go around for everyone. Right now I just want to bask in the joy of seeing my sons succeed – both personally and professionally."

"You're right, Dad; it was a heartfelt gesture. I'm sorry I over-reacted." Jon shrugged. There was no way of convincing the old man, so he might as well make the best of it.

"I'm glad we're in agreement, Jon. I wanted your mother's memory, the memory of our marriage—" Hank broke off. "To be passed on while I was still around to see it. Who knows how many days I have left on this earth, and to tell you the truth, without your mother, I wish there wouldn't be that many."

"Dad..." Jon felt his throat tightening with guilt. He'd been so preoccupied with his own affairs that it never even crossed his mind to think about how his father was coping with his wife's death. "Dad, you know that you are loved very much by your family; you are very important to us." Jon stopped short; he was a pro when it came to peddling corporate speeches in boardrooms, but when it came to speaking from his heart, he choked.

"I know, son." Hank patted Jon's hand. "Well, I'd better get out of your way. You've got a company to run."

"Okay, Dad. But you know that I'm always there for you, should you need to talk or anything..." Jon offered awkwardly.

"I know, son. I know." Hank turned toward the door. "And Jon…"

"Yes?"

"Remember what I said about your brother: he's got the potential to run the company as your partner. Help him realize it."

Jon nodded. "I will, Dad."

Once the door behind his father closed, Jon pressed his fists against his temples. He had enough worries keeping him up at night. Now, he also had to devise a way to involve his younger brother in the business while keeping him out of the loop on any matters of substance. God forbid Paul, with his Boy Scout mentality, should ever find out about the changes that Jon had implemented at the firm. His naïve, prudish brother would be the first in line to confess to the SEC and the Feds. Still, Jon had to admit that the old man did have a point. Rather than trying to keep Paul away, Jon should embrace his younger brother. This way, Paul would begin to trust him and consult with Jon on his decisions. In fact, if Jon had done just that, he could have anticipated Paul's stupid move of hiring that DA lawyer…

Speak of the devil, Jon thought, looking through the glass wall of his office. There was a reason why he had remodeled his office with glass walls. He had his eye on the trading floor at all times, and now he saw the pesky new lawyer heading from the Operations area carrying a stack of folders under her arm. Jon recognized the folders as client files because he had personally made a visit to the Operations area a few months back. He had given that woman Rosemarie a nice raise, and in return, she was to apply relaxed paperwork standards for certain clients. When Jon had intuited the new process to Rosemarie, he saw understanding flash in her eyes: she had an unemployed husband and three children to feed. Jon knew how to pick his employees. Of course, there was always a risk of the regulators snooping around, but Tom Wyman would take care of that. His law firm had excellent rapport with the SEC and the Feds. Jon

Bostoff had followed enough white collar crime cases to know that the only time the regulators ever caught on to anything was when things were leaked from inside, so he had made sure to pay the key people properly. And now, thanks to his brother, a former DA attorney was snooping around his firm. Jon picked up his phone and dialed Tom Wyman's number.

"Hi there, Jon," Wyman's voice boomed in the receiver. "Business going well? But then after the last deal you got going with Emperial, that's really a rhetorical question," Wyman smirked.

"Hello, Tom." Jon forced himself to ignore Wyman's cockiness. The man was a genius when it came to setting up schemes, but that did not give him the right to be so damn arrogant. "Thing are going well indeed."

"So, what can I do for you today, Jon?"

"You can help me keep an eye on that new hire my brother brought in. Have you met her yet?"

"Yes, as a matter of fact I gave her a brief orientation on Bostoff's corporate structure. Between you and me, I'd like to give her a lot more than that, but she seemed pretty uptight."

"You what?" Jon exploded.

"Hey, Jon, I was just kidding. Rest assured, Janet Maple's honor is safe from me."

"That's not what I meant, Tom. What was that you said about the orientation?"

"Well, I ah… I showed her the entities owned by Bostoff Securities. Paul said he wanted me to train her. I thought you knew. I thought you wanted to start doing some of the work in-house to save on legal fees."

"Tom, you know me better than that. I'm never cheap when it comes to matters like that. Do you know that Janet Maple used to work for the DA's office?"

"I know, but she got laid off. I checked her out – they kicked her out in the middle of an investigation. Seems she meddled in affairs that were above her pay grade. She was unemployed for several months before she landed here. After an ordeal like that, I doubt she has any affinity to her previous occupation. But in any case, I don't think she understood much of what I told her – she seemed completely overwhelmed."

"Once a snitch, always a snitch." Jon pressed his lips together grimly.

"And besides, the employment non-disclosure agreement she had to sign would prevent her from blabbing, anyway."

Jon made a mental note to obtain a copy of Janet Maple's signed employment agreement.

"That's a good point. Do me a favor, Tom, keep close to her, okay? I just saw her poking around in client files. I don't need a snitch in my house. And next time my brother comes to you with any new ideas, you be sure to let me know about it."

"I will, Jon. And don't you worry about Janet – it will be my pleasure to keep an eye on her."

After hanging up the phone, Jon Bostoff leaned back in his chair. He was feeling calmer now. If Tom said that Janet did not have a clue what Tom was talking about when he trained her, he had to be right - unless Tom was covering his tracks for having blabbed about matters he was not supposed to blab about, but then Tom was not one to be blamed for that lapse. Jon's brother was, which reminded Jon of his earlier resolution. If he wanted to keep Paul under control, he had to keep him close.

With a grunt, Jon rose from his chair. He could have his secretary schedule a meeting with Paul, but a personal visit would set the mood Jon was aiming for.

As Jon walked down the hall to Paul's office, he tried to conjure up a cordial and brotherly demeanor. Getting close to Paul was a matter of business importance, and when it came to money, Jon was willing to put his personal feelings aside.

Through the open door of Paul's office, Jon could see his brother peering at the computer screen with intense concentration.

Jon rapped his fingers on the office door, forcing hearty cheer into his voice.

"Hi there, Paul."

Paul lifted his eyes away from the monitor. "Hi, Jon." Paul's voice sounded unusually prim as he folded his hands neatly on his desk. "What can I do for you?"

With each day that prick gets more and more arrogant. Jon took a seat in one of the chairs facing Paul's desk. "Well, I just wanted to say congratulations again. This is such an exciting time for you and Lisa - an exciting time for all of us," Jon added hastily.

"Thank you, Jon. Lisa is a great girl, and I'm so happy that she's going to be my wife." Paul sounded a bit warmer now. "She's really bright, Jon, and I think she could take on so much more in the company. I was looking through our legal bills – Tom Wyman is charging us a fortune. If we got back to keeping more of the work in-house, the savings would be significant."

"Good thinking, Paul. But there are reasons why I employ Tom. Why don't we get together and go through them? In fact, I think we should have a standing meeting – every two weeks or so, to update each other on company developments and plans in our respective areas."

"Sounds great. I've got a lot of ideas I'd like to share with you, Jon," Paul was bursting with enthusiasm now.

"I'm glad to hear that, Paul. You know that Dad wants us to be partners in running this firm, and I, for one, do not intend to disappoint him."

"Me neither, Jon. I'm so glad we had this talk." Paul smiled.

"Me too, brother. How does every other Thursday sound for our meetings? I'm thinking we'll schedule them during lunch. This way we can grab a bite to eat and catch up."

"Sounds good."

"I'll have my secretary send you a planner. By the way, how is that new girl working out?"

"I think she's doing well. Lisa told me Janet was helping her with an audit."

"I like it – getting right to work." Jon rose from his chair. "By the way, I wanted to have a party to announce your and Lisa's engagement to the company. Nothing formal, just drinks and hors d'oeuvres at BLT?"

"Thank you, Jon." Paul blushed. "That's very generous of you…"

"It's settled then. Shall we say next Thursday?"

"Yes, well, I'd like to run it by Lisa first."

It took Jon all his will not to smack Paul on the head. What a sniveling blob his brother was! "Just take charge, Paul. I'm sure Lisa will appreciate the surprise."

"Oh, well, all right then. Thank you, Jon."

"You're welcome. I'll see you soon, brother."

Before heading back to his office, Jon decided to swing by the legal department – he remembered the directions well from his previous altercations with the firm's previous general counsel, Rossingram. Jon was sure glad to have gotten rid of the old goat, but now he was experiencing a déjà vu with a young female version of Rossingram.

On his way to Lisa Foley's office – the office that old Rossingram used to occupy - Jon passed by Janet Maple's office. He saw the girl hunched over the client folders, which were strewn all over her desk.

"Hello, Lisa." Jon knocked lightly on the door of Lisa's office.

Lisa perked up behind her desk. "Hello, Jon. What a pleasant surprise. What brings you to this neck of the woods?"

"Oh, I just wanted to say hello to my future sister-in-law." Jon swooped over to Lisa's desk and planted a kiss on her cheek. While performing this familial gesture, Jon shot a quick glance at Lisa's computer screen, which had Saks Fifth Avenue's website on it. Jon smiled. At least he did not have to worry about Lisa Foley's zeal – only when it came to her spurring Paul to become a business mogul.

"Thank you, Jon. That is so sweet of you!" Lisa flashed an embarrassed glance at her computer screen.

"And I wanted to tell you that we'll be having a company party for you and Paul next Thursday at BLT."

"That sounds great, Jon. I'll be looking forward to it."

"Great. That's all I had to say. And by the way, how's Janet Maple working out?"

"Wonderful, just wonderful. I asked her to look at the client forms for the upcoming SEC audit. I only wanted her to check the general wording, but she's actually gone further to check the forms we have on file to make sure all the documentation is complete."

"Ah, personal initiative – I like it. And by the way, did she sign all the new employment paperwork?"

"I'm sure she did. I'll double check with HR."

"Great. Thank you, Lisa."

As Jon turned his back to Lisa to exit her office, the smile left his face. If there was one thing he detested, it was employees who poked their noses into matters they had no business in.

Chapter Eleven

Seated behind the desk of his home office, which really was not an office at all but a nook with a desk crammed into it in his tiny studio apartment in Soho, Dennis Walker peered at his computer monitor. Finally, he had struck gold. The data Dennis was examining was a breakdown of commission revenue from Bostoff Securities' clients. It had taken Dennis a while to get access to the data. The accounting system was protected by intricate encryption software, but after several coaching sessions with IT specialists at the Treasury, Dennis was able to get through. The first few rows of the commissions did not indicate anything out of the ordinary, but as Dennis scrolled down the report, several numbers caught his attention. Emperial, Creaton, Rigel, Gemini, and Sphinx were being charged almost triple the going rate. All of these hedge funds were known for their so called aggressive investment policies, which really meant using collusion and market manipulation to reap high returns. There had to be a reason why Bostoff was charging these clients excessive commission, and Dennis was determined to get to the bottom of it.

There was a reason why Dennis was good at catching the bad guys: he had once been one of them. It had been an inadvertent mistake that had cost him his securities licenses. Such was the deal that Dennis had struck with the authorities for helping them bring down Vitaon, a corrupt hedge fund Dennis had foolishly accepted an employment offer from for a position of a trader. That had been five years ago, but there had not been a day that Dennis did not regret the wrong turn he had made in his career.

The son of a hotel manager and a grade school teacher from Park City, Utah, Dennis had grown up dividing his time between skiing in the winter and mountain biking in the summer. Somewhere in there school fitted in. Despite his mother's occupation, studies had not been important to Dennis in his early years, but that had changed later. Once he turned fourteen, Dennis started making an extra buck by working at the ski resort in the winter and caddying in the summer. Overhearing conversations between tourists from cities like New York and Chicago made Park City seem small, and Dennis started thinking about what life was like in other places. His studies became important then, as Dennis realized that if he wanted to do anything other than work in the service industry, college was his way out. Since his parents could not afford to pay tuition, scholarship was the only option.

When Dennis turned sixteen, his father got him a part-time job as a bellboy at the five-star hotel in Deer Valley in which Dennis's father had worked as a reception desk manager for close to fifteen years. Dennis's elder brother had just started his first year at the same hotel as a full-time employee, and Dennis's father saw no reason why Dennis should not follow his brother's suit. Hauling luggage and opening doors for the hotel's guests strengthened Dennis's resolve that much more. He was always courteous and diligent in his tasks, but deep inside he despised his job. By now his plan to leave Park City had acquired a definitive shape. He was going to go into finance. From the scraps of conversations that Dennis overheard at the hotel, he learned that a large part of the guests occupied positions in finance; there were also private business owners and corporate executives, but the finance people always booked the most expensive rooms, had the latest ski equipment, and the prettiest women with them.

In his senior year of high school, Dennis spent most of his time behind books. He subscribed to the Wall Street Journal and Forbes. Gradually, the articles he read started to make sense. He continued to work at the hotel a few hours a week for his pocket expenses, as his father did not believe in giving his kids an allowance. That winter Dennis happened to deliver luggage to the penthouse suite rented by Terrance Stanton. The name of the guest stood out in Dennis's mind immediately: he had spotted it in a Forbes article only a few weeks ago. Having served as a senior executive at numerous high-profile financial firms, Terrance Stanton had just been recruited as the CEO of Rossman Grozling, a major investment bank. Terrance Stanton was also a generous supporter of many charitable causes, including the famous four-year scholarship he awarded to several lucky students every year. Dennis had applied for the scholarship, but had yet to hear the results. As he wheeled the luggage cart in Mr. Stanton's suite, Dennis could feel his heart beating wildly. Most likely nothing would come out of it, but he was going to at least try. Before knocking on the door, Dennis straightened his uniform and puffed out his chest. As he had read in various 'how to succeed' books, personal appearance was the first thing people noticed about a person. Then Dennis rang the bell.

A woman so incredibly beautiful that Dennis had lost his ability to speak opened the door. She was in her early twenties, about five ten, with lanky legs, deep blue eyes, and long, blond hair. She was dressed in skinny jeans and a tunic of see-through material, under which Dennis glimpsed a lacey black bra.

"Come on in," the blonde said.

With a tremendous effort of will, Dennis recovered. "Thank you, ma'am. Where would you like the bags?"

"The foyer is fine."

Dennis lowered his eyes as he wheeled in the luggage. One more glance at the siren and his pants were bound to become dangerously tight.

"Terry, give the boy a tip, will ya?" The stunning beauty cast Dennis a bewildering smile before she disappeared in another room of the suite.

Just as Dennis finished offloading the last bag, a gentleman appeared in the hallway. Dennis recognized Terrance Stanton instantly from the photo he had seen on the scholarship application brochure. At fifty, Terrance Stanton had the lean, trim body of a man who exercised regularly. His strong features– a straight nose and firmly set lips - were accented by his pepper-gray hair, which was brushed back.

"Here you go, kid." Terrance gave Dennis a twenty dollar bill.

The generous tip set Terrance apart from the majority of the guests who, despite their wealth, were often stingy.

"Thank you, sir." Dennis bowed slightly. "And if I may, congratulations on your new job." Dennis held his breath. He had gone out on a limb, and the result could turn out to be disastrous. But Dennis was not kept in suspense for long. When he saw the smile on Terrance Stanton's face, he knew he had made the right move.

Terrance nodded approvingly. "I see you follow the world of finance. What's your name?"

"Dennis, Dennis Walker, sir."

"And what do you plan on doing with your life, Dennis Walker?"

If the question had come from anyone else, Dennis would have been annoyed, but now he was extremely flattered.

"I plan to go on to college and major in Finance, sir – I've applied to five schools."

"Oh, yeah? What schools?"

"Princeton, Duke, Harvard, Yale, and University of Utah."

"Good choices." Terrance grinned. "But those are expensive schools and hard to get into. What's your GPA?"

"Three point nine, sir." Literature had been the reason for Dennis's not having a four point zero GPA. He simply did not have the patience for words. Numbers were his game.

"Impressive. Any extracurricular activities?"

"I'm on the town's ski racing team, my school's debate team, and I'm also chair of the finance society, which I've started, sir."

Terrance whistled. "Do you know that I run a scholarship fund?"

"Yes, sir. I've applied, sir, but I haven't heard back yet."

"We'll be sending out responses soon." Terrance scratched his chin.

Just then a golden lab retriever bounced into the foyer, followed by the blonde Dennis had admired earlier.

"He doesn't listen to me, Terry!" The blonde complained. "We've got to get somebody to walk him while we're here."

"You just have to be firm with him, Cindy. Stand your ground." Terrance whistled to the dog. "Here, boy. Come here."

But rather than heeding his master's orders, the dog wagged his tail at Dennis and started to nuzzle his hands.

"I'm sorry I don't have any treats, boy." Dennis petted the dog. Ever since he was a kid, dogs had always liked him.

"He likes you." Terrance grinned. "Say, you wouldn't be interested in making an extra buck walking Grover, would you? I'll pay ten bucks an hour."

"Thank you, sir. I could definitely use the money, sir."

"Great, you start right now." Terrance Stanton thrust a dog leash into Dennis's hands. "And take your time: he needs an hour walking time every day."

"Yes, sir." Dennis put the leash on Grover and hurried out the door. From the way Terrance was eyeing Cindy, it was clear that the reason he wanted Dennis to take his time walking the dog was not Grover's wellbeing – at least not primarily.

For the ten days that Terrance Stanton stayed at the resort, Dennis walked his dog, but the initial cordiality that Stanton had shown to Dennis had been a one-time occurrence. Upon all the encounters that had taken place between them after, Terrance maintained a demeanor of polite and superior indifference. By the end of Stanton's stay, Dennis was regretting his agreement to walk the dog. Sure, the money would come in handy, but his dignity was worth more than a hundred bucks. Dennis had agreed to Terrance's offer because he had hoped to ingratiate himself into getting a scholarship – a foolish plan, he now understood, but it was too late now. His winter break had been wasted on walking Stanton's dog, and his friends, along with his brother, seemed to have an unending supply of jabs to dig at him for being a dog walker.

In the spring, Dennis received his acceptance letters. He had gotten into all the colleges he had applied to. Most awarded him scholarships, but those were not full scholarships, and University of Utah was the only option that would be fully paid for. Then, a few weeks later, just as he was about to send in his admission acceptance, Dennis received a letter from Stanton scholarship fund stating that he had gotten a full scholarship for four year tuition at any school that he chose to attend. The choice was easy: Dennis decided on Princeton, which was Stanton's alma mater.

During freshman orientation at Princeton, Dennis was not surprised to see Stanton as one of the speakers. The man was one of the most honored alums of the school, but Dennis was surprised to see Stanton approach him during the reception afterwards.

"I'm glad to see that you chose the right school, Dennis." Terrance greeted him.

"Thank you, sir. If it had not been for your generosity, I wouldn't be here."

"Nonsense, Dennis. You've worked hard, and if you continue the same way, you will reap the rewards."

Stanton's prophecy turned out to be true. Dennis did succeed, at least for a while. Stanton became Dennis's mentor of sorts. They did not have standing meetings or anything of the kind, but Stanton did get Dennis a summer internship at Rossman Grozling's offices in New York while Dennis was in college, and he even arranged for a room and board for him in the corporate housing. When Dennis graduated, he was hired by Rossman Grozling as a first-year analyst and began working through the ranks on a trading desk. The first year had been brutal, as Dennis worked eighty hour weeks. His duties ranged from getting the senior traders their breakfasts and coffee to doing the grunt work that was too dirty for the senior guys. He also studied for his securities licenses exams, which he passed on the first try.

The second year was much better. Gradually, Dennis started getting more meaty tasks, which gave him a chance to implement his understanding of the market. The market movements were like music to him: as he sat before his Bloomberg screen, eyeing the trading activity on all the world's exchanges, Dennis saw a pattern that could bring in millions of dollars in profits. All of his ideas were vetted by a senior trader, but Dennis still got the credit for generating record revenues as a junior associate.

Dennis repeated his success year after year, and three years later he was promoted to Vice President. Money was pouring in, and Dennis upgraded his lifestyle accordingly by moving out of the apartment he shared with a roommate in Hell's Kitchen into a swanky loft in a luxury building in Battery Park, which was only a ten-minute walk from his job. With the hours he worked, he could not waste any time on commuting. And then there were women... Dennis was not vain, but he was fully aware of his good looks. From his early teens, members of the female sex had found him attractive. The guys on the trading desk took Dennis to exclusive New York clubs frequented by models and starlets. At first, there was a nameless succession of beauties, but when he turned twenty-seven, Dennis zeroed his attention on Vanessa Cleary. Vanessa was a model and an aspiring actress: her resumé included a variety of commercials, but she was determined to get on the big screen someday. She had long legs, sandy-blond hair, and eyes as blue as the sky. She was the kind of girl Dennis Walker of Park City, Utah never imagined he would be with. It was not long before Dennis asked Vanessa to move in with him. He upgraded his apartment to a two-bedroom, and the two settled into a blissful life. Dennis was rarely home during the week, but weekends with Vanessa more than made up for his grueling days.

The tricky thing about money was that the more you made, the more you wanted to spend. Vanessa loved exquisite things, and Dennis loved giving them to her. He was making a good living, but he was hungry for more. When one of the senior partners of Vitaon hedge fund approached Dennis with an extremely lucrative offer of employment, he found himself saying yes. Working at Rossman Grozling had been great – Dennis had learned a lot, but he had also contributed a lot. His trading picks had generated stellar returns for the desk, covering for several traders' wrong picks. No matter how much money he generated for the firm, there was still a cap on the bonus. Sure, the bonuses were generous, but Dennis felt he deserved more. At Vitaon, traders were compensated on a percentage of what they generated: the more money you made for the firm, the larger your bonus would be. Perhaps Dennis would have reconsidered employment with Vitaon if Terrance Stanton had still been around at Rossman Grozling, but Dennis's mentor had been ousted in a corporate squabble a year before and had since retired.

During his first year at Vitaon, Dennis had reaped the largest bonus of his career. The day after he got his money, he proposed to Vanessa with a ten-carat diamond ring from Harry Winston. Vanessa squealed with delight. She was going to forget about acting – who needed all that traveling and constant dieting when one could focus on things that mattered, like being a wife and a mother? Dennis felt his pride swell. He had everything he had ever wanted, and he was just getting started.

Dennis still remembered the shock he felt when he discovered Vitaon's fraud. The hedge fund might have been booming, but its management was indiscriminate as to the sources from which its investors' money came, including terrorists and drug cartels. Dennis was shocked to learn that all the partners knew about the fraud. As a thank you for his remarkable performance, Dennis was promoted to partner and let in on the secret. Joy was not the emotion Dennis felt after his promotion. With his new title, he would be liable for the fraud that had been taking place at Vitaon long before he got there.

Dennis knew that he had to get out, but before he could circulate his resumé on the street, he was approached by the Feds. They were onto the whole scheme, and they were willing to offer Dennis a deal if he agreed to aid in the investigation. Dennis would have to give up all the compensation he had made at Vitaon and he would be barred from the industry, but he would not be prosecuted further. Should Dennis pass on the chance, the offer would not be extended to him again.

Terrified, Dennis said yes. For several months he wore a wire to work and downloaded hundreds of emails and documents to aid the Feds in their case. In return, he got to keep his freedom, but lost his livelihood.

The biggest blow was when Vanessa left him. At least she was decent enough to give him back the ring. As much as it had hurt him, Dennis knew that he would need every penny he could scrape. His father had proclaimed him a disgrace to the family. He had never objected to all those checks Dennis had sent back home, but now that the cash register was no longer ringing, Dennis had become the black sheep of the family.

In a gesture of generosity that was enough to break Dennis's heart, Terrance Stanton had come to his aid by hiring the best litigation lawyer to represent Dennis and make sure that the Feds would indeed keep the deal they had promised Dennis.

Terrance had wanted to pay the bills, but Dennis would not have that. With the sale of his apartment, Vanessa's ring, and other luxury items which had become irrelevant in his dire situation, Dennis was able to cover his legal costs.

When the whole ordeal was over, Dennis sat on the floor of his five hundred square feet studio in Soho. If he lived modestly, he had enough money in his bank account to sustain him for about a year, which was not much at all, as he had no idea what he was going to do now.

A knock on the door brought Dennis out of his reverie. When he saw Terrance Stanton on the threshold, he nearly burst into tears.

"I'm so ashamed," Dennis had whispered. "I'm so ashamed of what I have done."

"The only thing you are guilty of Dennis is being naïve. You have not done anything to be ashamed of – Vitaon's owners did."

"But I worked for them."

"You were young and hungry, and they lured you in. Part of it was my fault – I should have prepared you better for this life." Terrance looked away. "We all make mistakes, Dennis. I've made plenty myself. Have you ever wondered why I do all these things for charity? Why I run that scholarship fund?"

"Because you want to help people; because you are a good person, the kind of person I wanted to become, but failed."

Terrance sighed. "Ah, Dennis, do not be so hard on yourself. What do you really know about me? Do you know that I have a son who died from a drug overdose?"

Dennis shook his head, stunned.

Terrance looked down, as though afraid to meet Dennis's eyes. "I was not always the level-headed man I am now. The corporate game is a jungle, and if you're not careful, it will suck you right in. I had no time for my family, arrogantly believing that if I provided for them financially, that would be enough. But the truth of the matter was that my career was the focal point of my life. I was in the middle of a merger when Jack overdosed for the first time. He was sixteen years old at the time." Terrance shook his head. "I could not break away from the deal – I had to be at work. I thought I had fixed things when I got Jack into a first-grade rehab program. He seemed to get better, and then, one day, we got a call from the police. Jack had overdosed at a friend's party. He was eighteen years old."

"I'm so sorry, Terrance. I didn't know." Dennis was at a loss for words. His own torment seemed meaningless compared to that of his mentor's.

"You don't have to pity me, Dennis. I don't deserve it. I told you my story so that you would understand that we all make mistakes. You've made a mistake – a costly one, no doubt. The question is, what you are going to do now? You can make amends and put the whole thing behind you. You are very young, Dennis. You can start your life over."

The next day, Dennis received a call from the Feds offering him employment as a consultant for the white collar crime division. To this day, Dennis was not sure if Terrance Stanton had a hand in this offer, but when he received it, Dennis knew it was his chance at redemption.

He threw himself into the work relentlessly. His knowledge of the industry gave him an upper hand when it came to ferreting out frauds. Unlike the majority of the investigators, Dennis actually understood the complicated financial terms. For three years he toiled for the Feds. The pay was not much, but Dennis had preserved and amplified the savings he had from his days as a trader: he was no longer trading professionally, but that did not preclude him from managing his own investments, and his savings had grown nicely. When the Treasury started a new investigations unit, his supervisor at the FBI recommended Dennis for employment and he was hired as senior investigator.

He had reclaimed his place as a decent member of the society, but his downfall would always be a part of his past. His life was simple now, with two major principles: no lavish spending and no getting close to women. An occasional fling was a welcome distraction, but no woman would ever hurt him the way Vanessa had.

Dennis rubbed his forehead. It was almost one a.m. His eyes were burning from hours of staring at the computer screen, and his head was splitting from the memories of his haunted past. Dennis would see to it that Bostoff and his scheming clients got justice, if only to stop them from luring another hopeful, wide-eyed kid into working for them.

Chapter Twelve

Janet frowned at the client files on her desk. The clients that had caught her eye were Emperial, Creaton, Rigel, Gemini, and Sphinx. All five were hedge funds, and all five were missing address and ownership information. Janet had run background checks and found that every single one of these companies had pending litigation against them. Emperial appeared to be the most notorious of the group, with several financial blogs alluding to Emperial's having had a hand in the recent meltdown of several well-known stocks.

Janet was thinking of the best way to present her findings to Lisa. Lisa's initial assignment had only included checking the verbiage of the client forms. Through her own initiative, which she now regretted, Janet had unearthed deficiencies in Bostoff's operations. Now, she had to find a way to fix them, even if that meant upsetting Lisa's bridal mood.

The door to Lisa's office was closed. Janet was glad of the excuse to put off the unpleasant task, but to satisfy her conscience, she gingerly knocked on the door.

"Come in!" Lisa called through the door.

Janet forced herself to straighten her back and open the door.

Lisa was on the phone with her legs propped on her desk. She motioned for Janet to sit down.

"Yes." Lisa waved her hand impatiently. "I was calling to confirm my appointment for a facial – yes, today at five.

Perfect, thank you." With a groan, Lisa hung up. "These people have no idea of customer service. They charge five hundred dollars per visit and have the nerve to put you on hold!"

Janet nodded politely. She did not really have much to say on the subject of a five-hundred-dollar facial, but the mysterious processes it involved had to be worth it.

"I know – five hundred dollars is a lot, but they are really very good. It's this Japanese place, and after they do their magic, your skin literally glows. I only go there for special occasions, and next week is my and Paul's company engagement party. I would have preferred an appointment next week, but they only had a slot for today, so I'll sneak out a little early. You've got my back, right?"

"Of course."

"Thanks." Lisa sighed. "And here I was hoping that after I got engaged, I would not have to ask a question like that, but somehow Paul has gotten it into his head that I actually enjoy working here. He thinks I want to contribute to the company." Lisa rolled her eyes. "I guess I should take credit for that. I've always been a good actress. Remember the time I played Juliet in our high school play?"

"I remember." Janet struggled to keep a straight face: Lisa had recited her lines monotonously, but the low-cut bust line of her costume had more than made up for that lapse, at least with the male audience.

"Those were the days: we were so full of hope and promise..." Lisa looked away wistfully. "Well, I guess I'll just have to keep my act up until Paul and I tie the knot. Once I'm Mrs. Bostoff, I'll be home free. But enough about me. How are you doing? Everything okay?"

"Actually, Lisa, I wanted to talk to you about the client forms ..."

"Ah, yes, how's that going?"

"Well, I found some things that may be of concern..."

"Are the forms missing any items that we should be asking for?"

"The forms are perfect, but…"

"Whew, you had me worried there." Lisa mock-wiped her forehead.

"But some of the documents are missing," Janet continued. "I found five customer files that are missing addresses and ownership information."

"Only five? That hardly sounds alarming."

"Yes, but there is a pattern: Emperial, Creaton, Rigel, Gemini, and Sphinx are the hedge funds that we are missing this information for, and all of them have had regulatory sanctions in the past."

"Hmmm… It's probably nothing more than a simple omission. Have you talked to the Operations group about this? I think the woman's name is Rosemarie."

"I was going to talk to her next, but I wanted to speak to you first. Here is some information on these hedge funds that I found online." Janet handed Lisa the printouts.

Lisa glanced at the papers that Janet placed on her desk. "These days every firm on the street is getting smacked. Just remember that you don't work for the DA anymore, and in the real world things aren't always perfect. I'm sure there's a perfectly reasonable explanation for all of this. Just talk to Rosemarie, okay?" Lisa's tone sharpened, "I don't want this to become our problem. Let Rosemarie resolve it, got it?"

"Yes." Janet bit her lip. Without her boss backing her up, how was she to do her job?

"Oh, and Janet – did you sign your new hire forms? Jon was asking me about them."

"I meant to do that. I'll drop them off with human resources."

"Oh, I almost forgot." Lisa perked up. "This weekend, my folks are having a little party to celebrate my and Paul's engagement. You're coming, right?"

Janet nodded. She had told Lisa that she would be going to Long Island to visit her folks and there was no escape now.

"Great, it will be so much fun!"

"I'm looking forward to it already."

"Well, I'll be leaving soon – I need to run some errands before my appointment." Lisa reached for her purse.

After Lisa left, Janet headed for the Operations area, hoping that Rosemarie would have the answers she needed.

"Hey there, Janet." Rosemarie looked up from her desk.

"Hi, Rosemarie. I don't mean to bother you, but I'm still learning the ropes, and I had some questions I was hoping you could help me with."

"Sure, Janet, pull up a chair. What can I do you for?"

Janet took a seat. "I was looking through the client files and found that some accounts were missing some information."

"Which accounts are those?"

"Emperial, Creaton, Rigel, Gemini, and Sphinx are all missing ownership information, and addresses."

Rosemarie rubbed her neck. "These are major clients; I'm sure there's an explanation for each of them." Rosemarie punched in a few keys on her computer. "Just as I thought. The information has been requested from the clients. It's company policy to open an account while pending document submission."

"I understand completely. Big clients have to be accommodated."

Relief flashed in Rosemarie's eyes. "The kind of revenue we're getting from these boys warrants any number of paperwork exemptions, if you get my drift."

"Of course. They are major players in the market."

"That they are." Rosemarie pointed to the pile of paper on her desk. "These are the trades from last week. Just look at the volumes from Emperial."

The report had hundreds of entries, and Janet needed more time to make sense of it. "Do you mind if I take a look at these at my desk? I just want to make sure that there's nothing for the auditors to be alarmed by."

"Well, I need this copy, but Jon authorized your access, correct?"

Janet nodded. "I've been asked to help with the audit."

"The reports are saved on the Operations computer drive. It's password protected." Rosemarie scribbled the password on a Post-it. "Here you go. Make sure to commit it to memory. We would not want anyone who isn't authorized to get access to this data."

"Thank you, Rosemarie, you've been most helpful."

With her heart racing, Janet walked back to her office. She had not exactly lied to Rosemarie, but she did not tell her the truth either. The truth was that Janet was disobeying her boss's instructions.

"Busy day?" Dean Snider poked his head through the doorway of Janet's office.

At the sight of the unexpected visitor, Janet wished she had kept the door closed. "Um, yes. I'm catching up on some work, preparing for the audit." Janet hoped Dean would take the hint and leave. Under a different set of circumstances, chatting with the cute IT engineer would have been fun, but not when there were piles of confidential reports on her desk: reports she was not supposed to have access to.

"Sounds serious." Dean eased himself into Janet's office. "Wow, just think of all those killed trees." Dean clicked his tongue, eyeing the stacks of paper on her desk.

Janet blushed. Dean did have a point, but if he had any inkling about the kind of information she was looking for, he would understand that, although important in the grand scheme of things, environmental concerns were the least of her current worries. "I'll be sure to recycle when I'm done." Janet eyed the door pointedly, hoping that her insistent visitor would get the hint.

"You don't look like you're having a good day." Dean flashed Janet a smile that was intended to charm her, but instead annoyed her. Ignoring her mute stare, he continued, "I think I've got something to cheer you up. There will be a company party next week." Dean placed a color-printed leaflet on Janet's desk. "And I was hoping that you would agree to be my date."

Janet picked up the leaflet Dean had put on her desk: it was an invitation to Lisa's and Paul's engagement party. "I'll have to go. Lisa is my boss."

"And Paul is everyone's boss," Dean added. "So, yes, I think it's a good idea to attend, but that still doesn't answer my question. Will you be my date?"

Janet lowered her eyes. She wanted to say yes, but she had already promised Lisa that she would talk to Tom Wyman at the party. Not that Janet was particularly interested in keeping her promise, but she knew only too well that when Lisa had her mind set on something, she never took no for an answer. But just because Janet could not say yes did not mean that she had to say no, at least not exactly. "I didn't know it was necessary to have a date for a corporate party."

"Is that a no?" Dean's fallen expression made him look even more endearing.

"I didn't say that." Janet had to admit that she liked toying with him. "Tell you what – I am going to be there, and you are going to be there, so there's no reason why we shouldn't be able to have a drink or two, as coworkers."

"Coworkers." Dean mulled the word over. "I'll take that to start with, as long as you promise me a date in the future."

"The future is unpredictable," replied Janet. Dean Snider was bringing out the flirt in her.

"I'll take the absence of a definite no as a possible yes. And now I will let you get back to your work. I'll be looking forward to next Thursday," added Dean before closing the door behind him.

Me too, Janet thought. Dean Snider certainly was not nearly as dashing or successful as Tom Wyman, but there was just something about the guy that made Janet spark every time she saw him.

∞∞

Dennis Walker sat behind his desk with a smile glinting on his face. He had stopped by Janet Maple's office for a casual chitchat, but when he noticed the papers on her desk, Dennis knew he had struck gold. Dennis considered himself to be in possession of many unique and valuable traits, but the trait that had proven to be exceptionally beneficial to him was a photographic memory. He could literally glance at a page in a book and be able to reconstruct the image in his mind afterwards. This quality had been most useful in his college days and in his career as a trader, but it became invaluable in Dennis's role as an investigator.

As he pretended to look at his computer screen, Dennis reconstructed the details of the data he had glimpsed on Janet's desk. He had only managed to steal a few quick glances, but even that had been enough. Dennis remembered with vivid clarity the cluster of orders from Emperial, Creaton, and Rigel. They were all centered in the company had been in the news lately for sharp decline in its stock price. He had only seen a snippet, but he was fairly certain that the rest of the data would show a similar pattern.

Dennis had been trying to get his hands on this information for a while, but all his attempts to gain access to it had failed. Who would have thought that the firm's legal department would have access to such nitty-gritty data? Normally, the legal folks deemed themselves too important to mar their hands with anything other than legalese mumbo jumbo. Janet Maple, however, did not mind getting her hands dirty, which made Dennis like her all the more. Now, he had a valid reason to get to know Janet better.

Chapter Thirteen

Janet surveyed her reflection in the closet door mirror. The hour of Lisa's party was approaching. For as long as the two of them had been friends, Lisa had always had the spotlight. Not that Janet had any ambitions to outshine Lisa tonight. Even if she could, she would not want to, Lisa's engagement being the reason for the festivities and all, but neither did she want to be fading into the background.

"Hurry up, Janie, we don't want to be late!" Janet heard her mother's voice in the hallway.

A few moments later, Christine Maple appeared in the doorway. "Almost ready?"

Janet nodded. "What do you think?"

Christine walked into the room. "Classy, yet sexy," she proclaimed her assessment of Janet's figure-fitting black cocktail dress, navy pumps and matching clutch. "Oh, this is so exciting! I can't believe that Lisa is engaged. I still remember when the two of you were in grade school."

"That was a long time ago, Mom."

"I know, but as you get older time starts to fly. I'm so glad that the two of you remained friends. Wasn't it sweet of Lisa to get you the job?"

"Actually, Mom, I meant to ask you about that... Did you ask Lisa to get me the job?"

Christine looked back to Janet, bemused. "Well, yes, I did. Didn't she tell you? I ran into Lisa when she was visiting her folks, and I told her that you were between jobs... And like the good friend she is, Lisa came to the rescue. I thought you'd be pleased. I'm sorry – I didn't mean to upset you. Well, I sure hope that you're not mad at me now, especially since my plan worked after all."

"But next time, please talk to me first, okay?" Janet shook her head. She might have been unemployed with bleak career options, but that did not mean that she needed her mother to go around asking her friends to give her a job.

"Honey, what's wrong? You sound awful edgy."

"It's nothing." Janet sighed. "Just nerves."

"I think I know the reason. It's Lisa's engagement, isn't it?"

Janet lowered her eyes, feeling petty. Lisa was Lisa, but they were still friends, and friends were supposed to rejoice at one another's fortune. But in Janet's defense, it was difficult to feel happy about something that was constantly being rubbed into one's face, making one feel inadequate.

Christine patted Janet's arm. "Honey, it's all right; it's only natural to feel this way. "You'll meet someone special soon, I'm sure of it."

"I don't know, Mom. I'm twenty-nine years old; as they say, the clock is ticking. I thought Alex was going to be it... If I at least had a career, I could feel less of a failure."

"What do you mean, a career? Aren't you happy about your current job?"

"I loved my old job."

Christine shook her head. "Janet, honey, you've got to toughen up. I know you had all those dreams about bringing Wall Street to justice, but the truth of the matter is that you've got to keep your own bread buttered. You worked hard at the DA's office, and how did they repay you? By firing you and promoting Alex instead. Now, Lisa has gotten you a good job, and a well-paying job, I might add. What more could you possibly wish for?"

"Nothing." Janet shook her head. "It's a great job – I just need to get used to it."

"Honey, you've got to stop picturing the world as black and white. The truth is that it's mostly gray. No one is ever one hundred percent right, nor is anyone ever one hundred percent wrong."

"What about the crooks who gypped Grandpa out of his life savings? Wouldn't you say that they were one hundred percent wrong?"

Christine nodded. "Yes, they were, but that did not stop them from taking off with their loot and hightailing to Mexico or Ecuador or wherever it was those crooks went. They never got caught, did they?"

"No." Janet sighed. It was idealistic to the point of silliness, but her grandfather's having been a victim of a Ponzi scheme was the main motivation behind her pursuing a career in the DA's office. She wanted to catch the bad guys who had taken away her grandfather's earnings. Well, she had failed at that aspiration as well. By the time Janet started her employment with the DA, the case against the Ponzi scheme organizers who had swindled her grandfather and many others out of their lifesavings had already been closed, with all the guilty parties having made their escape to unknown locations. While at the DA's office, Janet made it her mission to prevent similar crooks from hurting any more trusting grandpas, like her own; she had worked hard, but instead of being rewarded, she got downsized. And now, in an ironic twist of fate, she found herself employed by a firm with suspect operations. Although she was fairly certain that Bostoff Securities was not out to rob widows and orphans, she had already gathered enough information about its operations to understand that they were far from kosher. She needed to figure out what to do next, and she needed to do it quickly.

Her mother's voice brought her back to the present, "Are you going to wear your hair like that?"

Janet sighed. Both her professional and personal lives were derailed, yet she was supposed to care about her hair.

Christine eyed Janet's French twist critically. "Men like it when women wear their hair long and loose."

"Then how come you're not following your own advice?" Janet looked at her mother's practical bob that she had been sporting for as long as Janet remembered.

"I'm married," Christine countered. "Before I met your father, my hair was shoulder-length. Unless I was teaching a class, I always wore it loose." Christine checked her watch. "Good, there's still time."

"Time for what?"

"To do your hair. Don't you move! I'll be right back."

"Come on, Mom. I'm really not in the mood for this."

Christine arched an eyebrow. "Young lady, how can you ever expect to find a man with such an attitude?"

Janet fell back into a chair with a resigned look on her face. By now her mother's incongruities had stopped to baffle her – having Ph.D. in English Literature and teaching Women's Studies as part of her course load did not prevent Christine Maple from maintaining somewhat outdated views on life. Apparently it did not matter how smart or intelligent a woman was: if she wanted to find a man, she'd better wear her hair down or risk remaining alone for all eternity. Still, a part of Janet had to admit that perhaps her mother did have a point. After all, her mother had already been married at Janet's age, and Janet had yet to find her match.

"I found it!" Christine Maple returned, carrying a long object in her hand.

"Oh, no – not that thing!" Janet shook her head after recognizing the alarming-looking contraption in her mother's hands as a curling iron. It was not just any curling iron, but the same curling iron Christine had used on Janet's hair the night of her high school prom.

"I promise I'll be more careful this time," Christine added sheepishly. "Come on, that was just a one-time accident; you can't hold it against me forever."

"You almost burned my scalp."

"Exactly, almost. But in the end no real harm was done, and your hair still looked beautiful."

There Janet had to agree. She had looked beautiful at her high school prom – a fact that would have been so much more worthy of remembering if she had been accompanied to this crucial event by a date she actually liked instead of a jock, Ted Hunter. Yet another disastrous date Janet had Lisa to thank for, only that one had been during one of the most important nights of her life, or so it had seemed at eighteen years of age. *But this really isn't the whole story, is it?* a tiny voice inside Janet's head whispered. *No, it isn't*, Janet admitted. Had she been surer of herself, she would have gone with Justin Trenner. Wonderfully sweet and witty Justin whom Janet had a crush on her entire senior year of high school, which was the year she and Justin worked on the editorial staff of the school newspaper together. Oh, well, these days Justin was happily married to another girl, Valery Meehan, who had been confident enough to be Justin's date that memorable night all those years ago. The past could not be helped, but that did not mean that it had to be given the power to take over the present.

Janet took a decisive look into the mirror. She liked the way her swept-up hair accentuated her cheekbones and showed off the green amethyst earrings she had picked specifically to play up the green of her eyes.

"Mom, I appreciate the effort, but I'm keeping my hair the way it is," Janet said firmly.

"It looks good this way too, baby; it shows off your long, lovely neck. You're going to be the belle of the ball." Christine shrugged apologetically. "I'm sorry, honey, I got carried away. I just wanted to relive the past a bit. I miss my little girl, you know?"

"I know, Mom." *I miss being her too*, Janet thought.

Chapter Fourteen

The Foleys' house was only three blocks away from the Maples' house. As Janet followed her parents along the familiar path, she was reminded of the countless times she had made these very steps: in middle school and in high school, sometimes almost hopping as she rushed to tell her best friend some piece of exciting news, sometimes dragging her feet, aching for consolation. In her own way, Lisa had always been there for Janet, and if she had not always given Janet what she needed or wanted, well, Janet's unwavering acceptance was as much to blame for the rift in their friendship as Lisa's self-centeredness. But while their friendship might not be what it once had been, tonight was Lisa's night, and that was important enough to put the old grudges aside.

"Please hold this, honey." Janet's dad handed her the carton with the chocolate praline cake intended for Lisa's party and rang the bell of the Foleys' house.

Janet twirled the carton strings. The cake, made by the local bakery, had been a staple at all the birthday celebrations she and Lisa had shared throughout the years. Not that Lisa was going to deviate from her strict pre-wedding diet and eat even a sliver of the delicious confection, Janet was willing to bet her life on it, but her dad had insisted on bringing the old favorite. Well, Janet just might have a piece or two herself. After all, she didn't have to worry about fitting into a wedding dress any time soon. No sour grapes, Janet smiled brightly. Tonight was going to be just like old times.

"Janet, dear!" Emily Foley answered the door. "Christine, Matt – come in, come in!"

"Congratulations, Emily." Christine extended her arms in a hug, which Emily reciprocated, air-kissing Christine.

"You look wonderful, Christine," Emily observed. "Any new beauty secrets you'd like to share with your friend?"

"Not particularly. Simply good genes, I guess."

"Just wait till I show you the new cream that we've come out with. I've got samples for you."

"That's very kind of you." Christine nodded politely, but Janet could tell that her mother was annoyed. Why was it that friendship with the Foley women was a never-ending ping-pong of snide comments and comebacks?

"Matthew, you suave devil! You're looking as handsome as ever!" Emily made her way to Janet's father and kissed him on both cheeks, leaving traces of her lipstick.

"Why, thank you, Emily." Matt grinned, wiping the lipstick off his face. "You'd better not let your husband hear you say that or he just might get jealous."

Emily beamed, but Janet's heart sprang with silent glee as she exchanged a silent glance with her mother. She knew her father well enough to recognize the veiled sarcasm in his tone.

"Janie, honey! How long has it been?" Emily placed her palms on either side of Janet's face. "Darling, what skincare line are you using? You have to be careful, you know – I can see those early lines are starting to come in."

Janet balked, Emily's hands clutching her face like a pair of pliers.

Emily clicked her tongue. "Well, never you mind. I've got just the thing for you."

"Janie!" Lisa appeared at the head of the foyer staircase. The girl knew how to make an entrance. As she made her way down the stairs, Lisa gave everyone an ample view of her party dress, and what a dress it was! A tailored lilac bodice of silk with a long, flowing skirt. Many women would run the risk of looking overdressed by wearing such an elaborate gown at a simple house party, but not Lisa. Instead, she made everyone else look drab.

"Darling." Clad in a charcoal suit, Paul had materialized just in time, holding out his hand for Lisa as she reached the bottom of the stairs – a scene so perfect, it made one think of old Hollywood movies.

"Thank you, darling." Lisa placed a demure kiss on Paul's cheek.

Then came the introductions, as Paul shook hands with Janet's parents and Lisa cast about proud and satisfied glances.

"Let's not stand around here," Lisa commanded. "The party is out in the backyard."

The Foleys' backyard had been transformed for the party into an open sky bar, complete with a catered bar station stocked with all kinds of liquor and a handsome bartender. But what caught Janet's attention was not the bar stand. She had seen plenty of those, but the abundance of the intricately laid-out plant and flower beds made the place look like a miniature farm.

Janet got a hold of Lisa's hand. "The yard looks amazing."

"So you like my garden, Janet?" Jack Foley appeared by Janet's side, holding three glasses of champagne in his hands. "It's good to see you, Janet. You look really well."

"Thank you, Mr. Foley. So do you." Janet had always liked Lisa's father. In contrast to his wife's larger-than-life persona, or maybe because of it, Jack Foley was a quiet and reserved man – character qualities that the Foley women could use more of. Now, he looked the same as Janet remembered – slightly older perhaps, but well put together in his conservative suit, collared shirt and tie.

"And you, my dear, look simply stunning." Jack admired his daughter's beautiful gown.

"Thank you, Daddy." Lisa ran her hand over her dress. "I thought it might be a bit much, but what the heck?"

"You look perfect, as always," Jack assured her. "A glass of bubbly to celebrate?" Jack offered a glass to Lisa and Janet.

"To my beautiful daughter and her lovely friend – for the happiness is so much sweeter to enjoy and the sorrow is so much easier to bear when you have friends to share them with."

"An excellent toast." Paul joined in, placing his arm around Lisa. "I'll drink to that."

"And to my future son-in-law," Jack added.

No sooner had they lifted their glasses that they were interrupted by the arrival of new guests: Joe O'Connor and his fiancée, Daphne.

"Joe, you came!" Lisa exclaimed as though she had known Joe her entire life. "And you must be Daphne!" Lisa exchanged kisses with Joe's fiancée, who was looking very much the way Janet remembered her – the same heavily made-up face, only now she was dressed in a barely-there spaghetti strap dress of crimson red.

Janet's lips tightened in a forced smile. It was just like Lisa to invite Joe and his fiancée without telling her. No sour grapes, Janet reminded herself. She could have had her chance with Joe in law school, but she had chosen Alex instead, and now it was too late for second guesses.

"Hi there, Janet." Joe stole a quick glance at Janet's outfit as he kissed her cheek. "It's always good to see you."

"You too, Joe."

"It's Janet, right?" Daphne stood vigilantly by Joe's side.

Janet nodded. "It's great to see you again, Daphne."

The party continued, with Lisa's aunts and uncles taking their turns to say hello to Janet, invariably remembering how 'adorable' Janet had been as a little girl and never failing to inquire whether she was seeing anyone 'special,' and upon hearing that she was not, consoling her that her 'big day' was bound to come soon.

After half an hour of such mortification, Janet decided that she needed a break. She still remembered the layout of the Foleys' house like the back of her own hand, so she crept out of the now crowded backyard and snuck into one of the guest bathrooms. There, in the tiled solitude, Janet turned her attention to the bathroom mirror.

Before she had arrived at the Foleys' house, Janet had felt confident about her appearance. She had been 'good' the entire week, consuming mostly salads and oatmeal, and shunning sweets, the diligent regimen resulting in her having shed two pounds. But now, all she could think of were the 'early lines' Emily Foley had warned her about. In the harsh light of the Foleys' bathroom, Janet saw two faint creases stemming treacherously from the outside of her nostrils to the corners of her mouth – smile lines. They were barely there, but they were there nonetheless, as were the two faint lines on her forehead from her habit of wrinkling her forehead whenever she was surprised or upset, and lately, she had plenty of things to be upset about. Well, she was already twenty-nine. In a year, she would be thirty. Perhaps Emily Foley's snide remark did have a grain of truth. Janet would look into a preventive skincare routine, but she'd be damned if she would turn to Emily Foley for advice. And in the meantime, there was the rest of Lisa's party to get through.

Janet pressed her forehead against her hands and closed her eyes, as she counted till ten, taking deep, even breaths. She opened her eyes and straightened her shoulders. She was as good as new.

"Janet, I was looking for you!" Lisa ambushed Janet in the hallway, ruining Janet's intention to rejoin the party inconspicuously. "Where have you been? There's someone I want you to meet."

"I had to pee," Janet lied.

Lisa wrinkled her nose at the excessive detail. "Never mind. Andrew is here. Remember him?"

Did she ever – Janet had to stifle a groan. "Vaguely."

"Well, he remembers you." Lisa beamed. "And trust me, he looks nothing like he used to, and he's single, with his own Internet business."

"What kind of business?" Janet asked out of politeness. Even if Andrew Foley became a millionaire ten times over, he would still remain the same pest she remembered him to be.

"It's a dating service, but what difference does that make? He's pulling in a seven-figure income, and the last time I heard, he was going for an IPO."

Great, Janet thought. The ghost of Lisa's horny younger cousin who had been the bane of her existence throughout adolescence had come back to haunt her, reincarnated as a dating service mogul.

"Let's go already. I can't wait for the two of you to see each other."

Neither can I. Janet shook her head, thinking that the only way this evening could get any worse would be if the party were to be raided by wild bears.

"Andrew!" Lisa squealed to the back of a tall, suit-clad man.

"Lisa!" The man turned around and Janet was in for a surprise. Andrew Foley had changed, and for once, Lisa had not lied. He looked nothing like Janet remembered him. The scrawny, sex-obsessed teenager had blossomed into a tall, broad-shouldered stud.

Janet stood back quietly, thinking that it would be unlikely for Andrew to remember her, but was surprised again.

"Janet, so good to see you." Andrew's eyes remained fixed on her face, which was a stark contrast to Janet's memory of Andrew's furtive glances directed at her boobs.

"Well, I'll leave you two to get reacquainted," Lisa excused herself.

"Could I get you a drink?" Andrew raised his glass, motioning to Janet's empty hands.

"Sure – a whiskey sour." Why not? Janet thought. This was a party, and she was finally starting to enjoy herself.

"So, what have you been up to, Janet Maple?" Andrew handed Janet her drink.

"Oh, nothing much – went to law school, got a job."

"I see." Andrew nodded. "Any interesting men in your life at the moment?"

Janet bristled. Apparently, Andrew Foley had not changed that much after all.

"A purely professional question," Andrew added in a voice that made it clear that these days he had no lack of female attention. "Did Lisa mention that I run a dating service?"

"Yes, she did. How did you get into that line of work?"

"It was a natural progression of things I suppose." Andrew touched his goatee in a pondering gesture. "As you remember, I wasn't exactly Mr. Popularity in my teenage years, so naturally, I tried all kinds of ways to get in with the ladies. When 'normal' dating failed to do it for me, I turned to online websites, and there, I finally struck gold. You see, the world of online dating is very different from the face-to-face dating. Online, you can be anyone you want to be. Before long, all my friends started coming to me for help to write their online profiles to get girls…"

"But the truth will come out once you meet the person face to face," Janet could not resist contradicting.

Andrew shook his head. "The whole idea is to get the person attracted to you before the face-to-face meeting. If the process is paced correctly, the two parties have already become so attracted to one another's online personalities that once personal contact takes place, their virtual attraction will render any of the real-world shortcomings inconsequential."

Janet humored Andrew by nodding. Clearly, he had invented his own dating reality.

Andrew continued, "That's the premise of my business venture. Date Magic dot com is an online dating space where people get the individualized attention they deserve. Depending on the level of membership, we offer services from writing your online profile to first-date coaching."

"Sounds fascinating," Janet managed.

"You should try it sometime. I can hook you up with a complimentary membership."

Janet forced a smile, wondering how she could ever repay Lisa for this humiliation.

"Just yanking your chain." Andrew chuckled. "Imagine what a pompous ass I would have been if I had actually meant it? Oh, I think that's the signal for the dinner seating," Andrew remarked, pointing at the trail of guests making their way inside the house.

The two of them joined the rest of the guests, and Andrew got hijacked by one of Lisa's aunts, who was intent on finding out whether Andrew's business catered to the fifty-plus crowd.

"What did I tell you – is he hot or what?" Lisa whispered into Janet's ear just as she was about to take her seat at the dinner table. "You can thank me later for the seating arrangements."

Before Janet could say another word, Lisa had vanished, leaving Janet all alone in the company of Lisa's great uncle who was seated to Janet's left. She glanced longingly at her parents who were seated at the opposite side of the table. This was going to be a long evening.

"What a pleasant surprise." Andrew took his seat next to Janet's. "Excuse me for being kidnapped by Aunt Agnes. She is getting over a divorce and is desperate to meet new men."

This time Janet's smile was genuine.

Surprisingly, his dating philosophy aside, Andrew proved to be a wonderful dinner conversationalist. Intercepting Lisa's meaningful glance, Janet had to admit that this time Lisa had finally come through. When she caught Joe O'Connor's eyes following her and glimpsed Daphne's sour expression, Janet's evening had become complete. She might be single, but she was still desirable.

Before long, the dinner was over. Guests lingered with after-dinner drinks, slowly starting to take their leave. The party was coming to an end, and so was her unexpected blind date with Andrew, if it could even be called that. Janet said goodbye to Lisa and Paul and Emily and Jack Foley. She was about to join her parents for the walk back to the house when Andrew caught up with her.

"Would you like to take a drive?" he asked. "I have a kick-ass car," he added.

"Sure." Janet smiled, and why not? The night, as they said it, was young. "Let me just tell my parents not to wait up."

"I'll wait in the driveway."

A few moments later, Janet found Andrew right where he had said he would be.

"I'm parked a few blocks down," he said.

Together they walked down the deserted sidewalk, the only light being that of the houses they passed on the way.

"Here we are." Andrew opened the door of his yellow Ferrari.

"You drive a Ferrari?"

"Do you think it's too much?"

"No, I don't. I think it's just perfect." Janet climbed inside the car. The low sports car seating exuded thrill and sex.

Andrew climbed in beside her and within moments, they were off.

"You're driving too fast," Janet shrieked.

"Are you worried I might get a ticket?"

"Maybe."

"That's very sweet of you, but you needn't worry. A very high-ranking officer of the local police is an old buddy of mine, and he's also a very good client."

"Really?" Janet's eyebrows rose in disbelief. "What's his name?"

"You'll just have to take my word for it. I can't reveal his identity. Professional confidentiality."

"Can you at least tell me where we're going?"

"You'll see." Andrew pressed on the gas pedal, making the engine roar.

"What is this place?" Janet asked after the car had stopped. It was dark, and she had a hard time making out their surroundings.

"Don't you remember?"

Janet squinted, the recognition coming to her in a flash. How could she have forgotten? This has been a popular make-out spot in high school, and probably still was for the kids who filled the school's halls these days.

"I just thought it might be fun to come here," Andrew offered.

Janet felt tension creeping over her; suddenly, the night had lost all of its charm.

"I really like you, Janet," Andrew murmured, moving in closer – so close that Janet could sense his breath on her neck. "I'd like to get to know you again."

Janet drew away. Again implied that they had known each other at some point in time, but aside from Andrew's lustful ogling, there had not been much interaction between them prior to tonight.

"There is chemistry between us, don't deny it," Andrew continued.

Janet lingered; yes, there had been something a few moments ago. Who knew, their banter might have even led to a kiss at the end of the evening, but now, all she felt was revulsion.

Before she could get out of his reach, Andrew's hand was on her waist, sliding down to her bottom, and his wet, sloppy mouth was covering hers. His tongue was making its way inside Janet's mouth like an eager lizard, as Andrew's hands unzipped the back of her dress with alarming deftness.

"Get away from me!" Janet shrieked. "What the hell are you doing?"

"What the hell are you doing?" Andrew snapped. "I thought you wanted this."

"Me?"

"Yeah, you. Why did you agree to go for a ride with me then?"

"I don't know; we were having a nice time. I just wanted to go for a drive. Did you think I was going to have sex with you in your car?" Janet wrapped her arms around herself protectively.

"Don't flatter yourself, honey. These days I don't have to beg for sex. Women are throwing themselves at me. Lisa had chewed my ears off with talks about how desperate you were to meet someone. You looked so lonely at the party; I just wanted to do you a favor."

"I don't need any 'favors,' especially from the likes of you." Janet hurriedly zipped up her dress. "Have a nice life, Andrew. I hope your IPO tanks."

"Hey, there's no reason to get all worked up about this. Come on, I'll drive you home..."

But Janet did not even bother to reply as she made her way uphill to the road. It was a half-hour walk to her parents' house, but she'd rather walk barefoot on broken glass than spend another second in Andrew Foley's car.

Chapter Fifteen

On Monday morning Janet sat in her office, tallying up the results of the weekend, which even taking her most humiliating adolescent memories into account had been the most embarrassing weekend of her life. Blankly staring into her computer screen, Janet compiled a mental list of all the indignities she had endured in the past two days: attending an engagement party as the only single guest under the age of fifty– check, being harassed by your friend's mother regarding your appearance – check, being badgered by the same friend's relatives about your personal life – check, and last, but by far not the least, becoming an unwitting object of lust of a formerly puny, sex-obsessed teenage pest, who had turned into a much better looking, but still equally sex-obsessed man.

Janet could not help a sad smile at her tally. Perhaps, she should start a dating blog about the mortifications of being single in your late twenties. Given the amount of single women in New York, it ought to be a popular subject. That would be one way of turning lemons into lemonade. If she got this second career off the ground, she would no longer have to worry about her employment at Bostoff Securities or the nature of Bostoff's business. For a moment the possibility seemed tempting, except Janet worried that most women would not relate, for she was beginning to suspect that she was an aberration when it came to her bad luck on the love front. She knew for a fact that in her entire life Lisa Foley had not encountered even a fraction of the embarrassment that Janet had suffered through this weekend.

But as much as she would have loved to wallow in self-pity, Janet had much more pressing matters to attend to: like the matter of her employment, which was as precarious as her love life. If indeed her research would confirm her initial suspicion about Bostoff Securities, she would have some very tough decisions to make. She was just about to focus on the report for Friday when there was a knock on the door. This time Janet had been vigilant enough to keep the door of her office closed. She quickly put the papers away. "Come in!"

"Am I interrupting anything?" Lisa sauntered in.

"Oh, no, I was just doing some research," Janet replied, her heart beating wildly. She wasn't lying, but then she wasn't telling the truth either.

Lisa rolled her eyes, indicating that such a subject was not worthy of her interest. "Janie, I'm so sorry about the party. What a jerk Andrew turned out to be! I meant to call you on Sunday, but Paul and I were busy looking at catering venues."

"How did you hear about what happened with Andrew?"

"The prick had the nerve to complain to me about it. He got all upset about me dragging him out for nothing. Apparently, my engagement is not worthy of his attention; he also had to score with you."

Janet's irritation spiked. Lisa's narcissism was unending. Never mind that courtesy of Lisa, Janet had been pawed by Lisa's sleazoid cousin in the middle of nowhere; in the end, Lisa was still the victim.

"What exactly did you tell Andrew about me, Lisa?"

Lisa fiddled with her blazer. "Oh, nothing much. That you were going to be at my party..."

"Are you sure? Then how come he knew about me being single? He also used the word 'desperate.'"

"Oh, I might have mentioned that you were single, but I never said a word about desperation. Clearly, you have no reason to be desperate."

There it was again: Lisa's old trick of switching the tables on you, but this time Janet was not budging. "Do me a favor, Lisa, stop setting me up on dates."

"Suit yourself." Lisa rose from her chair. "Don't forget about the company party this Thursday."

"I'll be there, but don't even think about setting me up with that Tom Wyman character."

"Not to worry. Your personal life is now solely in your capable hands. Rest assured, there will be no interference from poor, sloppy me." Lisa cocked her head as she began to slowly exit Janet's office.

Janet guessed from Lisa's measured walk that she was awaiting an apology, but remained silent. Her boss or not, there was a limit as to how much humiliation one person was allowed to inflict upon another.

Lisa stopped short before exiting through the door, and Janet's heart lurched. Could it be that Lisa was going to apologize? That would be an unprecedented occurrence worthy of the Guinness Book of World Records.

"Oh, and I almost forgot, I'm going to look at wedding dresses next weekend. I expect you to be there."

Janet nodded; a promise was a promise, and she had agreed to be Lisa's maid of honor. "I'll be there."

"Good." Lisa shifted her feet, clearly dissatisfied with the absence of an apology. "Well, I'll see you later."

₧₨

Dennis Walker sat in his boss's office for an urgently scheduled briefing. It was lunch-time, and Dennis had left his post at Bostoff Securities under a pretext of a doctor's appointment. When working undercover, he hated briefing meetings during business hours because of the risk of being tracked down, but his boss had made it clear that it was imperative for them to speak, and Dennis had no choice but to agree. He had been careful when he left Bostoff, and to his knowledge, he did not see anyone trailing him.

"Sorry I'm late, Dennis." Hamilton Kirk walked into the room, carrying a cup of coffee. At fifty-five, Ham Kirk was lean and trim, thanks to daily six a.m. workouts at the gym. As usual, he was dressed in a dark gray wool suit, white shirt, and argyle-patterned tie.

He must have an inexhaustible supply of argyle ties, Dennis thought of his boss. Today's tie was in a navy color scheme, but Dennis had witnessed Ham wear green, beige, and even maroon variations, but always in an argyle pattern and always accompanied by a dark gray suit, of which Ham too had to have an endless supply.

"Would you like a cup?" Ham offered with belated hospitality. "I could ask Linda to make another cup."

"It's all right." Dennis shook his head. He just wanted this tete-a-tete to be over with. As far as bosses went, Ham Kirk was generally a good boss, but he could be a real nuisance when he was in one of his sour moods, and by the prim expression on his boss's face, Dennis could tell that Ham Kirk was in one of his moods today.

"Well, then, let's get right to it, shall we?" Ham rested his fingertips on the coffee cup. "What have you got on Bostoff Securities so far, Dennis?"

Dennis had to make a mental effort to maintain a neutral expression. He had been sending regular updates to his boss, so why the silly spectacle?

"Well, sir, not much has changed since my last report," Dennis formed the sentence deliberately to pique Kirk.

"Not much, huh? Well, that's disconcerting. In fact, that's the reason why I called you in here today, Dennis."

"But sir, with all due respect, undercover work takes time. Now that I have access to Bostoff's data, I can confirm that Emperial, along with Creaton, Rigel, Gemini, and Sphinx are Bostoff's top clients. As you know, these companies have previously been suspected of organized market manipulation, yet the lack of concrete evidence prevented—" Dennis did not get to finish his sentence.

"Yes, I am very well aware of this fact, Dennis, but so is the FBI. I just got a call from their white collar crime desk this morning. Apparently, FBI's white collar crime desk has been doing some digging on Bostoff, and now, they are requesting assistance with the investigation from every regulatory agency. I'm afraid Bostoff is no longer our case. We've lost any chances for a lead that we had."

"But, sir, how can the Feds encroach on our case?" Dennis burst out, knowing full well that the question was rhetorical. After all, he had worked for the Feds for three years, and he knew that the eight-hundred-pound gorilla that they were, the Feds always got their way. "We've already done so much of the work. Granted, after we have gathered the information necessary for the investigation, we will pass it on to the Feds for criminal prosecution, but in the current state of the investigation, involving another party could put the entire operation at risk."

"What a smooth talker you are, Dennis, but I'm afraid you can't bullshit your way out of this one. The Feds are after glory. They've ballooned their staff, spawning all kinds of useless divisions, and now, they need to justify their existence with achievements, and what better way to do that than to snatch someone else's catch?"

"So that's it? We're done?"

A shrewd smile appeared on Ham's lips. "Not quite – I got us an extension. Three more weeks was all I was able to get. They agreed that if we're able to get the evidence to convict the buggers, we'll be the first to announce the results of the investigation, then hand it over to the Feds for further action."

"Three weeks," Dennis repeated grimly.

"And not a day more."

"Sir, I'd like to ask for your permission to recruit an internal source."

Ham's eyes glowed. "You found an inside source?"

"Yes, sir; a woman who works in Bostoff Securities' legal department—"

"Oh, Christ, Dennis, don't tell me that you're chasing skirts instead of doing your job."

"Sir, this is strictly professional," Dennis countered. "Although Janet Maple also happens to be quite an attractive woman, my interest in her is only driven by her potential value as an information source," Dennis replied, almost convinced by his own words.

"Fine, do whatever it takes, Dennis, but you'd better come through on this one. Don't make me regret giving the assignment to you instead of Laskin. I don't intend giving up my promotion to the Feds, and I presume, you do understand what's going to happen if I get passed on my promotion?"

Dennis nodded.

"That's right, you can forget about moving up in this place. You're dismissed, son. Now get back to work."

With as much dignity as he could master under the circumstances, Dennis bowed out of Ham's office.

Walking along the hallway, Dennis tried to regroup. His professional pride had been bruised by Ham's chewing him out. Sure, it was easy for Ham to rant. When was the last time the old goat had done any hands-on work? All he did was receive updates from his employees, basking in the glory of the accomplishments brought in by his charges. Dennis checked his watch: it was twelve-thirty in the afternoon, which left him just enough time to stop by the section of the floor where the junior analysts sat. As part of the mentorship program that had been recently introduced at the Treasury, Dennis had taken several pretty girls under his wing. At the moment, wide-eyed adoration was just what he needed to boost his bruised ego. But halfway before he reached his destination, Dennis was interrupted by yet another unpleasant encounter.

"Dennis Walker, what a pleasant surprise!" Peter Laskin greeted Dennis with affected cordiality. "How's life in the fast lane?"

"Hello, Peter. You're looking well." Dennis noted with satisfaction that Laskin's bald spot seemed to have grown bigger since he'd last seen him. "Is that a new haircut?"

"Why, thank you, Dennis, you're most kind." Laskin smoothed his hair, or what had remained of it. "It's been a while since we last spoke. You are a rare sight these days."

"Well, as you know, field work does not leave much time for loitering around the office."

"Ha-ha, very funny. I must say that I've been busy analyzing emails of Bostoff Securities employees, courtesy of your undercover work there. Are you sure they're not feeding you dummies, my friend? There's absolutely nothing there." Laskin raised his hands, spreading out his fingers for added effect.

"You just wait and see," Dennis replied. "There'll be plenty soon."

"From your mouth to God's ears," Laskin called after Dennis's irked back.

⁊⁃

"I'll be right there. Show them into the conference room," Jon Bostoff instructed his secretary over the intercom. He consulted his watch. David Muller, the Emperial honcho, was right on time for their meeting, but where was Tom Wyman? Irritated, Jon rose from his chair. He had rather expected Wyman to arrive ahead of time for the meeting, what with all the hefty fees Jon had been paying him. But now it looked like he would have to make small talk with Muller while waiting for Wyman to join them, and Jon Bostoff detested small talk.

"Sorry I'm late, Jon." Tom Wyman walked brusquely through the door of Jon's office.

"It's about time; Muller is here already."

Wyman nodded. "Where are we meeting him?"

"In the conference room downstairs. I didn't want him wandering around the trading floor."

"So, you're sure that we're bulletproof to go ahead with the arrangement?" Jon asked Wyman as they walked to the elevators.

"To the extent that the legal system allows, yes."

Blasted lawyers – always with the caveats. Jon resisted the urge to snap at Wyman; after all, it was not as though he were in a position to back out of the deal now.

"David, great to see you again." Jon shook Muller's hand heartily, feigning affability as best as he could. He detested the pompous prick, but now was not the time to show it, for Muller's scheme was bound to generate some serious cash.

Muller answered Jon's handshake with his lizard-like grip. "You're looking well, Jon. Have you been working out?"

Jon shook his head. "Nothing more than usual: just good, clean living."

Muller chuckled, shaking his longish blond locks. "Whatever it is, it's working. I've just started a new diet myself: no glutens, no carbs, and no dairy, and I've upped my gym time. I'm feeling super."

"You look great." Jon smiled obligingly. Muller was obsessed with healthy living. At six two, he did not have an extra ounce of fat on his bony frame. Did the guy want to become a skeleton?

"But as much fun as it is talking about fitness, that's not what we're here for," Muller cut to the chase, pulling out a chair at the head of the rectangular table and motioning for everyone else to sit down.

The pompous prick. Jon took his seat next to Muller, making a mental note to replace the rectangular table with a round one.

"So, what are your thoughts on my proposal, Jon?" Muller steepled his long fingers.

Jon exchanged a quick glance with Wyman, and after receiving a discreet nod, went ahead. "Bostoff Securities can commit to the volumes we discussed."

"Quit the cryptic speak, Jon. Are you in or what?"

"Yes, David, I'm in."

"Good. So here's what's going to happen. I've handpicked a number of stocks that are ripe for the picking. They are overvalued and overpriced, and we're going to bring them to the levels where they belong and make a ton of money in the process."

Jon adjusted his cufflinks nervously. "You're not going to do anything too obvious, are you? We would not want to get spotted by Market Watch, would we?"

"Not to worry, Jonnie – we've got everything covered. You don't think I'd be going into this sort of thing alone, do you? There are some very big names involved besides me, and the targets we picked do not have the clout to retaliate. Take this one for instance: Date Magic dot com - an online dating site going public! Their offering price is thirty-five dollars, and analysts are predicting first-day trading price of forty. That's an overly optimistic prognosis for a site that caters to fat, single people, don't you think?"

"There's a dating site dedicated to fat, single people?"

"I was speaking metaphorically, Jon. I don't know whether they are fat or thin, but they are bound to be losers to have to use the Internet to get dates. Anyway, I'd say the true price level should be somewhere at ten, don't you think? Bulls get rich, bears get rich, but pigs get slaughtered. Well, the dumb hogs who invested in this crackpot of an IPO belong in a slaughterhouse. And trust me, even if any of the investors or so called 'company management' were to raise a peep, the stock price decline would be attributed to another capricious market turn."

"It certainly sounds like you thought everything through," Jon conceded, assuring himself that the business structure that Tom Wyman had set up for him would provide iron-clad cover.

"Gentlemen, I look forward to doing even more business with you." David Muller rose from his chair. "You'll be hearing from me soon, Jon."

"That guy doesn't beat around the bush," said Wyman once Muller had left the room.

"Are you sure we're covered on all fronts, Tom?" Jon locked Wyman's glance, determined to get a concrete answer this time. This would not be the first time for Bostoff Securities to be accepting questionable orders from Muller and his posse of shark hedge fund managers, but it would be the first time for doing it on such a massive scale.

"You can sleep soundly at night, Jon; you're covered. Unless someone gets their hands on the formation documents, there's no way to tie Bostoff Securities to Impala Group. And to get those, they'd have to break into my office: an undertaking that has about the same probability of success as hacking into Fort Knox."

"Thank you, Tom. I knew there was a reason for footing those hefty bills of yours – it's called peace of mind. By the way, how's that new girl in Legal doing?"

"I haven't seen much of her lately, but I can't imagine anything to worry about."

"Do me a favor, Tom. Stick close to her at the party this Thursday. I want you to make sure she's not suspecting anything."

"There's a party this Thursday?"

"Didn't you get the invite? It's my brother's engagement party."

"I'll be there, Jon."

"And do me a favor. From now on, don't say a word about company business to my brother unless you discuss it with me first."

"Sure thing, Jon. We've already been over this. I thought that you wanted Janet Maple to lighten the bill load, so I've given her a very basic overview of the structure; she couldn't have possibly made much sense out of it, but I'll be sure to keep an eye on her."

Chapter Sixteen

While on his way to Janet Maple's office, Dennis Walker was thinking of a pretext for stopping by. He would start on a light note – something along the lines of Monday blues, and from there he would progress to having a drink after work. Ordinarily, he would have waited until the office party that was to take place on Thursday, but with the new condensed timeframe given to him by his boss, time was a luxury Dennis did not have.

He was just about to stroll into Janet's office when he heard her voice coming through the doorway. She was on the phone. A little eavesdropping never hurt anybody. He pressed his back against the wall and strained his ear to hear Janet's conversation. It would not do to get caught red-handed, so in case anyone were to pass by, he had a manila folder filled with important-looking office papers loosely positioned in his hand, ready to drop to the floor at any moment.

"Hey, Katie. Yes, it was pretty awful. Yes, Andrew was there – Lisa's horny, geeky cousin. Yes, I'd love to have a drink after work – six o'clock sounds great."

Where? Dennis thought desperately. *Six o'clock where?*

"Perfect. I'll see you at the Blue Orchard at six."

Dennis heard the sound of the telephone receiver being replaced and tiptoed down the hall. When it came to establishing contact, accidental encounters were so much better than arranged dates.

Dennis Walker arrived at the Blue Orchard at five-thirty. He figured that would give him enough time to get a spot by the bar and find a pretty girl to chat up. If his plan were to work, he had to look like he actually had a reason to be there other than stalking Janet. He loosened his tie and hung his shabby suit jacket over the back of his chair. This Dean Snider routine was getting tiresome. Well, at least he was wearing a decent shirt, and his natural charm would just have to compensate for the rest of his appearance. However, the fake glasses went into Dennis's jacket pocket. Dean Snider's drab persona had not gotten him very far, and since his boss had just upped the stakes, Dennis Walker was going to change the rules and infuse some much-needed swagger into Dean Snider.

Dennis eyed the bar crowd, skimming past the usual suit types and eagerly smiling career women who accompanied them. He soon found what he was looking for – a pretty blonde by the other side of the bar. She was typing on her Blackberry intently, no doubt simply keying in gibberish while she waited for her friends to arrive so as not to appear unoccupied. Dennis slunk off his chair and made his way to where the girl was sitting. As he approached her chair, Dennis got a quick glimpse of her Blackberry screen. His hunch had been correct; the screen was filled with meaningless lines of letters and numbers. He pulled the chair next to the girl, but she was too intent on trying to look busy to notice him.

"Apple martini," Dennis said.

"Excuse me?" the girl's tone was chilly.

"Your favorite drink – it's apple martini, isn't it?"

The blonde's eyes widened. "How did you guess?"

"I have a gift." Dennis grinned. This was ridiculously easy. He signaled to the bartender. "Two apple martinis, please."

The girl put her Blackberry away and eyed him appraisingly. Dennis watched her eyes linger undecidedly over his jacket, grow warmer on his shirt, and finally flash with approval upon reaching his face. He was a handsome-looking fella, even if he did say so himself.

"To unexpected encounters." Dennis raised his drink.

"To pleasant unexpected encounters." The girl ingested the majority of her drink in one gulp.

Dennis took a tentative sip. He sincerely hoped that he had not been mistaken in his mark. A loud drunken scene would ruin his plan. "And may I ask what a pretty girl like yourself is doing all by herself in a bar?"

"Who said I was by myself? I could be waiting for my boyfriend," the girl added playfully.

Dennis relaxed. He had not been mistaken after all. His plan was to flirt with the blonde long enough for Janet to notice him. Once the blonde's date would arrive, Dennis would safely excuse himself and exhibit great surprise at running into Janet, saying something to the effect of this being a small world. "Secretive, huh? Well, may I at least know your name?"

"Summer."

"That's a beautiful name. I'm Dean."

"No, it isn't. My mom was a rock star groupie and I think she was high when she named me." Summer finished the rest of her drink. "Do you believe that people's names determine their destinies?"

"I can't say that I do," Dennis replied distractedly. His attention was occupied by the sight of Janet Maple walking into the bar. Her usual no-nonsense business suit and put-up hair made her stand apart from the rest of the women with their décolletage and tangled manes.

"Well, I think it does. Take me for example. My name is Summer. What does Summer stand for? Crazy, fun time, which is exactly what men want from me, and once they get it, they just keep on moving along. Do you know that I've never been in a relationship that lasted longer than a month? That is if you can even call a one-month affair a relationship."

"I'm sure you could call it that," Dennis conceded.

"And you were right," Summer burst out. "I am here alone because my date bailed."

Dennis blinked, unsure of how to react to Summer's candidness. Truth be told, he didn't really care. By now, Janet Maple had been joined by a friend – a tall, lanky redhead. What Dennis really wanted to do was to eavesdrop on their conversation, which was impossible due to yet another flaw in what was now turning out to be a hastily and poorly designed plan: he had expected Janet and her friend to sit by the bar, but the two women chose to sit at a table instead. The only solution was to quickly disengage himself from Summer and think of a way to join Janet and her friend.

Summer kept droning on, and Dennis was starting to lose his patience.

"Take my mother for example, she has been married three times, and each time she changed her last name. No wonder she has no direction in life. I mean, how could she possibly become her own person? She's had so many last names, it's dizzying!" Summer's voice grew dangerously acrimonious. "You're not really listening to me, are you?"

"Yes, I am listening," Dennis replied distractedly. He really could not care less about what Summer thought. He had noticed Janet and her redheaded friend glance at him surreptitiously and whisper excitedly afterwards, and he wanted to know what they were saying about him.

"What did I just say then?" Summer demanded.

"Excuse me?" Dennis nearly snorted his drink through his nostrils. This was getting perilously ridiculous.

"You heard me. What did I just say?" Summer placed her hands on her hips.

Dennis tried to bring Summer's exact words to memory, but failed – she had been babbling something about her mother... "Your mother has been married three times," Dennis finally remembered.

"Is that fella bothering you, sweetheart?" A middle-aged playboy squeezed his trim body next to Summer's chair.

"He's doing quite the opposite; he's ignoring me."

"A beautiful girl like you? How's that possible?"

"Yes, he is." Summer pouted, no doubt hoping to elicit jealousy from Dennis, a ploy that under normal circumstances might have worked, but now it only provided a much-needed means of escape.

"I'm afraid I was," Dennis admitted. "But I'm sure a gentleman such as yourself will appreciate Summer for the entertaining conversationalist that she is. Summer, it was a pleasure meeting you." Dennis tossed two twenties on the bar stand, and, without waiting for a response from Summer, he started to make his way to Janet's table. His face had already assumed an expression of surprise at running into a coworker so unexpectedly: it was a small world indeed.

ഇൗ

Janet took a long swallow of her martini. After the traumatizing weekend, she needed a drink.

"So, let me get this straight," Katie said after she had downed some of her whiskey sour. "You got pawed by Andrew Foley – Lisa's sex-obsessed cousin who used to ogle you when you were teenagers?"

"Affirmative." Janet took another long swallow of her dirty martini and popped one of the blue cheese-stuffed olives into her mouth. "These are delicious."

"And then what did you do?"

"I told him that he was a jerk and walked to my parents' house."

"I meant did you tell Lisa that she's an idiot for setting you up with him?"

"I did tell her to stop setting me up on dates." Janet reflected on that morning's conversation with her boss. In all the years she had known Lisa, it was the firmest stand Janet had ever taken with her.

"And what did she say? Did she at least apologize?"

"In her own way," Janet answered evasively. As annoyed as she was with Lisa, she was not in the mood for bashing her. After all, the two of them were bound by many ties. Lisa was still her boss, and Janet was going to be the maid of honor in Lisa's wedding to Paul Bostoff.

"And how are the wedding plans progressing?" Katie asked, as though reading Janet's thoughts. "Has she got you running around on a twenty-four-hour itinerary, catering to her every whim?"

"Look, Lisa can be unreasonable at times, but I'm not going to complain about the wedding. She has asked me to be her maid of honor and I agreed. Let's leave it at that." To indicate that this topic of conversation had been closed, Janet bit into another olive, but the sight of the dark-blond man by the bar made her choke.

"You okay?" Katie pushed a glass of water toward Janet.

Janet thankfully gulped the soothing liquid. "Don't look now, but there's a guy from work by the bar."

"Is he cute?" Katie whispered conspiratorially, her eyes darting to the very place where Janet told her not to look.

"Don't stare at him!"

"Geez, relax, will ya? There's a huge crowd – I don't even know which one he is."

"The tall one, in a blue shirt."

"The James Dean look-alike with the slutty blonde?"

"Yeah, that's him."

"He's cute," Katie pronounced her verdict after a momentary deliberation. "What does he do?"

"He is in IT."

Katie nodded approvingly. "A solid and practical profession. I'm getting sick and tired of dating lawyers. They are the most self-absorbed and narcissistic bunch of men on the planet. Litigation lawyers are the worst – so pompous. Don't ever date a lawyer."

"Oh, I think I've learned my lesson on that one," Janet replied, wondering if Katie had forgotten about Alex.

"I'm sorry, Janet. I wasn't thinking," Katie instantly caught on. "But back to the present. What's the story with the cute IT guy?"

"No story." Janet finished the last of her drink. "We chat at work sometimes."

"We chat at work sometimes? Come on, Janet, it's me you're talking to. Do you like him or what?"

Janet nodded. "He is kind of cute, but…."

"But what?"

"Dating at work could be complicated, and I don't want to complicate things too much now," Janet added quickly. She certainly had plenty of things to be anxious about at work without having to worry about Dean Snider.

"Things are always complicated—that's the nature of life. Sounds to me like someone is being a chicken."

"Sounds to me like someone is being overly nosy," Janet shot back, already regretting having mentioned Dean. "Besides, he's clearly not interested in me: as you can see, he's got a date."

"A date, please! I'm sure it's some girl he just met at the bar. Speaking of which, there's an interesting development." Katie's eyes darted toward the bar again.

Even though she knew she should not, Janet let her eyes follow the direction of Katie's glance.

"Looks like our Romeo has a rival." Katie grinned.

Janet could not resist a smile. It was amusing to watch Dean Snider being forced out by a middle-aged Burt Reynolds look-alike. Apparently Dean's date preferred older men, and even though Janet did not have any plans for herself and Dean, she was glad to know that at least for tonight he too was single. Unless, of course, he managed to pick up another girl, which given Dean's good looks and the fact that the night was still young was quite a viable possibility. Oh well... Janet stole one last glance at Dean to wish him a mental good night, but she had not been quick enough. Their eyes locked, and Dean's hand rose in a wave of recognition, as he started to advance in the direction of their table.

"Quick! Look the other way," Janet whispered. "He is walking over here."

"Oh, goody." Katie rubbed her palms excitedly. "This is going to be fun."

A moment later, Dean was smiling at her with that charming smile of his, his blue eyes shining with a mischievous spark. "Janet – fancy meeting you here!"

Janet noticed how different he looked outside of the office. He had taken his glasses off and loosened his tie – insignificant alterations, but somehow his whole demeanor channeled a sexy and mysterious vibe.

"Dean, what a surprise!" Janet's voice sounded much more eager than she had planned. "Do you come here often?"

"Not really. Just stopped by for a drink after work, and now that I've run into you, I'm glad that I did." Dean smiled.

Before Janet could think of an equally flirty remark, Katie cut in, "Your date gave you the slip, huh?"

"You could say that." Dean grinned, not flustered in the least. "I think she prefers older men," he added.

"I love a man who can be a good sport about being rejected," Katie approved.

Wishing Katie would be quiet, Janet made a belated introduction, "Dean, this is my friend, Katie Addison."

"It's a pleasure to meet you, Katie." Dean smiled. "May I join you ladies for a drink? I'm in need of recompense after tonight's fiasco," he added. The tone of his voice, however, was anything but embarrassed; on the contrary, it was playful.

He is used to randomly picking up girls at bars and replacing them just as frequently, Janet thought, concluding that it would be best for everyone involved if Dean would just leave, but before she could voice her opinion, Katie interjected.

"By all means." Katie motioned to an empty chair. "You don't mind, Janet, do you?"

"No, of course not," Janet conceded, darting an askance glance at Katie. No doubt Katie thought she was doing Janet a favor, but she would not be the one having to face Dean at work day after day. From now on, when it came to coworkers, Janet wanted to keep things purely professional.

Dennis settled into a chair next to Janet. "Drinks are on me. What will it be?"

"Whiskey sour for me and a dirty martini for Janet." Katie beat Janet to the punch, nixing her plan to avoid alcohol. Dean's proximity was inebriating enough. What with his charming smile and baby-blue eyes, Janet's head was already swimming.

"Excellent choice." Dean signaled for the waitress and placed the order, adding a vodka martini with onions for himself.

"So, Dean, it sounds like you're a man of the world, and I was wondering if you could help Janet and me settle a little dilemma we've been struggling with."

Dean leaned in closer, propping his elbows on the table. "I don't know about the man of the world bit, but I'll give it my best."

"What's your opinion about dating coworkers?" Katie asked innocently.

Suppressing the urge to strangle her friend, Janet kicked Katie's foot underneath the table.

"Excellent question." Dean nodded. "An issue that has been raised numerous times by various media sources, including such paragons as Marie Claire and Cosmopolitan."

Katie raised an eyebrow. "You read Cosmopolitan?"

"I read all kinds of magazines," Dean deadpanned back.

Mercifully, the waitress arrived with their drinks, and Janet prayed that the subject of the conversation would be forgotten, but her hopes were fruitless.

"As I was saying," Dean continued, taking a drink of his martini, "numerous opinions have been voiced on the subject, but none of them were conclusive. My personal view is that one never knows when Destiny might knock on one's door, so I say, if you hear your Destiny knocking, open the door," Dean concluded with a sidelong glance at Janet.

Really? Janet thought, could this guy get any smugger? First he invites himself over to our table and now he's making suggestive innuendos. But, then, she could not very well blame him for the latter since Katie had pretty much invited Dean's remark with her impertinent question.

"Well said." Katie nodded. "Don't you agree, Janet?"

This had done it. "I think that it's important to look who's at the door first, or risk opening one's door to a burglar."

"Ah, but the search for love implies danger. Without risk, reward cannot be gained." Dean grinned.

"And on that note I'm going to leave you two." Katie rose from her chair completely ignoring Janet's outraged look. "I've got to prepare for a deposition tomorrow."

Deposition? Janet nearly spurted her drink through her nostrils. Katie would not know how to depose a witness to save her life. Her legal work had always been behind the scenes, but she clearly was intent on playing Cupid tonight, and there was no stopping her.

"You're a lawyer?" Dean asked.

"Guilty." Katie smiled.

"I didn't know you transferred into litigation, Katie." Janet gave her friend a pointed look.

Katie waved her hand. "It's just happened – I'm helping out a new partner. Well, gotta run. Dean, it was a pleasure meeting you."

"Very nice to meet you, Katie."

Janet nodded silently as she watched Katie take her leave. From her behavior, one would think that Katie was an expert on dating, but as far as Janet knew, her friend's love life situation was about as dire as her own. Speaking of which, now that she had been involuntarily set up with Dean Snider, she had to think of something to say. She could not very well just sit there like a fish.

"So, how do you like working at Bostoff so far?" Dean asked.

"It seems that every time you see me, you ask me this question," Janet pointed out, immediately regretting her snippiness. The guy was just trying to make conversation. "It's all right," she added hurriedly. "I'm still feeling my way around things, but it's coming along." She smiled, thinking that she was putting up a very good front.

Dean's eyes lingered on Janet's as though evaluating the sincerity of her answer. "Good." He nodded. "I'm glad."

"How do you like it?" Janet asked.

"Oh, you know, aside from hating my boss and my work, everything is peachy. I'm just kidding," Dean added. "It's a job– it pays bills."

"Yep. That's the important part." Janet finished the last of her martini. She decided to abstain from eating the olives in front of Dean.

"Aren't you going to eat the olives? That's the best part."

"That's my favorite part too," Janet confided, picking up the toothpick with the olives skewered on it. "Would you like one?"

"Sure." Dean nodded. Then he did something Janet did not expect him to. He took her hand into his and directed it to his mouth, leaning in to scoop an olive off the toothpick.

Janet blinked. This was certainly forward of him.

"Aren't you going to eat your olive?" Dean asked, as though nothing was the matter.

Why the heck not? Janet thought. She did like the guy, and for all she knew, she might not be employed by Bostoff that much longer anyway, which made the issue of Dean being her coworker irrelevant.

Chapter Seventeen

"May I walk you home?" Dean asked.

They were standing outside the bar. It was a beautiful, romantic night.

"Sure." Janet was flattered by Dean's old-fashioned remark. This guy was full of surprises. "I'm on Ninetieth and Second Avenue."

"I'll get us a cab." Dean moved to the curb.

Us, Janet felt an involuntary jolt of pleasure at Dean's choice of words.

After several off-duty cabs had passed them by, Janet offered, "Let's take the bus instead."

They walked to Madison Avenue for the uptown bus. Just as they got to the bus stop, they spotted a bus that was about to depart. They raced after it and, laughing hysterically, jumped through the bus doors.

Her heart pounding, Janet threw her head back. "We made it."

"Yes, we did." Dean paid the bus fare for both of them.

They sat by the window. "There's something special about riding the bus at night, isn't there?" Janet said.

"I like riding the bus at night too. I think it has to do with having a space that's normally so crowded all to yourself." Dean eyed a sleeping passenger in the far corner. "Well, almost all to yourself." He grinned. "When I was a kid, I used to sneak into my school building at night. There was just something special about seeing the space that was bursting with people during the day all peaceful and quiet at night. It was my sanctuary when I needed a quiet place to think."

"Sometimes, when I'm riding the bus at night, I like to pretend that I'm lost at sea and that the bus is a lifeboat that's been sent to save passengers from a shipwreck. Somehow, it always makes me feel better." Janet halted, unsettled by her own candidness. She barely knew the guy, and here she was, opening up to him for no particular reason other than the fact that they were riding the bus together after having had a few drinks.

"I know what you mean." Dean nodded. "Sometimes I think that life itself is like being lost at sea, paddling your way to the shore."

Janet looked away. She did not know Dean well enough to reveal any more of herself to him.

There it was: an uncomfortable silence. But when Janet looked back at Dean, she saw him smile back, letting her know that it was completely all right not to have to say a thing.

Janet's stop was coming up, and she signaled for the driver to stop.

The bus came to a halt, and Dean held out his hand to help her out of the bus. His grip was firm and warm, and Janet felt both flustered and excited as her fingers touched Dean's.

"Well, thanks for the bus ride. I'm all the way on Second Avenue," Janet added, giving Dean a way out to say goodnight.

"What kind of a guy do you think I am? I said I'd see you home, Janet. Besides, it's a wonderful evening for a walk."

Janet felt a surge of flattering warmth run through her: this was turning out to be a surprisingly exciting Monday night. She was about to thank Dean for his gallantry when she had a feeling of things being amiss. She checked her watch. It was a quarter after ten. Suddenly, she remembered that she had forgotten about picking up Baxter from her neighbor, who had agreed to dog sit for her. Janet felt her face flush with guilt. There she was flirting with Dean while Baxter was waiting for her.

"Is everything all right?" Dean asked.

"I have to pick up my dog from my neighbor and I'm late."

"Well, then, we'd better walk fast."

Fifteen minutes later, Janet rang her neighbor's door.

There was a sound of clicking heels from behind the door, after which the front door opened, and Mrs. Chapman appeared on the doorstep. Mrs. Chapman was a widow. She was in her seventies, but maintained that age was just a number and insisted on acting accordingly. True to her usual self, she was wearing a patchwork-patterned tunic and leggings, complete with pompom adorned pink kitten mules. Her bright red hair framed her face in taut ringlets – it was a new hairstyle.

While trying not to look too shocked by the fiery red of Mrs. Chapman's extravagant tresses, Janet was about to introduce Dean to her neighbor, but was interrupted by Baxter, who pushed through the door crack and started pawing at Janet's legs.

"Good evening Mrs. Chapman," Janet managed to say as she tried to keep Baxter from ruining her tights.

"Hi, there, Janet. Baxter is sure glad to see you." Mrs. Chapman chuckled, patting her hair.

"New hairstyle," Janet remarked obligingly. "It's very much you."

"Why, thank you, dear. At first I thought it was a bit much, but it's starting to grow on me now." Mrs. Chapman changed her hair at least once a month, saying that at her age she was lucky enough to have hair left on her head and she might as well have fun with it. "I don't know about Baxter, though – I don't think he likes it."

As if in confirmation, Baxter sat up on his hind paws and barked.

"Baxter!" Janet pressed her hand to her mouth to stifle a laugh, but Baxter's attention had already drifted elsewhere, as he began to warily sniff Dean's trousers.

"And who is your friend? I didn't realize we were in male company." Mrs. Chapman adjusted her hair again, peering at Dean curiously.

"Dean, Dean Snider," Dean beat Janet to the introduction. "We work together," he added, anticipating Mrs. Chapman's next question.

"Well, Janet, I dare say your new job must be fun," Mrs. Chapman remarked. "But look at the time… I've got to run; it's getting late, and I want to be up bright and early tomorrow to start working on the aria from Madame Butterfly. Goodnight, you two. Oh, and Janet," Mrs. Chapman added, throwing a side glance at Dean, "I didn't get around to Baxter's evening walk, so you'll have to take him. Sorry about that. Toodles."

"Madame Butterfly?" Dean raised his eyebrows quizzically.

"Mrs. Chapman used to be an opera singer."

Dean whistled. "I didn't know you had celebrity neighbors."

Janet shook her head. "Mrs. Chapman sang small opera parts, but mostly she worked as a librarian until she got married. She loves opera – it's a big part of her life."

As if to confirm Janet's words, there was a sound of singing notes coming from behind Mrs. Chapman's door.

"It sounds like you don't have any lack of entertainment." Dean glanced at Mrs. Chapman's door, which was adjacent to Janet's apartment door.

"It has its pluses and minuses." Janet grinned. Baxter tugged at his leash, reminding Janet of his presence. "Well, I've got to walk Baxter; thanks for seeing me home."

"You mean to tell me that after rushing like crazy to pick up the little fella, I don't get to come along for the fun part?"

As if siding with Dean, Baxter barked, waving his tail. Dean reached down and rubbed Baxter behind his ear, in response to which Baxter licked Dean's hand.

"I think he likes you." Janet grinned. "He usually doesn't like guys." This was true – ever since Janet and Alex had broken up, Baxter had taken a dislike to all members of the male sex, as if blaming the entire male gender for Alex's abominable behavior.

"Dogs usually like me." Dean smiled at Baxter. "And I like them."

"In that case, Baxter and I would be delighted if you joined us for Baxter's evening walk."

Dean held the lobby door open for Janet as they exited onto the street. Baxter pulled at his leash anxiously, eager to explore the street. Janet smiled to herself, her initial suspicion confirmed: Mrs. Chapman had set the entire thing up. If Baxter had not been walked, he would have been preoccupied with matters of greater importance. Janet peeked at Dean's handsome profile and mouthed a silent thank you to her neighbor.

They headed for Carl Schurz Park. It was an ideal night, with the moon hanging low in the inky sky and a breeze coming in from the water. The perfect setting for a kiss, Janet mused. Not that she was going to act on her thought, but a girl could dream. Baxter, however, seemed to be unfazed by the romantic atmosphere, as he tugged at his leash, heading in the direction of the dog playground.

"He sure knows what he wants out of life." Dean grinned at Baxter's determination.

"Do you mind if we stop by the dog playground?" Janet asked.

"Not at all."

Janet usually brought Baxter's toys along with her, but tonight she had left them at her apartment. Baxter looked up expectantly at her, waiting for the usual ball toss.

"Sorry, Bax – not today." Janet shrugged. "I left your toys at home."

"I think we can figure something out." Dean picked up a stick from the ground.

Baxter's hind legs twitched with anticipation, his tongue hanging from the side of his opened mouth.

"Here you go, boy, fetch!" Dean threw the stick to the other side of the playground, and Baxter stormed after it.

"Do you have a dog?" Janet asked. She knew next to nothing about Dean, and yet there they were, walking Baxter together.

"No." Dean shook his head. "But I used to walk a dog for someone when I was a kid."

Janet felt a warm tingling in her chest. How could a girl resist a guy who loved dogs?

By now Baxter had returned and placed the stick at Dean's feet, breathing heavily with expectation. Dean threw the stick again, and Baxter stormed after it.

"Dean?"

"Yes?"

"How long have you been at Bostoff Securities?"

"Not that long," Dean answered slowly. "Just a few weeks longer than you."

"Do you find anything odd about the place?" Janet asked before she could stop herself. There was something about Dean's demeanor that made her want to trust him, almost uncannily so.

Dean shrugged. "Every place has its own quirks. Why, what have you noticed?"

Janet hesitated. She was the one who had started the conversation, but until she got to know Dean better, she was not going to say a thing more.

"Oh, there were a few outliers I found while preparing for the audit, but nothing completely out of the ordinary. I just meant that it's kind of odd that the whole family is involved in the business – Bostoff Senior and his two sons, and now my boss, Lisa, is engaged to Paul Bostoff..."

"These things can get tricky," Dean cut her off, and she thought she saw a shadow of disappointment on his face. "Well, it's getting late. I'd better get going. I'm all the way down in Soho."

Janet felt the air grow rigid between them. She had a ridiculous sensation that Dean guessed exactly what it was that bothered her about Bostoff.

"I wish it weren't Monday night," Dean added quickly. "I'll walk up to Second Avenue with you and catch a cab there. I'll see you tomorrow?"

"I'll be there." Janet felt her ease returning to her. She had imagined the entire thing. Dean was just tired.

♞❦♜

Back in his apartment, Dennis draped his jacket over the hanger and loosened his tie. It was almost midnight, and he had to be at Bostoff at seven thirty a.m. tomorrow – the same time he was always required to come in, lest some dimwitted trader need help to turn on his computer. Judging by the quality of traders that Bostoff hired, it was no wonder that the company had to cater to corrupt hedge funds. The kind of dullards Bostoff hired were no doubt cheap, but they were also incapable of generating any respectable business. But then, Jon Bostoff was not interested in respectable business, so he hired the kind of people who would not bat an eyelash at the slimy schemes Dennis suspected Bostoff Securities was engaged in. If only Hank Bostoff knew about the sort of outfit Bostoff Securities was turning into under his son's stewardship…

By now, Dennis knew enough about Bostoff's business to understand that the corrupt direction in which the firm was heading was all Jon Bostoff's doing. While still nominally in charge of the company, Hank Bostoff had little idea about his son's business methods, and Paul Bostoff had no business in the world of finance. This realization saddened Dennis. He could only imagine the disappointment Hank would endure once the investigation would commence – the same kind of disappointment Dennis had, albeit unwittingly, caused his own mentor in what now felt like a different life, many years ago.

Dennis turned on the shower and stood under the pulsating stream of water, willing his brain to go blank, but failing. Bostoff Securities investigation was proving to be much more difficult than he had expected. Since he had started working for the Feds and then the Treasury, Dennis had relentlessly plowed away with the assignments put in front of him. An investigation was just that: an investigation. It was Dennis's duty to bring the culprits to justice to atone for his own mistakes: mistakes that continued to haunt him, no matter how many crooks he caught and how many schemes he exposed. Dennis closed his eyes and turned his face under the water stream. Janet's face hovered before his eyes, reminding him just how hopelessly naïve he had been. An investigation – any investigation – involved people, and Janet Maple was among the people who would get hurt once Bostoff's corrupt operations were exposed.

Dennis wanted to protect her, but the only way for him to do that was for Janet to become his ally. By now, Janet Maple had to be on to Bostoff; Dennis was sure of it. He had sensed that she had wanted to share her suspicions with him tonight, but had changed her mind at the last minute. She did not trust him enough yet. He needed to build his trust with Janet slowly, something that was easier said than done because of the deadline that his boss had given him – three weeks before the Feds would take over the case. Take it easy, Dennis thought. How difficult could it be to become Janet Maple's confidant? It was obvious that she liked him. The only problem was that he liked her too.

Chapter Eighteen

Paul Bostoff rose from his chair and adjusted his tie. The prospect of a lunch meeting with his brother made him nervous. Jon and Paul were not the kind of siblings who shared boyhood memories: the nine-year age difference between them was partly to blame for that, but mainly it was the difference in their characters and temperaments. His whole life, Paul remembered Jon treating him with veiled disregard: Paul was always too slow, too weak, too young to warrant Jon's interest. And even now, as adults, they were anything but close: a situation that proved to be all the more problematic since they were working for a family business. Paul could understand Jon's reasons for not taking him seriously. After all, Paul had not exactly been a paragon of business astuteness; he had majored in acting at Vassar, selecting marketing as a second major to appease his father. After graduating, Paul ran with the actor crowd for a while, landing small parts in off Broadway theaters – the kind of theaters that had folding chairs for the audience to sit on and nothing but the bare floor as stage decorations. But Paul did not mind; in fact, he thought of those years as the happiest in his life. Unlike Jon, he had never hungered for money or prestige. Granted, both brothers had grown up in a well-to-do household, but Jon seemed to have been born with insatiable ambition. Even in his boyhood years, Paul had noticed a look of vague dissatisfaction on his elder brother's face. No amount of money would ever be enough for him and no social position sufficiently high enough. Paul, however, was the complete opposite of his brother. As much as he would have liked to please his father by showing some of Jon's business rigor, he came up flat. Business did not interest him, which was a difficulty that could be easily overcome by perseverance, but Paul's predicament ran much deeper than lack of effort. He had no acumen for the world of finance. Numbers held no allure for him, leaving his head heavy with headache and confusion. He was an artist, not a number cruncher like his father or brother.

But while Paul longed to see his name heralded in film and stage credits, he learned that the entertainment business was anything but easy to break into. There, again, ambition prevailed, and he lacked the killer instinct that had propelled his more tenacious friends into stardom. When Paul's acting aspirations failed to blossom, he had been content to channel himself into marketing. At least, there was some aspect of creativity to it. He had wanted to strike out on his own. He had an offer to join the marketing department of a reputable magazine, but his father had insisted that Paul join Bostoff Securities as Chief Marketing Officer. Embarrassed by the pompous, nepotism-procured title, Paul worked hard. He wanted to prove to everyone, and most of all to himself, that he was more than just his father's son. He had succeeded: his advertising campaigns for Bostoff Securities were original and innovative. His father was pleased, and so were his colleagues, with the exception of his brother who considered marketing to be a sham of a profession. No matter; Paul was too old to need his brother's approval. He had been perfectly happy with his newly-found niche in marketing when his father insisted on transferring him into the business side of things and making him chief operating officer or COO at Bostoff Securities.

What did a COO do, anyway? Paul had no idea, and his father was not that keen on educating him, leaving the task to Jon, who was anything but helpful. So Paul fumbled along, doing his best to appear competent and constantly terrified of his pretense being exposed. Not that his father would notice. Ever since Paul's mother had passed away, Hank just was not himself: he was distracted and aloof, his presence in the office being a mere formality while Jon took over the reins. And Jon certainly did not have any interest in Paul becoming a competent COO, as he had no regard for his younger brother's input when it came to business or any other subject, for that matter. Things might have continued this way had it not been for Lisa. At the thought of his tantalizing fiancée, Paul felt his spirits lift. Lisa was one of the most exciting women he had ever met. She was so driven, so determined: a refreshing change from his own attitude; a spirit he could look up to. For as ashamed as he was to admit it, Paul knew that while he worked hard, his work was generated by the sense of duty and expectation of the others rather than his own ambition. Lisa, on the other hand, was different: she had real hunger for things, an urge for success that Paul had never managed to arouse in himself. From the very start, Lisa had become interested in Paul's position in the company and advised him to persevere in growing into a fully-fledged partner in the business: to become Jon's equal.

Paul sighed. He had worked hard to live up to Lisa's expectations. Staying up late at night, he pored over Bostoff's revenues and expenses, trying to come up with ways to cut costs and increase profits, but when he tried to contribute by expanding the internal Legal department instead of outsourcing all the legal work to that Tom Wyman slickster who charged the company an arm and a leg, Jon blew a lid. Just what was it that upset his brother so, Paul could not understand.

Well, this meeting was bound to clear things up. There were several questions that Paul had for Jon as well. Over the past months, he had noticed increased revenues coming in from several hedge funds, Emperial being the highest. Interested in the identity of the high revenue-generating client, Paul did some digging and found that Emperial's reputation was notorious to say the least. Paul remembered Hank Bostoff's long-standing reluctance to go after hedge fund business, but Jon, on the other hand, was eager to open the doors to just about any client that paid good commissions: a notion that did not sit well with Paul at all.

Paul checked his watch; he would have to hurry. With all his brooding, he had lost track of time, and he knew only too well how much Jon despised tardiness.

₧₨

At the sight of his brother entering the restaurant, Jon Bostoff finished the rest of his scotch. Normally, he never drank during the work day, but today he had a good excuse. The first tranche of orders for the Impala Group had come in this week, generating a nearly seven-figure commission in just one day. The prospect of the money that was to come made Jon giddy with anticipation. Finally, he was getting to the station in life he had been destined to occupy. Now, all he had to do was make sure that his buffoon of a brother did not mess things up by poking his nose where it did not belong, and to do that, Jon would have to make Paul feel like he was part of the game. He needed to come up with a project to keep his brother busy and make him feel useful.

"Paul." Jon willed his lips into a smile. Deciding that a handshake would be too formal and an embrace too filial, he patted his brother heartily on the shoulder.

"Sorry I'm late." Paul stiffened. "I was just finishing up some reports and lost track of time."

"No worries." Jon smiled. "I think our table is ready."

As the pretty hostess led them to Jon's usual booth, Jon eyed her perky behind undulating pleasantly on her long, slim legs. Jon Bostoff liked pretty women just as much as he liked money, and he strove to possess top tier in both categories. He had managed to do so in the first category: to his mind, all women paled in comparison next to his wife, and he was finally well on his way to realizing his ambition on the business front of things.

Jon took a seat. "Would you like a drink?" he offered Paul.

Paul lifted his eyes from the menu. "I don't usually drink at work."

"Neither do I," Jon retorted, "but this week calls for a celebration." Without waiting for Paul's response, Jon ordered two gin martinis.

Paul took a sip of his water. "Speaking of which, I noticed an increase in the commission numbers this week."

The sneaky bugger is not as dumb as he looks, Jon thought, conscious of keeping a hearty grin all the while. "That's exactly it, brother, we're finally breaking into the big leagues."

"By taking orders from hedge funds with questionable reputations?"

Somebody is getting feisty, Jon thought, barely resisting the urge to reach across the table and smack his brother for old times' sake. Unfortunately, they were no longer kids. The smacking around would have to be confined to verbal parries. "What do you mean by questionable reputations?"

"Do you want me to make a list? Emperial for one, and just this week, some entity called Impala Group of which I've never heard before."

Jon gulped. He had not expected such business dexterity from his younger brother. Clearly, the louse could be quite tenacious when he wanted to. "Would you call a hedge fund paying its investors eight percent per year questionable?"

"If the return is generated illegally, yes." Paul fixed his eyes on Jon. "Dad always stood away from the hedge fund business. You are completely ignoring his wishes."

"Dad has been out of touch with the business reality for some time," Jon snapped. "Have you looked at the company finances recently? The only way to make any money these days is through volume. Going after hedge funds is the way to do that. And as far as Emperial goes, nothing has been hung on them yet, and as long as that's the case, they are a good client to me."

"Well, I suppose you have a point. Nothing has been proven against them," Paul trailed off.

Mercifully, the waitress arrived with their drinks.

Jon took a long swig of his martini and placed his order: cheeseburger with American cheese and French fries. He had to take another swallow of his drink when he heard Paul's order: a salad for Christ's sake! What a pansy his brother was.

"Lisa and I are trying a new diet," Paul added almost apologetically. "It's based on the fact that meats and poultry are highly acidic foods and vegetables are alkaline. Consuming alkaline foods boosts your metabolism and flushes out the toxins."

Jon nodded. "I applaud your self-control, brother, but I'm too much of a carnivore to give up meat. I figure hitting the gym every morning ought to do it."

"It's more of a solidarity gesture for Lisa on my part, really."

How lame, Jon thought, but nodded approvingly. "I like that; that's the key to a strong marriage. Getting back to our conversation... I understand your concerns, Paul, but even the U.S. justice system says that one is innocent until proven guilty. And I might add that these days you'd be hard-pressed to find a financial institution that did not have a run-in with a regulator at some point of its existence."

"I suppose so." Paul lowered his eyes, taking a drink. "I don't want to fight with you, Jon. I just don't want Dad's legacy to be tarnished, that's all. Heck, truth be told, I went into the business because Dad wanted me to: he's got this idea that we should be working together, and I can clearly see that you don't want that."

Damn straight, I don't, Jon thought, but out loud he purred, "That's not true, brother. I want us to be a team, but you have to trust me. I know you're anxious to contribute to the business, and you have already done a great deal, but you have to give it time to acquire an understanding of the company before jumping to conclusions. Let me be your mentor. I promise I will guide you through this maze called finance, and then, we can really be a team."

Paul nodded. "I'd like that. To be honest, I was quite happy to be on the marketing side of things, but Dad wanted me to be involved in the business more."

"And who said that marketing is not important?"

"Do you really mean that?"

"Of course, I do!" Jon almost burst from the effort of containing his smirk. "It's one of the most important functions in the company. It presents our face to the outside world."

"I had no idea you thought so."

"I'm sorry if I was unclear about it. In fact, that's one of the topics I wanted to talk to you about today. Now that Bostoff Securities is going to become a more prominent financial player, we need to up our publicity profile. I was thinking something along the lines of a charity event. What are your thoughts?"

"We could organize a charity sports tournament."

"A splendid idea! That's exactly what I'm talking about, Paul. We are a team. What kind of tournament?"

"It could be golf or tennis."

"Tennis – I like that – more original than golf. How long do you think it would take to put one together? How does two weeks' time sound?"

"Oh, I don't know, Jon. That's pushing it real tight. We might not get anyone from outside to participate on two weeks' notice."

"Who says we need to get anyone from the outside? We can make it an employee only function. We'll have several rounds, with the firm making a donation to the charity choice of the final winning employee. Can you get it started?"

"Well, sure, Jon. I'll get right on it."

"Great, I'm looking forward to it, Paul. And don't forget about your engagement party tonight." Jon wiped the grease off his mouth. The burger had been superb.

Chapter Nineteen

Janet perched on a bar stool at BLT and twirled the olive-studded toothpick in her martini glass. There were few things she would describe as being torturous, but sitting alone by the bar at a corporate function definitely rated in the category. Janet caught a glimpse of her reflection in the bar mirror: her hair covered her shoulders in loose, soft curls: she had snuck out at lunch to get it styled at the nearby hair salon, and she had to admit that it was a welcome change from her usual French twist. She wore a fitted black sheath with a matching jacket, which she had taken off and hung over the back of her chair, leaving her arms and neck exposed and flatteringly offset by the black material of her dress. All in all, she looked good, even if she did say so herself. Of course, she had hoped that Dean Snider would be there to take notice of this fact, but so far, he was not in attendance.

She checked her watch: it was only five-thirty, and people were just starting to arrive. She wished Dean would hurry up already. But then she was the one to blame for her current predicament: Dean had asked her to be his date for the corporate party several times, and not wanting to make a big deal out of the whole thing, she had evaded a reply. Truth be told, she had been tempted to accept Dean's invitation all week. Ever since their accidental outing on Monday night, Janet had become intensely conscious of Dean's presence at Bostoff Securities.

Suddenly, he was in the hallways, in the kitchen, in the cafeteria; wherever Janet went, Dean seemed to materialize out of the thin air. These coincidental encounters were more than welcome on Janet's part, as the two of them joked, laughed, and flirted, filling the grayness of the workdays with sparks of excitement from each other's company. Well, at least that was true in Janet's case, and she hoped that Dean felt the same way. She had been looking forward to tonight all week, imagining herself cozying up to Dean by the bar, her face being tilted at a seductive angle and her smile playing on her lips just so as she looked into his eyes, listening to his deep voice recounting yet another anecdote about some dim-witted trader being unable to turn on his computer. There was no denying it: despite her determination not to get involved with coworkers, Janet was ready to break her own rules for Dean Snider. The only question that remained was whether Dean was interested in turning flirtatious banter into something more: a question that was difficult to answer since Janet herself had difficulty defining just what she meant by 'more'.

Janet stole a glance at her watch: a quarter to six and still no sign of Dean. Irked, she took another sip of her drink. That was the law of things: the minute one started wanting something, it was bound to become unattainable. All week long, Dean kept popping up before her with his uninvited banter, and now, when she finally decided to give the bugger a chance, he was nowhere to be found. But then perhaps it was all for the best. It was not as though she could afford the luxury of wasting her brain cells on flirting. If she was ever going to figure out what exactly was going on at Bostoff Securities, she had to keep her head cool.

"Is this seat taken?" A male voice woke Janet up from her reverie.

Janet turned around and saw Tom Wyman leaning against the chair next to hers. As always, he looked impeccable. His tailored suit did not have a crease out of place, and his tie immaculately matched his shirt: an intricate ensemble that he no doubt had spent some time putting together. Perhaps Janet imagined it, but it seemed to her that Wyman's entire demeanor oozed with self-satisfaction. He looked like a cat that had just swallowed a canary.

Wyman took the seat next to her.

"So you're a martini girl," Wyman observed Janet's choice of drink. "That's my kind of girl."

"I'm glad to know that." Janet took a sip of her drink. She was not particularly happy to see Wyman at this very moment, but Wyman was at the heart of Bostoff's business. If she was ever to get to the bottom of Bostoff's operations, Wyman was the key.

The rail-thin brunette who was tending the bar zoomed over to Wyman, batting her eyelashes at him.

How was it that fashionable restaurants always had rail-thin women hosting, serving, and tending the bar? Were these stunning, but undoubtedly famished representatives of the female sex not tempted by the food that surrounded them at their places of work? Janet pondered while Wyman ordered himself a dirty martini.

"What can I get you, sir?" The bartendress's misty gaze made it clear that she would be more than happy to oblige Wyman's needs beyond the cocktail menu.

After a much deliberated measuring, stirring and pouring, the bartendress finally placed Wyman's drink before him, and after casting one last longing look at Wyman and a fleeting look of menace at Janet, departed to address the needs of other customers.

"Cheers." Wyman raised his glass.

"What are we celebrating?"

"Lisa's and Paul's engagement, of course." Wyman smiled with an open look of a man who had nothing to hide.

"Yes, of course." Janet returned his smile. She knew that Wyman would be a tough nut to crack, but it never hurt to try.

"Do you have any other reasons in mind?" Wyman made a barely perceptible shift in his seat, sliding closer to Janet.

"It looks like business is picking up," she observed nonchalantly just as Wyman's hand brushed against her bare arm.

Wyman stiffened. "Yes, indeed. From what I hear, the revenues are up. Of course, I'm not involved in the day to day operations, so you would probably know more than me. What have you seen on your end?"

"Oh, I just overheard the traders talking in the hallway. They sounded really excited about the business picking up," Janet replied. She was not about to admit to the fact that she had been combing through the firm's records.

"Another drink?" Wyman offered.

"I don't see why not." Janet pushed away her empty glass.

"Janet, Tom!" Lisa's voice rang in the air. Janet had been so intent on observing Wyman that she had failed to notice Lisa Foley and Paul Bostoff walking toward them.

"Hello." Janet slid off her chair to reciprocate Lisa's embrace-outstretched arms. The gesture was surprising given the fact that aside from exchanging a few terse phrases, Janet had barely seen her boss all week. Lisa was still sore at Janet's refusal of her matchmaking.

"I see you found Tom. Isn't he great?" Lisa whispered, planting an air kiss on Janet's cheek.

"You look wonderful, Lisa. Congratulations to both of you." Wyman smiled officiously.

"Why, thank you, Tom!" Lisa leaned on Paul's arm. "Don't you think it's time you tied the knot?" Lisa's glance alternated between Janet and Wyman.

"Not all of us are as lucky as Paul here," Wyman countered. "I'm still waiting for the right girl to come along."

"Well, Tom," Lisa smiled meaningfully, "perhaps you should open your eyes – or you just might miss her."

Lisa's remark made Janet wish she could fall through the ground. Unfortunately, she was standing on a floor of solid wood.

"Congratulations!" Jon Bostoff joined the group. He shook his brother's hand and kissed Lisa on both cheeks. "Janet, it's a pleasure to see you again. How are you finding it at Bostoff?"

"Wonderful, thank you," Janet replied, taken aback by Jon Bostoff's unwarranted attention. As far as she was concerned, she was but a mere speck on Jon Bostoff's landscape.

"Janet is a tremendous asset, Jon," Lisa cut in. "She's done so much already."

Jon Bostoff's eyes lingered on Janet. "Great. I'm glad to hear it. Tom, make sure you show Janet the ropes."

Wyman's glance darted back understandingly. "I sure will, Jon. Not to worry."

"Well, I'll leave you to it." Jon smiled. "Paul, Lisa – the guests of honor must do the rounds."

Lisa lingered behind. "I'm keeping my fingers crossed for you and Tom," she whispered to Janet.

Janet merely nodded. Annoyed as she was by Lisa's remark, she was in no position to address it with Tom Wyman standing in front of her.

"So how about that drink?" Wyman motioned at the bar.

"Don't mind if I do," Janet conceded. She did not intend to have another drop of alcohol, but she needed the pretense to get Wyman to talk.

"So, Janet, tell me about yourself." Wyman raised his glass in another celebratory gesture.

"Oh, I think you pretty much know everything already. I spent the last four years at the DA's office, went to Columbia Law…"

"That's not what I meant, Janet." Wyman reached for Janet's hand, covering it with his wide palm. "I'd like to get to know you as a person." He fixed his gaze on Janet's eyes, waiting for her reaction. "Don't you think it a pity that we so often know next to nothing about the people we work with? People we spend so much of our time with…."

Janet paused demurely. This was her opening, her chance to get him to talk.

"Yes, Tom. For instance, I hardly know anything about you, and I'd like to learn a great deal," she purred.

"What is it that you'd like to know?" Wyman's voice swelled with his ego.

"Well, you see, I'm still learning the ropes at my job, and it all seems so complicated to me. I would so much appreciate it if you could walk me through Bostoff's business model and all the complicated things that you do for the firm." Janet fiddled with her cocktail glass. "You've showed me a great deal already, but I must admit that it all seemed so complicated that I'm afraid I need another lesson."

Wyman stroked his chin. "Sure, Janet, I'd be glad to. But first, what do you say we get out of this place and go somewhere quiet for dinner?"

"Why, yes, Tom. That sounds like a splendid idea."

"After you, my lady."

Janet started walking toward the exit. Her heart was beating wildly. Playing detective was fun, and it would be even more fun if she did not risk being implicated in the very scheme she was trying to unravel.

Tom followed Janet, but had to rush back to the bar to retrieve his laptop case that he had stowed under his chair.

"Almost forgot the darn thing," he muttered. "It's been a hell of day."

Janet eyed Wyman's laptop case from under her lashes. She would love to get her hands on the files that he kept there.

&ⱭᏨ

Dennis Walker was hurriedly making his way through the crowd. He could see Janet by the bar. He had not missed his chance after all. In a few moments, he would reach her and apologize, citing an important work assignment as the cause of his delay. In reality, it was his boss's micromanagement that had made him late. With so much riding on the Bostoff investigation, Hamilton Kirk had turned into a nervous Nellie and demanded daily updates from Dennis. Ham had stipulated that these updates be face-to-face, and for the past week Dennis had found himself rushing to see his boss at all kinds of hours. Usually their meetings were either early in the day or late in the evening, but today Ham had insisted that they meet at five-thirty, claiming that he could not stay late due to a family function. Oh, well, when it came to his boss's whims, there was little that Dennis could do.

At least Ham had managed to get a one-week extension out of the Feds, which left Dennis with a total of three weeks to work the case, as one week, Dean was chagrined to admit, had already gone by. Dennis could sense that something big was brewing at Bostoff. With Janet's help, he could solve the case much faster. All week long, he had gone out of his way to run into Janet in the hallways and the cafeteria. They chatted and laughed. She liked him, he could tell. All he needed now was a little bit more time to make her trust him, and tonight would provide the perfect opportunity for that.

As he got closer to the bar, Dennis halted in his footsteps, realizing that Janet was not alone. Bostoff's attorney, Tom Wyman, was hovering over her like a bee over honey, and Janet seemed to be welcoming his advances, leaning toward him at angles of alarming proximity. At the sight of this display, Dennis froze in place. Dennis was certain that Wyman was the link that connected Bostoff to Emperial and the rest of the hedge fund piranhas that filled Bostoff's client list. If Janet got close to Wyman, she could find out all sorts of useful information from him. But if Janet genuinely liked Wyman - if she were to become his accomplice - she would be of no use to Dennis. Even more unsettling was the possibility of her becoming something more than Wyman's ally. The thought made Dennis's fists curl involuntarily. His reaction scared him; this was a job, not a game of hanky-panky. Dennis needed to secure Janet's affection, but he needed it to procure evidence from her, not to indulge his own emotions.

Deliberating his next move, Dennis shot another glance at Janet. She looked positively glowing tonight. Her chestnut hair draped her shoulders, adding a new kind of attractiveness to her face. Her entire demeanor seemed more relaxed, exuding a new kind of appeal. Was it merely the change in her hair style or was it Wyman's presence that was responsible for this change in her? Dennis wondered. The thought of Tom Wyman as a rival for Janet's attention undid the last remnants of Dennis's resolve. He wanted to rake his fingers through the rich mane of Janet's hair, to cover her inviting mouth with his lips, to trace the outline of her body with his hands. While Dennis struggled with his fueling desire, Wyman leaned in closer to Janet and whispered something into her ear. She nodded and smiled, shrugging her shoulders coquettishly. Before Dennis could make up his mind whether to approach the cooing couple, the decision was made for him. Seething inside, Dennis watched Wyman get up from his chair and usher Janet toward the exit. As they passed through the crowd, Dennis ducked against the wall, but the precaution had been unnecessary. Janet's eyes were glued to Tom Wyman.

Chapter Twenty

Janet stared at the computer screen in her office. Last night had been fun. A bit too much fun, she had to admit, but, boy, it felt great to be basking in its afterglow.

After they had left the corporate party, Wyman took her to Gilt – the swanky restaurant located in the historic Villard Mansion in midtown, Manhattan that was designed for seduction. No doubt Wyman had taken many of his conquests to that very place, but he did not get his way with Janet last night. She could sense his expectant, self-assured gaze on her throughout the meal He was the kind of man who was used to women succumbing to his charisma, which made it so much more delightful for Janet to say no. Not that she was impervious to Wyman's charms – she was only human, but now that she had a different purpose in mind, Wyman had become a tool in her plans. Last night she was seducing him as much as he was trying to seduce her, only Janet's objective was information, while Wyman's aim was a bit more carnal.

However, Janet had to admit that Tom Wyman would be a tough nut to crack. She had spent the entire evening trying to get Wyman to open up about the work he did for Bostoff Securities. She had employed admiration, flattery, and simple naïve curiosity, but Wyman had remained bullet-proof, only allowing the most general of statements. Yes, he had helped incorporate entities for Bostoff, and yes, he drafted contracts for the firm, but other than that, Janet was none the wiser today than she had been the day before.

With a sigh, Janet grabbed her cell phone and dialed Katie's number. After all, Katie worked for a law firm, and she might be able to help her.

"Hello, there," Katie's voice rang cheerfully in the receiver. "It's about time you called."

Janet felt an instant flash of guilt: she had not spoken with Katie since the evening Dean Snider had interrupted their girls' night out. "I meant to call earlier, but it's gotten so crazy at work…"

"So, how is Dean in the sack?"

"Katie!" Even though it was impossible for anyone to hear them, Janet blushed. "What are you talking about?"

"Not what, but whom, and you know damn well whom I'm talking about: that handsome IT guy from your job. Dean. You could at least thank me for tactfully leaving the two of you to enjoy each other's company."

"Thank you. And by the way, how was the deposition?"

"What deposition? Oh, never mind; there was no deposition, and you know it. Now, dish the goods."

So much for talking about the stuff that matters, Janet thought. Katie was an excellent lawyer, but lately she had been placing personal matters over professional ones.

"Well, if you must know, nothing happened: he saw me home, and then we walked Baxter together."

"A real gentleman," Katie sighed. "Last night, my date insisted on coming up to my apartment as payment for walking me home, and he did not even buy me a drink. We met at an open bar, which does not even make him my date; he was just some guy I picked up at a legal seminar. God, those things are awful, as awful as the men who attend them. See how I've fallen? And there you are, with a perfectly fine specimen of the male gender vying for your attention…"

"I'm sorry." Janet stifled a smile. Katie had such a sense of the dramatic. "But I'm afraid my life is not as exciting as you think. We were supposed to go together to the corporate party for Lisa's engagement, but he never showed."

"That doesn't sound good. Did he actually ask you to be his date?"

"Sort of, but I never committed."

"Sounds to me like someone is having commitment issues, and now you're upset that he didn't show up? Next time he asks, you'd better say 'yes.'"

"Okay, Dr. Phil," Janet conceded. Katie did have a point. "But seriously, I called because I wanted to talk to you."

"We are talking."

"About something important."

"Are you telling me that having a sex life is not important? Keep thinking like that and you'll never get one. Take it from the expert in the area."

Janet was about to blow her fuse. "Can you meet me for a drink after work tonight?"

"No can do. I've got a date. And I suggest you get one too by asking Dean out - men like it when women show initiative."

Janet was just about to come up with a retort, but Katie beat her to it.

"Sorry, hon, I've got to run. My boss is on the other line, but call me tomorrow, and we'll dish."

Janet stared at her cell phone. Katie had given her an idea. Perhaps she should talk to Dean after all. Not about their failed 'date' of course, but about her misgivings regarding Bostoff Securities. She had almost brought up the topic the evening they had been walking Baxter together, but never had worked up the courage to say anything of substance. After all, she could not very well voice her suspicions to someone she barely knew. Yet, something in Dean's expression had made her think that perhaps she had been wrong. Perhaps, like her, Dean suspected that all was not kosher with Bostoff's business, and maybe together they could get to the bottom of things.

෮෬

Dennis Walker looked aimlessly at his desk. There were things he could be doing instead: things he had to get done, like preparing memos for his boss or scouring for any suspicious events on Bostoff's trading floor, but he found it impossible to concentrate on any of his tasks. His mind was occupied by thoughts of Janet Maple. The sight of her leaving the party last night with that dog Wyman hung before Dennis's eyes: what could she have possibly seen in that creep? But then Dennis was not blind to his opposition. There were plenty of things that made Tom Wyman, Esq. attractive to women. His lucratively paying job for one, his polished manner and sharp clothes — all of those were the advantages that Tom Wyman had over the persona of Dean Snider.

God, Dennis was sick and tired of this charade! For the first time since he had begun his career as investigator of financial crimes, Dennis found himself on the brink of quitting a case because of a woman. It was immature, he knew, but his desire for Janet and his competitive spirit towards Wyman were getting the better of him. Dennis adjusted his tie, loosening the collar of the cheap shirt that was making his neck chafe. Once the Bostoff case would be over with, he would burn all of Dean Snider's clothes in a celebratory bonfire.

He had to think calmly. Quitting was not an option. He owed it to his boss to finish the case. Ham Kirk could be a pain in the ass, but the man did put considerable trust in Dennis. Successful completion of the Bostoff Securities investigation would finally bring Ham the promotion the old man had been coveting all these years, and Dennis, sure as hell, was not going to backstab Kirk by ruining his chances. Besides, there was no proof that

Janet had actually fallen for Wyman's charms. Yes, the two had left the party together last night, but for all Dennis knew, their subsequent rendezvous could have ended with Janet throwing a drink in Wyman's face. He should go and see her to explain his missing her at the party last night. After all, he had promised to meet her there, but thanks to Ham Kirk, Wyman had beaten Dennis to the punch.

Dennis was about to get up from his desk when he noticed Janet walking in his direction. His pride swelled at the thought that she was coming to see him. He had been right. That pig Wyman had nothing on him. Quickly, Dennis opened a random program on his computer and started typing away feverishly, doing his best to appear intensely busy.

"Hello, there." Dressed in a wrap dress that hugged every single one of her tantalizing curves, Janet smiled at him.

Dennis looked up from his screen. "How is it going?" His voice came out terser than he intended. He could not help it: he was still mad at her.

"Good." She looked slightly perplexed. "It's Friday," she announced the obvious, no doubt hoping for him to save the conversation.

"Yes, it is," Dennis confirmed.

"I missed you at the party last night. I thought you were going to be my date."

"I got held up at work. But it looked like you did not have any shortage of dates," he added dryly. Shut up, you moron! Just shut up, his reason screamed, but it was too late – he was beyond common sense.

"You were at the party? Why didn't you say hello?"

"Because you were busy flirting with Tom Wyman. I didn't want to interrupt you." What are you doing? Dennis thought frantically. You're ruining it!

"We were just having a friendly conversation."

"I saw you leave with him." Might as well add oil to the fire, Dennis thought. It was as though a flood gate had broken inside him.

Janet reddened. "Well, I never... Clearly, you're having a bad day; we'll talk some other time." Janet swung around and started walking away from his desk.

"Janet!" Dennis kicked his chair back as he rushed after her. "I'm sorry." He touched her arm. "I don't know what came over me. I'm under a tight deadline. That's why I was late to the party last night..." Dennis broke off, wondering if he could still salvage the situation.

"That's all right, I understand."

"Could I make it up to you? Let me buy you dinner tonight."

She paused momentarily, weighing his offer.

"Purely as a peace offering," Dennis added.

"All right, but we're going to split it. How does six o'clock sound?"

"Sounds great. Do you like Indian food?"

"I love Indian food." The tone of her voice made it clear that his transgressions were forgiven.

"Great. I'll make a reservation at Tamarind restaurant for six o'clock. I'll meet you in the lobby at five thirty?"

"I'll see you there."

"See you there," Dennis mouthed as he watched Janet walk away.

Once he saw Janet leave the floor, Dennis grabbed his cell phone and rushed downstairs. He needed to secure his boss's permission to recruit an inside source.

Chapter Twenty-One

Janet looked at Dean walking beside her. At first, she had been hesitant about accepting Dean's dinner invitation. His earlier outburst at having seen her at the corporate party with Wyman had taken her aback. But then everyone was entitled to blowing a lid now and then, and Dean did have an excuse. He was under a lot of pressure at work, and Janet could only guess that dealing with the trading types at Bostoff day in, day out was no walk in the park. Besides, she had to admit that, as childish as it sounded, Dean's reaction was also flattering. If seeing her with Wyman had upset him that much, he had to see her as more than just a coworker. This realization brought a smile to her lips. Dean did like her after all. But then she had guessed it all along– had sensed it from their first meeting when she had found him in her office, fixing her computer, but now she knew for sure. And from the way Dean spoke about Tom Wyman, it was obvious that Dean owed no loyalty to Wyman or his machinations, which meant that she could speak freely to Dean about her suspicions of Bostoff. Maybe he would help her decide what to do next.

She had wanted to bring up the subject of Bostoff Securities during dinner, but somehow the right moment never came up. Dean had been his charming self, making Janet laugh hysterically at work war stories he was so apt at telling, but when he thought she was not looking, Janet noticed a worried look stealing over his eyes. She had wanted to ask him what was on his mind, but thought better of it. After all, they were merely coworkers, hardly close at all.

Now, as they approached her building, Janet could sense the earlier unease coming over Dean again. It was as though he wanted to tell her something, but could not get the right words to come out.

Janet lowered her eyes. They were about to say good night. She had missed her chance to talk to Dean, unless...

"Would you like to come up for a drink?" Janet offered, almost instantly regretting her invitation. She did not want Dean to get the wrong impression, but neither did she want to say goodbye to him just yet.

He seemed to sense her hesitation, so he made his reply casual. "Sure. A drink would be great. All that spicy food made me thirsty."

"Follow me."

"I already know the way."

"That's right." She smiled. "Baxter will be very excited to see you."

While they rode up in the elevator, Janet tried to remember the contents of her bar, or to be more precise, the section of the cupboard in her kitchen that served as a bar. She had a bottle of Jameson she had bought specifically for the times that Mrs. Chapman stopped by, as a way to thank her neighbor for walking Baxter. There ought to be something left on the bottom of that one, Janet thought. She was not a big whiskey fan, but Mrs. Chapman was quite a whiskey aficionado. There was also some Apple Sour Martini Mix, but no vodka to mix it with, and two bottles of Sam Adams in the fridge. Janet had been meaning to restock her supplies, but now it was too late to retract her invitation. She just hoped that Dean was not much of a drinker.

"Here we are." Janet slid her key into the front lock. Instantly, Baxter's barking, accompanied by the sound of his paws scraping against the floor, exploded from behind the door.

"Baxter can't wait to see you," Janet grinned, wishing the lock would open already. All this noise was liable to stir Mrs. Chapman out of her apartment. Ever since Dean's visit earlier in the week, Mrs. Chapman had been peppering Janet with questions about the charming young man from her job.

As if on cue, her neighbor's door opened, and Mrs. Chapman shuffled into the hallway, carrying a garbage bag.

"Oh, hello there, Janet." Mrs. Chapman peered at Janet and Dean with a sly smile on her lips.

"Good evening, Mrs. Chapman." Janet inwardly cursed the finicky door lock. It had been jamming for the past few weeks, and she had meant to talk to the super about it, but had never gotten around to it. "This is Dean – my coworker."

"Good evening." Dean smiled.

"Yes, I remember." Mrs. Chapman nodded. "Well, I'll be on my way." Mrs. Chapman headed toward the garbage room.

Finally, the lock clicked. Janet cracked the front door open and was instantly ambushed by Baxter.

"Hello, Baxter." Dean bent down to pet Baxter. At the sign of this attention, Baxter abandoned Janet and ran toward Dean, barking excitedly.

"He remembers you!" Janet observed, inwardly assuring herself that she was not hurt by Baxter's defection.

"Of course he does." Dean scratched Baxter behind his ear, the latter being frozen still in mesmerized ecstasy.

"Make yourself at home." Janet motioned to the living room. "I'll go see about that drink."

"Great. I'll keep Baxter company."

Janet's apartment had a galley kitchen open on either end, and as she inspected the contents of her cupboards, she caught a glimpse of Dean walking into the living room. Baxter's tiny footsteps followed his new subject of adoration and stopped as Dean took a seat on the couch, showering Baxter with compliments like "good boy" and "smart fella." Apparently, even Baxter, who was usually extremely skeptical of strangers, was helpless before Dean's charm. Janet opened the cupboard that held the liquor and inspected the contents of the Jameson bottle. She had been overly optimistic in her expectations, as Mrs. Chapman's last visit had left the bottle only one quarter full. Still, that would probably be enough. And then there were two bottles of Sam Adams in her fridge.

Janet joined Dean in the living room. Baxter who lay curled up by Dean's feet, merely acknowledged her entrance with a slight wave of his tail. "I'm afraid I don't have much of a variety."

"I'm easy." Dean grinned. "Anything you've got will do."

"Jameson or Sam Addams?"

"Jameson, neat."

"One Jameson coming up."

Janet returned to the kitchen and poured a liberal portion of whiskey into Dean's glass and added a splash into her own glass.

"Here you are." Janet placed Dean's glass in front of him.

"Cheers." Dean raised his glass to his lips.

"Cheers." Janet took a small sip, resisting the urge to grimace at the whiskey scent tickling her nose. She glanced at Dean. His drink was half-empty: most likely he would not stay for another one. She had to ask him now. "Dean?"

"Hmm?"

"Last time, when we were walking Baxter, you asked me if I noticed anything suspicious at Bostoff…"

"Yeah, what about it?"

"I noticed a few things that are funky to say the least."

Dean looked at her expectantly, waiting for her to continue.

"Well, for one thing, their client base is anything but stellar. Emperial, Creaton, Rigel, Gemini, and Sphinx are Bostoff's biggest clients."

"I remember reading about them in the papers. They were accused of being, what's the term, market raiders. But then nothing has been proven against them."

"That's true. Still, many firms would not sign up such clients, but Bostoff has been most lenient: they have incomplete files for all of them."

"That could be a coincidence."

"A very convenient one at that. I've seen the trading these guys do—they can tank a company in a matter of days. Don't tell me that that's a coincidence too."

"Were all these trades from the hedge funds you mentioned?" Dean asked.

"Up until recently, yes. But now, there's this new company—Impala Group, and it's sending the same volume of trades that Emperial used to send, but Emperial is hardly trading at all now." Janet paused. "Something tells me that Emperial is connected to Impala group."

"Janet," Dean halted, reaching out to touch Janet's arm.

"Yes?"

Dean took a deep breath. "I need to tell you something. You might not like it. In fact, you might throw me out of your apartment for telling it to you, but I need to tell you anyway."

Janet's eyes widened. "What is it?"

"I am not really an IT specialist," Dean said.

"You're not?"

"No." He shook his head. "That is, I'm pretty good with computers, but it's not what I do professionally."

"What do you do?"

"I work for the Treasury Investigations department."

"What?" Janet had to make a physical effort to keep her jaw from dropping. "And you're telling me this now?"

"Our department has been investigating Bostoff Securities for several months. Once we secured a court order to go undercover, I was put on the job." Dean spoke matter-of-factly, impartially, as though he were a different person from the man Janet had just had dinner with. "The reason I'm telling you this is that Treasury would like your assistance with the case. I have cleared it with my supervisor. If you decide to aid us in the investigation, no charges will be brought against you personally for the duration of your employment with Bostoff. It sounds to me like you have already got quite a bit of information that we could use. If you agreed to cooperate with us, you would be a great asset to the investigation. You don't have to answer me right now, but I would appreciate an answer by Monday morning."

"By Monday morning?" Janet sank back into the couch, pressing her hands against her face. Instantly, her own doubts about Bostoff Securities became irrelevant. Those were based on the information obtained by means she was entitled to have access to. Well, maybe not entirely entitled to have access to, but still, her actions paled in comparison to Dean's. The seemingly charming, witty Dean she had fantasized about kissing was an undercover rat, propositioning her to become a snitch. He was a cold-hearted snoop, on the hunt to shut down the firm and ruin the lives of the people who worked for it. But worst of all was his leading Janet to believe that he was actually interested in her, while all he wanted was her help in getting dirt on Bostoff.

"Well, I'll be going now." Dean rose from his seat. There was no hesitation in his movements or his voice. Each had been deliberately calculated, just as his previous interactions with Janet had been.

Baxter tiptoed after Dean and barked in a farewell salute, ignoring Janet's command to stay by her side.

As if in a dream, Janet heard Dean's footsteps and the sound of the front door shutting behind him.

Baxter returned and lay coiled by Janet's feet.

"Now you come back?" Janet looked at Baxter who barked and looked back at her unflinchingly. But then she herself had been a victim of Dean's charms, so how could Baxter be expected to fare any better? "Well, Baxter, it turns out your judgment of character is as bad as mine," said Janet, as she stared into the ceiling, wondering what to do next.

ౠఆ

Once inside his apartment, Dennis Walker grabbed a beer from the fridge. He lay down on the couch, contemplating his behavior with Janet Maple and wondering what on earth had possessed him to breach every line of protocol he had abided by in his investigative career up until now. He knew how to get an inside source to collaborate: he had done it so many times, it became a routine. You got some dirt on them first, making it impossible for them to turn down the deal and thus securing their collaboration. Did he have any dirt on Janet Maple? Not in the least: all he had was his hunch that she suspected that something was wrong with Bostoff and that, like he, she did not approve of it. He wished he could have waited to get closer to her, but time was a luxury he could not afford. He needed answers yesterday. He had three weeks left to work the case, and he was nowhere near a good starting point. Meanwhile, Bostoff was getting away with this scheme, aided by that scum of a lawyer, Wyman. Janet was the key. She could get close to Wyman. If she agreed to help Dennis, together they could solve this scheme.

Janet's got to say yes, Dennis thought. She had to, or Dennis would be in deep trouble. His having revealed the truth behind his employment with Bostoff Securities gave Janet the upper hand. Dennis had not thought of that when he had been in the heat of the moment, confessing to her, which, in hindsight, made him a pretty bad agent - a rookie, really. It would have been easy to plead this excuse, but Dean knew the true root of his predicament. He was a pro at the investigation game. What he was a rookie at was having feelings for a woman. It had been a long time – not since his fiancée had deserted him. Now, Dean was troubled to admit that Janet Maple had somehow managed to stir emotions in him that he thought he would never feel again.

Chapter Twenty-Two

"Full skirt or figure-fitting?" Lisa's voice pierced through Janet's thoughts.

They were at the Vera Wang salon on Madison Avenue, Upper East Side. Janet stared at the blindingly white fabric. Betray your friend and save your own skin, or go down with the sinking ship, was all she had been able to think of since Dean had dropped the bomb on her. The charming IT guy was not charming at all. In fact, he was a deceitful snake, and Janet was an idiot to have fallen for his act.

"Full or fitting? Wake up, Janet!" Lisa added imperiously. "God, if this is how you are now, what's going to happen to you when the wedding plans will be in full swing?"

That's just it, Janet thought glumly. If Lisa knew what she knew, she would not be worrying about the wedding - she would be worrying about her fiancé's being investigated by the Treasury and possibly the SEC, as these days regulatory agencies jumped on the bandwagon of one another's investigations. Janet knew. She had worked for one. She had to tell Lisa. Granted, Lisa had done many things during the course of their tumultuous friendship that could justify revenge, but the decision that Janet had to make now was beyond revenge or loyalty. It was about being a decent human being. Janet might have fallen victim to Dean Snider's conniving schemes, but she was not about to become a backstabbing snoop herself.

"Lisa, I think they both look great. You've got a figure that can carry off any dress," Janet added. Anything to get out of the stupid bridal salon so that they could finally talk about things that mattered.

"Now, Janet, do you really want Lisa to merely 'carry off' her wedding gown?" Emily Foley clicked her tongue. "A bride is the center of the wedding. She is supposed to shine in her dress, not carry it off."

Janet reddened. She was, after all, the maid of honor, even if there were much more pressing matters at hand, extremely pressing.

"That's not what I meant, Emily. Both dresses are lovely; it's just a matter of preference."

"Lisa has a small frame. A full skirt will drown her, but a fitted gown will accentuate her figure." Emily Foley pointed to a column dress of ivory silk. "How about this one, Lisa? You will look like a Grecian goddess!"

"Yes, Mother, I like it," Lisa acquiesced. "But I also want to try the full-skirted one. I've always dreamed of wearing a full-skirted gown at my wedding."

Emily pursed her lips. "But, honey, there's just too much material in that dress. It will overpower you. Listen to your mother. Mother knows best."

"I want to try the full-skirted one." Lisa pouted. "Janet liked it, and I trust her judgment."

At the sound of Lisa's words, Janet lowered her eyes. Would her friend still be of the same opinion if she knew what Janet knew?

"Speaking of Janet." Emily swung around. "We might as well start thinking about the maid of honor and the bridesmaids' dresses. "Janet, how about this one?" Emily selected an off-the-shoulder gown in pale lavender. It was simple, but graceful.

Janet exhaled with relief. She had seen some truly horrible bridesmaids' dresses, but at least, she had been spared in this regard. Mrs. Foley had too much taste to mar her daughter's wedding with bad fashion. Bridesmaids dresses! Janet wanted to pull her hair out as her mind returned to matters of real importance. She had a major decision to make, and she was worrying about bridesmaid dresses.

"What size are you?" Emily eyed Janet as though she were a specimen under a microscope.

"I'm a six," Janet announced self-consciously. Six was a perfectly good size, but next to Lisa's dress size two, it sounded ginormous.

"Ah, well, that will probably make you a ten in Vera's dress size chart." Emily made a prompt calculation.

Janet had been wrong. Emily Foley might be too classy to clad her daughter's friends into unflattering fashions, but she had plenty of humiliating tricks up her sleeve.

"Lisa, what about your bridesmaids? I know they couldn't make it to today's fitting, but what size do they wear?" Emily asked.

Lisa stalled. "Oh, I'm not sure. Janet, what size does Katie wear?"

"A six also."

"Ah, that makes it easy: size ten all around, with the exception of our Lisa, of course. Janet, let me see if the store has a size ten for you to try on in that lavender dress, and then we'll get things moving!" Emily waved at the rail-thin sales attendant who had been standing by attentively ever since the three of them had been ushered into the salon.

Seizing the distraction, Janet tugged on Lisa's arm. "I need to talk to you."

"What about?" Lisa perked up. "Let me guess. Wedding shoes. That's next on the agenda."

"Actually, it's work-related; it's really urgent."

"Janet, you need to learn to relax. It's Sunday, for crying out-loud," Lisa groaned, holding up her hand in protest. "I have an important favor to ask you. It's about Katie. I haven't exactly asked her to be my bridesmaid, but I'm sure she'd want to be in the wedding, right?"

"I'm sure she would, but Katie's calendar is pretty busy. She's got depositions scheduled back to back," Janet rattled off the first excuse that came to mind.

"Perhaps you could ask her for me?" Lisa smiled sweetly.

"Oh, I don't know. I think it would sound better coming from you."

"And I thought you were my maid of honor! Can't you do this little thing for me?"

Janet gulped. Bridesmaid recruitment was not exactly part of the maid of honor's responsibilities – at least not the way she understood them.

"Look, Janet, you know that I don't have that many girlfriends, but I've got to have bridesmaids in my wedding party. Now, I realize that Katie is your friend, but couldn't you get her to be in the wedding for my sake?" Lisa's voice was almost pleading, as she shot a worried look at her mother who was busy questioning the sales attendant.

"Oh, all right." Janet caved in, weighed by the heavy guilt of the monstrous secret she was harboring, albeit unwillingly. "But first, can we please talk about that thing I mentioned..."

"Oh, thank you!" Lisa interrupted. "And why not invite Joe's fiancée as well? What was her name? Daphne – yes, I think that's it. She would round off the wedding party nicely, don't you think?"

Immediately Janet regretted her impulsive weakness. That was classic Lisa: give her an inch, and she would take a mile.

"Lisa, I really need to talk to you about work: it's important," Janet tried to make her voice sound steely.

"What's that I hear? Talk about work during a wedding dress fitting?" Emily Foley cut in. "Into the fitting room, you two. Janet, I'm afraid they don't have a size ten on hand, so you'll just have to try on a size four. That's the largest size the store had for this dress, but if the overall shape fits, we'll go ahead and order the correct size."

"Thank you, Emily." Janet eyed the tiny gown, thinking that most likely it would not even slide past her hips.

"This way, please." The sales clerk carried the gown into the fitting room. "Would you like assistance with the dress?" The skeletal blonde eyed Janet almost fearfully.

"I'll call you if I need you," Janet snapped. There was only so much bullying a girl could take in a day.

Once alone in the fitting room, Janet stood in her tights, eyeing the dress with the grim determination of a soldier contemplating the enemy. At least she had been proactive enough to wear control-top underwear. That ought to ease things up by a few inches. Gingerly, Janet pulled the zipper on the gown. Here I come. Janet stepped into the silky skirt, cautiously pulling it up her legs and towards her hips, ready to cease at the slightest resistance.

A few tense moments later she exhaled with relief. Her hips had made it into the dress without any trouble, and she was even able to get her arms into the bodice of the gown. The blasted thing was on. Now, all she needed was to zip it up. If such a feat were possible.

"A little assistance please," Janet called out, hoping that the sales girl would come to the rescue.

"Janet, how is it going in there?" Emily Foley's voice pierced the dressing room silence.

"Fine, almost done. I'll be out in a minute. I just need help zipping this thing up."

"No matter, it's good enough that you were able to get into it. Come on out, let's have a look at you!" Emily urged.

Can this day get any worse? Oh, yes, it can – just wait until your friend hears what you have to tell her and calls you a backbiting snake, Janet answered her own question, hobbling out of the fitting room. She might have been able to squeeze herself into the dress, but walking in it was an entirely different matter.

Emily Foley eyed her appraisingly. "Under the circumstances, I'd say the result is much better than expected." Mercifully, Emily's observations were interrupted by Lisa stepping out of the fitting room. "Oh, my!" Emily gasped, bringing her hand to her mouth. "You look stunning."

"Don't I?" Lisa's eyes lit up as she twirled the heavy skirt around her.

"Like a princess," Lisa's mother confirmed.

"I told you that Janet wouldn't steer me wrong. Don't you think the dress looks great, Janet?"

Janet nodded. "I do." As she looked at Lisa standing there starry-eyed, clad in a strapless gown of silk and chiffon, Janet felt an involuntary lump in her throat. This was Lisa's big moment, but all Janet could think of was the ultimatum Dean Snider had given her on Friday night: I would appreciate an answer by Monday morning, he had said, as though two days were all it took to make up one's mind about stabbing one's friend in the back.

"And you look great too," Lisa offered. "Lavender is definitely your color."

Janet eyed her reflection in the full-length mirror. The dress was supposed to be a flowing off-the-shoulder gown, but instead, it fitted her like a sausage casting. Still, despite the wrong size, the color was flattering.

"The next time we come in, please make sure to have this dress in Janet's size," Lisa instructed the sales assistant.

"Of course," the assistant nodded stiffly. "Would you like to try the next dress now?"

"I don't know," Lisa deliberated. "I think this is the one."

"We could always come back to look at more dresses," Janet offered, thinking that if she would not get to talk to Lisa soon, she was liable to burst from all the tension that was mounting up inside her.

"Do try the one I picked out for you, honey," Emily urged.

"All right then." Lisa smiled brightly. "This is fun."

An hour and half and five dresses later they had finally emerged from the bridal salon. Much to Janet's relief, Lisa had not committed to a dress, but had decided to come back for additional fittings. The way things were going, Lisa might need the money she intended to spend on the designer wedding gown for her lawyer fees, but Janet did not want to think about that just yet. She wanted to believe that there was still a way out.

"Well, Janet, I'm afraid we must leave you now," Emily Foley announced. "Lisa and I have a spa appointment."

"Lisa, I was hoping we could have a quick word?" Janet eyed her friend meaningfully.

"What time is our appointment?" Lisa asked her mother hesitantly.

"I'm afraid there's no time. Your conversation can wait until Monday, but Lisa's cellulite treatment cannot. She's got to get in top shape for the wedding. Unless, of course, Janet you'd like to come along?" Emily eyed Janet's hips. "I could make a call and squeeze you in."

"No, thank you." Janet shook her head, eager to bid goodbye before she lost her much-abused temper and strangled Lisa's mother.

"Thanks for everything, Janet," Lisa mumbled sheepishly. "We'll talk on Monday, okay?"

"Sure." Janet nodded. Short of yelling at the top of her lungs, a different reply was not an option.

ഇൗരു

Back in her apartment, Janet opened a bag of Doritos and slumped onto her couch, ignoring Baxter's pleas for a treat.

"You should have thought of your loyalties before sucking up to that snitch Dean Snider, Mister."

As if shamed by his past conduct, Baxter lowered his head and growled.

"Oh, fine, here you are." Janet extended a Doritos chip to Baxter, which he immediately scooped up from her hand. She was pretty sure that Doritos were not part of a healthy canine diet, but the same could be said about the human diet. At the sight of Doritos, Emily Foley would probably run for the Stairmaster the way a priest would run for holy water to ward off forces of evil. Having a mother like that explained many of Lisa's shortcomings, and in her softer moments, Janet was only too eager to make excuses for her friend, but there was a limit to the amount of softer moments one was entitled to, and right now, Janet felt pretty pissed off. There she was, worrying her head off about Lisa, while Lisa was happily prancing about with her wedding preparations. And how about the fact that it was Lisa who had gotten Janet into the whole Bostoff mess to begin with? Granted, Janet had been unemployed, but from where she stood now, it would have been far better to remain unemployed than work for a corrupt firm that was being investigated by the Treasury.

The facts of the matter were that both Lisa and Janet were in a fix, and even though Lisa had gotten them both into the mess, she was not going to be much help getting them out of it. Janet would have to figure a way out all on her own. She had to make sure that innocent people did not get hurt in the Bostoff investigation, for, while Janet had no doubts about corruptness of Jon Bostoff and Tom Wyman, she was just as equally sure that Lisa and Jon's brother, Paul Bostoff, were innocent bystanders, dragged along in a scheme they had little understanding of. What Janet was not sure of was Dean Snider's view on the matter. Regulators were human too. They could be just as vain and career-hungry as any Wall Street raider. Only the regulators had the excuse of upholding the 'law.' She had seen innocent people swept under the rug in the heat of an investigation by regulators who were eager to make a name for themselves, and a man as calculating and cunning as Dean Snider had turned out to be struck her as just such a type.

Janet picked up the phone and dialed Dean's number. She knew exactly what she was going to say. She would be brief and to the point, leaving him no ground to stand on.

"Janet?" Dean's voice sounded almost relieved. "How are you?"

"Hello, Dean," Janet replied coolly. The bugger was not going to get any small talk out of her. "I thought about your offer, and I'm going to accept, but on one condition," Janet paused for emphasis. "No matter what the investigation reveals, Lisa Foley and Paul Bostoff are not going to be implicated in any of this. They walk away free and clear."

There was a brief silence on the other end of the line. "Janet, I can't promise you that. I'm pretty sure that I could strike a deal for Lisa, but Paul... He is the COO of the company; he will have to be questioned."

"This is my offer. Take it or leave it. And mind you, I don't even have to cooperate with you. It's not as though you've got any proof to speak of."

"No," Dean's voice turned rigid. "But if you refuse to cooperate, the conditions of the deal that I offered you are off. I don't believe that I need to remind you that the New York Bar Association is most strict when it comes to licensed lawyers being implicated in fraudulent schemes."

Blackmailing bastard. Janet clenched the telephone receiver in her hand, but then what did she expect – a knight in shining armor?

"So do we have a deal?"

"For Lisa, yes, but I can't promise anything for Paul."

"Fine. Let's compare notes on Monday." Janet pressed the off button on the phone, barely resisting the urge to smash the receiver against the wall.

Chapter Twenty-Three

Janet had been waiting for Dean to knock on her door since the morning. It was four o'clock now, but there was still no sign of him. She had not seen him in any of the usual places where their paths had crossed so effortlessly just a week ago. He was not in the cafeteria or the kitchen, and even when Janet ventured to the trading floor, she did not see Dean at his desk. Could it be that the deal he had offered her was off? Perhaps he had already found all the evidence he needed and was sharing his findings with his boss at the Treasury this very moment. Who knew? The Treasury might then choose to involve the SEC, and the SEC could pull in the FBI. It all depended on how much information Dean had dug up and how career hungry the people involved were.

Unexpectedly, Janet found herself defending Bostoff Securities. She did not condone Bostoff's machinations, but she thought that Dean's technique was equally detestable. In fact, she thought it was much worse. Crooks were expected to act like crooks, but those serving the law were supposed to act with dignity and honor. It did not matter that the Treasury had obtained a court order for undercover surveillance of Bostoff Securities and assigned Dean to the case. What mattered was that he chose to lie to her and manipulate her emotions to get close to her. And what made it worse was that he had succeeded. Even now that Janet knew what a treacherous worm the man was, she could not help feeling palpitations at the thought of seeing Dean again. At first glance, hers was a legitimate enough emotion since Janet's own future and that of her friend's now rested in Dean's hands, but as annoyed as she was at herself, Janet had to admit that hers were not tremors of dread, but of excitement. Despite everything she had learned about the man, she could not squash her attraction to Dean Snider.

At four o'clock the suspense became unbearable, and Janet headed for Dean's desk. She needed to know where she stood. Her pulse quickened as she spotted him behind his desk, typing away busily on his keyboard. He was all concentration and diligence. One would never suspect that Dean Snider was, in fact, a mole.

"Good afternoon." Janet flashed him a brusque smile.

"Ah, hello there," Dean answered with a distracted air of someone engrossed in his work.

"I am having problems with my computer; I was wondering if you could help me with that."

"I'll be right there," Dean replied, still typing. "Just give me about twenty minutes."

"Thank you."

Perplexed, Janet walked back to her office. For someone who had been so eager to get her help, Dean showed a startling lack of enthusiasm.

Janet closed the door of her office and sat down behind her desk. She looked at the reports she had been poring over all day. The orders from Impala Group continued to flood in, and the prices of the targeted stocks were plummeting. The most prominent price decline was in Date Magic dot com: a recent IPO that had started trading at thirty five dollars, but was now as low as twelve dollars.

Date Magic. Janet raked her memory. The name sounded familiar. She searched the company name on the Internet and was instantly reminded why. Andrew Foley's face beamed at her from the company's website. He was the company CEO. Normally, Janet would have said that the sleazeball got what he deserved, but in this case Andrew Foley was not the only victim. There were the company employees and the shareholders to consider. The memory of Janet's recent disturbing encounter with Andrew Foley aside, this was a strange development. Why would Jon Bostoff want to drive down the price of the company stock owned by Lisa Foley's cousin? After all, they were practically family.

Janet checked her watch. It was twenty after four. Dean was certainly taking his time. Just then there was a knock on her door and she nearly jumped from the tension that was wound up inside her.

"Come in," Janet called out in what she hoped was a calm voice.

"Hello, Janet." Dean walked inside her office. She expected him to close the door behind him, but he left it open. "What seems to be the problem?"

For a moment, she stared at him wide-eyed, wondering whether Dean had been stricken by a severe case of amnesia. Then she understood: he was maintaining his cover.

"Like I said, my computer is malfunctioning."

"Let's have a look." Dean walked over to her desk and stood close to her chair – way too close for her taste.

"I wanted to talk to you," Janet whispered, bewildered by the idiocy of the situation. Why was she whispering in her own office?

"Not here," Dean replied, his tone even. "I'll meet you at your place at eight o'clock tonight."

Janet's eyebrows shot up from this brashness. The nerve of the guy. Did he think that along with her cooperation in the Bostoff investigation he was also going to receive the added bonus of getting into her bed?

"We need a quiet place to talk," Dean whispered, as if reading her thoughts. "You could come over to my place instead. Or have you got any other suggestions?"

"My place is fine. Eight o'clock. You already know the directions," Janet conceded. At least she would be dealing with the snake on her own turf.

"See you then," Dean mouthed, and then added in a loud voice. "It's all fixed now, Ms. Maple. Once your machine reboots, it will be good to go."

ꕥ

At eight o'clock sharp, the doorbell of Janet's apartment rang. Janet went to answer the door. Dean was standing at the threshold, a bottle of Jameson in one hand and a laptop case in the other. He was dressed casually in a pair of jeans, Henley shirt, and a brown leather jacket. Unlike the ill-fitted suits he wore at work, the outfit did justice to his tall, lanky physique, making Janet do a double take.

"I think I depleted your supply the other night," he announced jauntily, making his way inside the apartment.

"I don't really drink whiskey. It's for the times that my neighbor visits," Janet retorted. The guy sure did not miss a thing.

"I'll do better next time."

Janet placed the bottle of Jameson in the kitchen cupboard. There would be no social drinking tonight.

Dean took a seat on the couch, directing his attention to Baxter, who was barking happily at his arrival.

Traitor, Janet thought, watching Baxter wag his tail at Dean. Never before had Baxter's radar been so off.

"I think we should get right to it," Janet announced.

Dean placed his laptop on the coffee table, looking at her expectantly.

Janet bit her lip, realizing that the first person to speak was bound to be in a weaker position, but she had set up her own trap.

"Do you promise the terms that I've asked for?"

Dean nodded. "Almost all of them. I met with my boss today and he agreed to keep Lisa out of it. From what I've seen of her in action, she has no idea about the operations of Bostoff Securities anyway, but Paul Bostoff's role in the company is too senior to grant him protection. Unless, of course, his brother were to say that Paul had nothing to do with the scheme. In that case, Paul would most likely be excluded from the investigation, but I doubt that Jon Bostoff would be that magnanimous."

"So that's it? That's your final offer?"

"It is. And I dare say that it's a damn good one. Look, Janet, I know that I'm no hero in your book, but Jon Bostoff is a crook, and Emperial's owner, David Muller, is an even bigger crook. The only reason we went after Bostoff was to get to Muller. We need to prove that the two have been operating a coordinated market manipulation scheme, and then we will be able to get the whole gang."

"What about Creaton, Rigel, Gemini, and Sphinx?" Janet rattled off the other hedge funds that were prominent clients of Bostoff.

"Them too, but they are small fish compared to Emperial. Emperial is running the shots. You worked for the DA's office. You used to catch the bad guys. I imagine it would not be that difficult for you to get back into the game again."

"I never pretended to be someone I was not, and I never snuck behind people's backs."

Dean nodded. "I guess I've earned that one. Look, I know you must hate my guts right now. I wish things could be different, but they're not. Help me with the case, and I promise you that your employment record will remain unmarred. The same goes for Lisa."

"Are you going to bring her in on the case?"

"Of course not. She's too close to Bostoff. Her loyalties are obvious. It goes without saying that you must not tell Lisa or anyone at Bostoff about your involvement in the investigation. If you do, the deal is off, and you'll be added to the suspects list for obstructing the investigation."

"Gee, thanks for the warning." Janet dropped her face into her hands. How was she supposed to go on sneaking behind Lisa's back for weeks to come and live with herself?

"Janet, I know it's hard, but you're getting a pretty good deal. Neither you nor your friend will be implicated in the investigation."

"Lisa got me a job at Bostoff in the first place, and this is how you want me to repay her? By sneaking around behind her back while her fiancé could face serious legal action against him?"

"I never said this would be easy, but let's evaluate the facts. For one thing, if Lisa weren't such a dingbat, she wouldn't be working at Bostoff in the first place. You were there for only a few weeks and you instantly saw that things were off, so really, it's because of her that you're stuck in this mess in the first place. And as for Paul – he's a nice enough guy from what I've seen of him, but he doesn't have the backbone to stand up to his father or brother, and sooner or later one pays the price for being a pushover."

"You've got an explanation for everything, haven't you?" Janet slouched in resignation. How easy it was for Dean to justify betrayal, but then what did she expect from a man who clearly had no moral principles?

"We could argue for hours, but I didn't come here to argue. I came here to ask you if you were on board. Are you on board?"

"Yes," Janet gave the only reply she had the option to give.

"Good. Moving on to step number two – developing a game plan."

"I thought you'd never get to that part," Janet could not resist poking at Dean's smugness. If Mr. In-Control had all the answers, then why did he ask for her help? Because he needed her, that's why, so he'd better get used to not being the boss with her. "These are the reports from last week." Janet pointed to the papers she had laid out on the table prior to Dean's arrival. "There is a clear pattern of orders from the Impala Group: the stocks they targeted plummeted in price. So far, the most noticeable impact has been on Date Magic, a recent IPO that started trading at thirty-five dollars, but closed at twelve dollars today."

"Let's see here." Dean punched a few keystrokes on his laptop. "Date Magic CEO, Andrew Foley…" He stared at Janet. "He wouldn't by any chance be related to Lisa Foley?"

"You never miss a thing, do you? He's her cousin."

"Nature of my job. Why would Jon Bostoff want to manipulate his brother's fiancée's cousin's company stock?" Dean shook his head. "That was a mouthful, but do you get my drift? I think this means that Jon Bostoff is merely taking orders from Impala; he's not the brains behind the operation. He didn't even bother to do the homework to see what stocks were being targeted."

Janet nodded. "I hadn't thought of that." And indeed she had not. Well, at least things were starting to look a little less dire. Bostoff taking fraudulent orders was still bad, but it was not nearly as bad as originating the orders.

"Now all we need is to find out who's behind the Impala group, and we've got our case."

"Something tells me that Impala and Emperial are connected– if only from the fact that orders from Emperial have dropped to almost nothing and orders from Impala keep pouring in."

"Yes, well, a mere coincidence is not going to help us. We need evidence."

"I've looked through Bostoff's legal files – nothing there. I bet Tom Wyman has all the answers we need. If only we could get to his files," Janet added wistfully. "But he guards his laptop like a hawk."

"We'll think of something."

"We've got to. Wyman handles all of Bostoff's legal affairs. Lisa doesn't know a damn thing, and frankly, I don't get to do much either. Wyman keeps it all under control. But it was not always like that...."

"What do you mean?"

"Wyman's predecessor, Fred Rossingram, used to be the general counsel for Bostoff Securities before Jon Bostoff started employing Wyman's services. I found several of Rossingram's memos on the Legal drive. The last one was dated right about the time that Jon Bostoff took over the business for his father."

"Shared Legal drive," Dean mused. "I missed that one."

"I guess you can't sift through everything," Janet could not resist jabbing him.

"Well, then, we've got to pay Fred Rossingram a visit."

"How do you propose we do that? I don't know anything about the man besides his name."

"In the age of the Internet, no search is insurmountable." Dean reached for his laptop. After a few moments of his fingers typing feverishly, he exclaimed triumphantly. "Found him." Dean turned the laptop screen towards Janet.

"Fred Rossingram – Estates and Wills, Prenuptial Agreements and Divorces," Janet read. "Must be a big change from being a general counsel of Bostoff Securities," Janet observed, noting Rossingram's address, which was all the way on York Avenue.

"I think we should pay the old man a visit."

"How do you know he is old, and under what pretext are we going to visit him?"

"The first one is easy." Dean flipped to the About Us section of Rossingram's website, showing a picture of a gray-haired man in horn-rimmed glasses. "We'll just have to come up with a pretext to visit him." Dean drummed his fingers against his chin. "We'll say that we need a prenuptial agreement."

"Can't you think of a better cover-up?"

"This one is perfect: a nice young couple seeking an old man's advice – just the thing to drop his guard."

"But we'd be imposters. Isn't that illegal?"

"I don't see anything illegal about inquiring about drafting a prenuptial agreement."

"You're the boss." Janet leaned back against the cushions of her couch, feeling as though she had sunk into a deranged thriller movie. "Can I ask you a question?"

"By all means."

"Do all Treasury investigators operate by such unorthodox means?"

"Nope – just me, but then I'm not your average investigator."

"What makes you so different?"

"If we solve this case, I promise I'll tell you."

Janet shrugged. She already knew the answer anyway: extreme arrogance and smugness. Oh, and deep blue eyes, a strong chin, well-defined nose, and broad shoulders... Snap out of it, she kicked herself. Dean Snider was the enemy, and one could not lose one's guard around the enemy.

Dean looked at his watch. "I think that's it for tonight. I'm glad to see that we're making progress already. I'll see you tomorrow: same time, same place?"

"You know the address."

"Janet, if we are to solve this case, we've got to move fast. My boss gave me an extension to a three week deadline, and week one started today."

"I got it. I'll do what I can."

"That's a girl. It's good to have you on my team, Janet Maple."

"Good night." Janet headed for the foyer and held the door open for Dean. He would not fish any compliments out of her.

"See you tomorrow."

🕳🕴

Back at his apartment, Dennis pulled a beer out of his fridge and gulped down half a bottle with satisfaction. Finally, he was getting somewhere. Granted, he had assembled most of the picture already, but having Janet help him on the case made things easier. Janet's access to the data on Bostoff's trades helped fill in the blanks, and he couldn't have gotten this data without her help. Sure, Dennis had wired her computer, but Janet had told him that the trade reports were saved on the shared computer drive. She was printing the reports without saving them to her computer, which was why the tracking software had missed the files.

Dennis was glad that Janet had agreed to help him. He was even gladder that he had been able to talk his boss into granting protection for her. Ham Kirk had been most cantankerous about the notion, but he had finally caved in, telling Dennis that his head was on the line. Well, Dennis Walker was used to taking risks, and he was not about to stop now.

Chapter Twenty-Four

Janet exited the cab on York Avenue and Ninetieth Street. A sign on the corner building with ground floor offices read, Fred Rossingram: Suite 1A. She looked around, searching for Dean. They had an appointment with Rossingram at six o'clock; it was six o'clock on the dot. The sound of hurried footsteps made her turn around. Dean was walking toward her. He had his work clothes on: another variation of a suit that was two sizes too big for him.

"Sorry, I got held up at work."

"Let me guess, another nincompoop who could not turn on his computer?" Janet felt a pang of sadness, remembering how Dean's jokes about his job used to make her smile when she had actually thought that IT Specialist was his real job and that his interest in her was genuine.

"You hit the nail right on the head. Shall we?" Dean offered his arm to her.

"You know, it's not too late to call the whole thing off. It has disaster written all over it. If Rossingram's got at least half a brain, he's bound to see right through us."

"And what makes you say that?" Dean put his hands on either side of Janet's shoulders, steering her toward the glass door of the building, in which she could see their reflection. He leaned in closer to her. "I think that we look compelling as a couple."

Janet felt her face flush. Dean was kidding, of course, but for a moment, the possibility had crept into her thoughts.

"Fine. Let's get it over with."

"That's my girl." Dean pressed the intercom button. The door buzzed open, and together, they walked into the building lobby.

Rossingram's office was on the ground floor to the right. Janet felt nervous jolts run through her body as Dean rang the doorbell. She made a mental tally of their story to Rossingram. They were an engaged couple on the brink of tying the knot, and they needed a prenuptial agreement. Nothing fancy, just the bare bones to protect Dean's inheritance. At least she was glad that Dean had spared her the role of the rich heiress. There was no way she could have carried off that charade. It was Dean's idea, so let him do the crazy bit. Yet, mixed in with her nervousness, there was excitement too. She had never done anything like this, and if it had not been for Dean, she probably never would.

"Good afternoon." A man in a tweed jacket and wool slacks opened the door. He was in his mid to late sixties, with gray, slightly balding hair. He had pudgy cheeks, a gray mustache and horn-rimmed glasses. "Jeff Amble and Jacky Stein?"

Janet blinked, remembering the pseudonyms Dean had come up with for their visit to Rossingram.

Holding her arm at the elbow, Dean nodded. "That's us."

"Come on in." Rossingram stood by the door. "This way, please."

The office consisted of two rooms: a foyer with a receptionist desk and a room in the back that contained Rossingram's desk and law reference books.

"Please have a seat." Rossingram motioned to two chairs that stood opposite his desk, as he took a seat in the worn swiveling chair behind his desk. "So, I understand that you are looking to draft a prenuptial agreement?"

"Correct." Dean patted Janet's hand, sending shivers up her spine. "It's my family. They are very conservative. I told Jacky that I trusted her completely, but you see, my mother will not have it any other way. You do understand, honey?" Dean cooed at Janet, and it took all of her self-control not to burst into laughter. What was this guy doing working for the Treasury? His calling was on Broadway.

"Yes, dear." Janet looked at Dean with what she hoped was convincing affection. "You know that I do."

"Good." Dean exhaled as though an incredible weight had been lifted off his shoulders.

"Very well." Rossingram eyed them curiously. "I am going to need some information about your employment and assets. Have you brought the paperwork I've asked you to complete?"

"Yes." Dean put a manila folder on Rossingram's desk. "Everything is in there."

"Let's have a look." His expression perfunctory, Rossingram began reviewing the files. When he reached the part about Janet, or Jacky Stein, as Dean had decided to name her, Rossingram's expression clouded. "You work for Bostoff Securities?" He peered at Janet over the rim of his glasses.

"Yes." Janet swallowed. Her throat had suddenly gone dry under Rossingram's piercing gaze.

"Jacky recently joined their legal department," said Dean. "Of course, I keep telling her that there's no need for her to work, but she is so independent," Dean exclaimed with the authentic disdain of someone who never had the need to work. "But all of this is going to change once we get married, right, honey?"

"We've talked about this," Janet retorted, aware that her acting was nowhere near on par with Dean's. "Now is not the time to discuss it." She blushed. This was a natural reaction, but she hoped that it would add credibility to her words.

"There, there." Dean took her hand and pressed it to his lips–an unnecessary action in Janet's opinion, but apparently, the gesture produced the desired effect on Rossingram, as the lawyer looked at Janet with a mixture of sympathy and concern.

"Young lady, and may I add that I use the term in the most endearing sense of the word – I've got a daughter of about your age, Ms. Stein." Rossingram cleared his throat. "I suggest that you listen to your fiancé and quit your employment at Bostoff Securities immediately."

"Why would you say that?" Janet asked, prompted by the pressure of Dean's fingers on her hand.

"That place is a boiler room," Rossingram snapped, halting immediately, as though frightened by his own blunt admission. "I have not spoken about this matter to anyone for years, but I suppose there is no harm in me telling you. The two of you seem like such a nice couple... I was the general counsel of Bostoff Securities for almost twenty years. Hank Bostoff and I were good friends, but when his son, Jon, took over, everything changed. Bostoff had been one of the most respected shops on the street for years, but the markets began to change, and the profits started to dip. The fact that Hank's wife passed away didn't help the matter either. Slowly, Hank began to give more and more authority to Jon, and the business of Bostoff Securities began to change. Jon started signing on shady hedge funds that Hank would have never let within two feet of the front door. I tried to reason with Jon, but he would not listen to me. Instead, he cut me out of the loop completely, contracting all the legal matters out to Ridley Simpson law firm. I believe the fella's name was Tom Wyman ..."

At Rossingram's mention of Wyman, Janet nearly jumped out of her seat, but was steadied by the touch of Dean's hand. Thankfully, Rossingram was too engrossed in his own memories to notice her reaction.

"I tried talking to Hank, but he waved me off, saying that we were too old to understand the new markets, and that it was time for him to pass the business over to his sons, Jon and Paul. But Jon was the one running everything. Paul's involvement was limited to marketing and PR. He did not really have a head for business." Rossingram took off his glasses and rubbed his eyes.

"It was a difficult decision to make. Over the years, I had come to think of Hank Bostoff as a friend, but there was nothing I could've done to help him. Jon had taken over completely, so I resigned. Now, I do estate planning and prenuptial agreements to keep myself busy."

"This sounds like a detective novel!" Dean exclaimed. "What exactly was going on at this firm while you were there?"

"I couldn't tell you the specifics, as Jon had cut me out of the loop. I bet the lawyers at Ridley Simpson have the whole picture, though. Jon started using them once I told him that I didn't agree with his 'business model.' He knew that I would tell Hank about the kind of business he was bringing into the firm, which I did, only Hank didn't listen to me…"

"So, Jon Bostoff outsourced everything to Ridley Simpson law firm?" Dean prodded.

"Yes. I'm sure there's another reason why he did it. If Bostoff Securities were ever to come under an investigation, attorney/client privilege would be impenetrable, unless waived by Bostoff. It's much easier to pressure a firm into disclosing its communications with the internal counsel, versus outside law firm." Rossingram shook his head. "I sure hope it will not get to that. I would hate for Hank to see his life's work covered in shame… I wish I could have helped, but Hank would not listen to me, and with the kinds of clients Jon was signing on, I knew that nothing good would come out of it, so I resigned, and I advise the same to your fiancée."

Janet looked at the sadness in Rossingram's face. The old man had been completely honest with them, and they had repaid him with ridiculous lies.

"Thank you, Mr. Rossingram. I'm going to follow your advice."

Rossingram nodded. "Wise decision; the place is a volcano waiting to explode. Feel free to mention me as a reference if you'd like."

"Thank you for that, but I would not want to trouble you."

Rossingram sighed. "It's no trouble. I would hate to see a young girl like you get caught up in their schemes. Sooner or later, those hot-shot hedge funds Jon Bostoff had signed on are going to get busted, and Bostoff Securities will go down with them. I just hope that Hank Bostoff will not be there to witness it."

"Thank you for your time, Mr. Rossingram. I think we'll be going now." Dean stood up from his seat.

"But what about the prenup?" Rossingram asked, surprised.

"Oh, I've changed my mind about that," Dean was quick to respond. "I don't want to put Jacky through this nonsense. She's got enough to worry about already. Mother will just have to accept my decision."

"How much do we owe you?" Janet asked. The least they could do was compensate Rossingram for the time he had spent with them.

Rossingram waved his hand. "It's free of charge. I didn't give you legal advice."

Once they were several blocks away from Rossingram's office, Janet glared at Dean.

"I'm never doing anything like that again."

"What's the matter with you? We've got a ton of valuable information from the man."

"I felt horrible sitting there and lying to his face, while he was being honest and genuinely concerned."

"Well, wouldn't you agree that there are genuine reasons for his concern? Last time I checked, you were still an employee of Bostoff Securities."

Janet balked; she had forgotten about that part. Dean might be spending ten-hour days on the trading floor of Bostoff Securities, but in the end, he was only pretending to be an IT Specialist at Bostoff Securities, while she was the one who was employed by the dubious firm, and she was the one putting everything on the line – her employment record, her reputation, and her future.

"Perhaps I should take Rossingram's advice and quit."

"Don't do this to me, Janet. We're so close to solving the case – we're almost home."

"It's easy for you to say: you're not the one sticking your neck out."

"If you resign, you can still be subpoenaed to testify about the events that transpired during your employment at Bostoff. The protection offered to you by the Treasury for your cooperation with the case would be voided the moment you resign from Bostoff."

"You knew about this, didn't you?" Janet stared at him in disbelief. Was there anything that was more important to this man than his career?

"These are standard terms; I thought I had made that clear. If not, I apologize."

"Thanks."

"Look, Janet, we've almost got them. Already, we have enough evidence to demonstrate that there is manipulative trading being conducted by the Impala Group. Bostoff Securities has failed in its due diligence and oversight obligations by taking the orders from Impala. These are strong charges, but to really corner the case we need proof of organized market manipulation."

"I think you forgot to say that we've gotten this far thanks to me," Janet sniffed. She was the one who had done the painstaking task of piecing all the trades together, deducing a pattern, and identifying the stocks that were being targeted. For the past few nights, Dean had been a constant guest in her apartment while she explained her findings to him.

"Yes, you've done an amazing job, and I've informed my boss of your valuable input to the investigation. Rest assured, when the time comes, your contribution will be recognized. This is why we cannot quit now; we are too close. The only missing piece is Impala Group and its connection to Bostoff. Once we get that, we'll hit a home run."

"And how do we get that?" Instantly, Janet wished she had not asked, for she already knew the answer: Tom Wyman.

Chapter Twenty-Five

Janet eyed the phone on her desk. The normally benign apparatus looked as menacing as a torture device. The task that loomed before her, compliments of Dean Snider, was as bloodcurdling as being subjected to waterboarding. Well, fine, maybe not that horrific, but it was certainly up there. Janet pulled out Tom Wyman's business card from her Rolodex and looked at it in calm determination. It was just a phone call – how bad could it be? All she had to do was to convince Tom Wyman to visit her at the office and have a drink with her afterwards.

That was the order Dean had given her, not that she was taking orders from Dean. Well, actually, she was, but it was too late to cry about it now. She was in this mess up to her neck, and the only way out was to complete the task she had signed up to do. As if being tormented by a guilty conscience were not enough, keeping the investigation secret from Lisa had made it almost impossible for her to face her friend, resulting in Janet's conjuring up various excuses to abstain from being involved in Lisa's wedding: the wedding that could possibly be ruined by the outcome of the case Janet was helping Dean to solve. Horrible, Janet felt horrible, but at least she had managed to secure protection for Lisa, although she was certain that once this truth were out, this fact would buy her little credence in Lisa's eyes. Perhaps it was only fitting that, as punishment for going behind her friend's back, Janet had to charm a sleazebag like Tom Wyman.

Janet picked up the receiver and punched in the numbers of Wyman's direct line. Just like ripping off a Band-Aid, calling Tom Wyman was best to get over with quickly.

"Tom Wyman," Wyman's brusque voice answered after the first ring.

"Tom, hi, this is Janet, Janet Maple from Bostoff Securities…" Janet made sure to introduce herself in abundant detail, not wanting to tax Wyman's memory.

"Janet," Wyman's voice instantly warmed up by several notches. "Of course – I was wondering how you were. We had such a nice time at the party, and then, I don't hear from you for days…"

Janet ignored Wyman's dig. If he had wanted to see her, he could have called her, but this was just his style. Men like Tom Wyman expected women to go after them.

"Oh, Tom, it's so good to hear your voice. I've been crazy busy working – I hardly had a spare minute of free time."

"Oh, yeah? Anything I can help with?"

"I'm so glad you asked," Janet paused. "I was hoping you could come over to the office so that we could talk…."

"I've got a better idea – why don't we meet for drinks after work instead?"

Janet hesitated. This was not the exact plan, but she had to go along with it…

"Sure, that sounds good too. How about Georgiana? They've got a nice bar." She was determined to insist on the bar Dean had instructed her to pick. He had said it was extremely important.

"Sounds good. They are on Fifty-Seventh and Third, if memory serves me right?"

"That's right."

"How does seven o'clock sound?"

"Sounds good; I'll see you there."

"I'm looking forward to it, Janet."

Janet replaced the receiver on the phone and stared at it. Of late, her life had turned into a bizarre thriller. She had become an impersonator, a liar, and a corporate spy. Her new reality was terrifying, but she had to admit that it was also exhilarating – well, at least at times when she managed to forget that she was still employed by Bostoff Securities. Dean had promised her that she would not be implicated in the investigation, and she certainly hoped that he would keep his word. Common sense told her that she should have hired a lawyer to protect her interests, but the reality was that she could not afford one. At a minimum rate of five hundred dollars an hour, one was liable to end up in bankruptcy unless one's bills were being picked up by a corporate expense account. Borrowing money from family and friends was not an option, as she saw no realistic way of repaying it: not when her future career prospects seemed dubious at best. She had gotten herself into this mess, and she would get herself out. If the worst came to the worst, she was a lawyer: she could represent herself.

Think of the Devil: there was a light rapping on the door of her office. Janet looked up and saw Dean standing in the doorway.

"How did it go?" Dean asked, closing the door behind him.

"How do you know that it went anywhere? Are you tapping my phone now?"

"You know better than that; you told me you were going to call Wyman first thing in the morning."

"And I did. He's going to meet me for drinks at Georgiana's at seven."

"He's not coming into the office first?"

"No, I tried to get him to come, but he said his day was full. I didn't think it was a good idea to blow him off for drinks. At least we got part of the plan in the bag."

"Yeah, that's better than nothing. I just hope he brings his computer with him – otherwise, it will be a wasted evening."

"So what's the plan?"

"You meet him there, and I'll join you shortly afterwards. We'll use the two coworkers run into each other at a bar routine…"

Janet blinked, reminded of Dean's accidental appearance during her night out with Katie – the night that now seemed to be eons ago. At the time, she had actually believed that running into Dean had been an accident, but now she knew better.

"Fine. How do we get him to talk?"

Dean looked over Janet's outfit. She was wearing a button-up blouse and a pencil skirt.

"Well, if you show up wearing this, he will not talk. Please, do me a favor and change before you go to meet him. You can leave the rest up to me."

"I'm not putting out to get him to talk. That's where I draw the line."

Dean pressed his lips together. "What kind of person do you think I am, Janet?"

Janet lowered her eyes. That was just it. She had no idea. There were so many different sides to Dean Snider.

"All I am asking you to do is to talk to the man."

"And wear a skimpy outfit while doing it."

Dean groaned. "All I asked was that you change into something a bit more intriguing for tonight. No one has ever been harmed by looks, or am I mistaken? But you don't even have to do that if you're that uncomfortable." He glared at her. "Besides, I'll be there to make sure that nothing bad happens to you."

At ten after seven, Janet walked into Georgiana's. To gratify Dean's request, she had changed into a violet wrap dress with a deep v-neckline and black pumps. At the moment, her sex-kitten outfit was concealed by a trench coat, as the fall weather was now in full swing.

Janet scanned the bar; it was crowded as usual, but it did not take her long to spot Tom Wyman. His tailored suit and immaculate haircut stood out among the sea of less elegant men.

Janet tapped his shoulder.

"Hello, Tom. I'm sorry I'm late." Slowly, she took off her trench coat; the effect on Wyman was as though she were stripping.

"Some things are worth waiting for." Wyman got up to his feet to help her with her coat. "Should we get a table? I could go for a bite to eat."

"Maybe later. Right now, I really want a drink."

"What will it be?" Wyman asked.

"A dirty martini," said Janet, remembering Dean's instructions.

While Wyman repeated her order to the bartender, Janet was relieved to see that Wyman's laptop case was underneath his chair. Dean would be pleased.

"Here you are." The bartender placed the drink before her. Janet took a sip and gasped from the powerful mixture going down her throat. The bartender was more than generous with the vodka. She wondered what Dean's plan was. At this rate, she would be under the table after two of these babies.

"God, I've had an awful day." Wyman pushed his nearly-empty glass out of the way and motioned for another drink. "But let's not talk about work; let's enjoy ourselves."

Janet raised her glass to her lips, barely taking a sip. Where was Dean, and what was she supposed to do next?

Dean must have read her thoughts because a moment later, she heard his voice behind her back.

"Janet, fancy meeting you here."

"Dean!" Anxious to surrender the reins to Dean, Janet suppressed the excitement in her voice. "Dean Snider, Tom Wyman," she made the introductions, "Dean is an IT Specialist at Bostoff."

"Pleasure to meet you, Dean." Wyman extended his arm for a handshake. "I'm Tom Wyman; I do some legal work for Bostoff."

"Very nice to meet you, Tom." Dean struck out his hand, knocking over Janet's drink. Both Janet and Wyman jumped up from their seats, the spilled liquid miraculously missing them.

"Oh, that was very clumsy of me. I'm so sorry," Dean apologized. "Please let me make it up to you. The next round is on me."

"There's no need, really," Wyman replied dryly.

"Please, I insist." Dean nodded at the bartender and asked for three martinis.

Several moments later a drink was placed before Janet. She took a sip and almost spat it out: it was vermouth and olive juice and no vodka.

"That's a good drink," said Wyman after a long swallow. "The kind of drink a fella needs after a hard day of work. I've had two of these babies already, but this one really hits the spot."

"Cheers." Dean held up his glass, downing it in three gulps.

Wyman followed suit. "So, Dean, how is it that you know Janet?" Wyman asked, his words coming out a little slower now.

"We'll get to that." Dean smiled. "But first, another round."

Janet saw a twinkle in Dean's eyes. Then it hit her: Dean must have made an arrangement with the bartender.

"I can waaaalk on myyyy ooowwwn," Wyman protested, as, a short while later, Dean and Janet steered him out of Georgiana's and into the street. A cab was standing by the curb.

"We're in luck," said Dean. "Tom, we'll drop you off first."

Wyman shook his head. "I don't wanna trouble ya."

"It's no trouble," Dean replied.

Together, Dean and Janet shoved Wyman into the back seat. Janet sat next to Wyman and Dean sat next to her, placing Wyman's laptop case under the seat.

"Where do you live, Tom?" Janet asked.

"Seventieth and Madison," Wyman slurred.

Dean repeated the address to the cab driver.

"Got it." The cab driver looked back over his shoulder, an expression of alarm spreading over his face. "Watch your friend. He pukes, I'm kicking you out of the cab."

"No worries, chief; he can handle his liquor," Dean reassured the cabbie.

Feeling the pressure of Wyman's head on her shoulder, Janet was not so sure – she maneuvered her body away from Wyman, but miscalculated, and Wyman's head ended up on her breast. Shortly afterwards, a sound of light snoring ensued.

Bewildered, Janet stared at Dean.

"Just leave him be," Dean whispered. "We're almost there."

Easy for you to say, Janet thought. You're not the one with someone else's head on your boob.

Five martinis must have done him in because Wyman slept like a baby through the entire drive. Finally, the cab stopped in front of Wyman's address.

"Tom," Janet nudged Bostoff's inebriated legal counsel, "wake up, this is your place."

"What?" Wyman snorted. "Wanna come up for a nightcap?"

"Maybe some other time. I had a lovely time, but I'm really tired now."

Reluctantly, Wyman lifted his head off Janet's breast. "Next time, then." Wyman started to shuffle out of the cab.

Dean was already waiting by the door. He offered his arm for Wyman to lean on and walked him to his building. There he surrendered Wyman to the care of the doorman and rushed back to the cab.

Dean gave Janet's address to the cab driver. "Step on it," he added.

The cabby looked over his shoulder and eyed Janet's low-cut dress peeking through her unbuttoned trench coat. "I got you man – I'd be in a hurry too."

"I'm sorry," Dean whispered.

Janet groaned. By now she was getting used to being treated like a piece of meat.

Fifteen minutes later, they were in Janet's apartment.

"Quick," said Dean. "We don't have much time. Wyman could sober up at any moment."

"You think?" Janet shook her head. "What did you tell the bartender to put into those drinks?"

Dean beamed. "That was clever – admit it."

Janet crossed her arms. "I'm not admitting anything."

"You take the fun out of everything." Dean took Wyman's laptop out of its case and pushed the power button. "We got what we needed, didn't we? And back to your question, I had a little talk with the bartender beforehand and asked him for special drinks – all vodka for Wyman and Vermouth and olive juice for us."

"But the first drink I ordered was strong – real strong."

"That was before I got there. Why do you think I knocked the thing out of your hand?"

"Thanks. If you hadn't gotten there in time, I might have ended up like Wyman. Do you think he'll be okay?"

"He'll be fine. Nothing that a cold shower and a few aspirins wouldn't fix." The entire time Dean had been speaking with Janet, he had his eyes on the screen of Wyman's laptop. "Let's see here," said Dean, as the password screen came up. After several keystrokes he was in. "Not a very complicated password system," Dean remarked, examining the documents list on Wyman's laptop. "Aha!" he exclaimed triumphantly, "found it."

"What is it?" Janet's felt adrenalin pulsating in her blood. She still could not believe that she had helped Dean to practically drug Bostoff's outside legal counsel, and now, the two of them were rummaging through Wyman's laptop. Well, technically, Dean was doing all the rummaging, but she was standing by, being a willing accomplice.

"Damn. I knew it couldn't be that easy. The files are password-protected." Dean attacked the keyboard with redoubled efforts. After several minutes of intermittent cursing and mumbling, he exhaled victoriously. "Got it." His eyes focused on the text on the screen as he read every word hungrily.

Janet stood behind Dean's shoulder, following him word for word. What she saw defeated all of her expectations. Impala Group was a Cayman Island company owned by Bostoff Securities.

"So Bostoff owns the Impala Group?" Janet stared at Dean in disbelief. This was bad. She had expected Emperial to be behind Impala, in which case Bostoff Securities would still be on the hook, but not nearly to the extent that the company and its senior staff would be liable now.

"Looks like it." Dean rubbed his hands in excitement. "And look, there's more." Dean opened another document. "Looks like an agreement between Impala, Emperial, Creaton, Rigel, Sphinx, and Gemini for services to be performed by Bostoff Securities. Or should we say payment for aiding market manipulation?"

"Why would Bostoff want it in writing?"

"I guess Bostoff was worried that Emperial and the rest of the gang would not pay, so he wanted assurances. He couldn't very well foresee that I'd get access to Wyman's laptop." Dean grinned smugly, glancing at his watch. "It took me a total of forty-five minutes to break into it. Not bad for someone who doesn't do computers for a living." Dean reached into his pocket and produced a flash drive, which he inserted into the laptop to copy the files. "Let's hope the laptop does not have protection software banning external devices," he murmured.

"Damn it," he cursed a moment later, "of course it has external devicc protection software." Again Dean attacked the keyboard, alternating between swift keystrokes and concentrated stares on the computer screen. "Bingo." Dean grinned. "We'd better copy these files quickly. I wouldn't want to be caught red-handed with Tom Wyman knocking on your door."

Janet shook her head. Dean's paranoia was unnerving. "I'm sure Tom Wyman is passed out cold right now. Besides, he doesn't know where I live."

"Didn't the two of you have dinner after the party last week?"

Janet sighed. Nothing ever escaped Dean's attention. "Yes, we did. He dropped me off in a cab afterwards, but I hardly think that he memorized my address."

"I beg to differ." Dean's eyes were locked in on the computer in concentration. "There, all done." He placed the jump drive into his pocket and closed Wyman's laptop. Then he got to his feet, and Janet felt herself lifting off the floor as Dean's hands encircled around her, lifting her into the air. "We got them, Janet, we got them!"

"Put me down, Dean!" Janet laughed, unable to resist the glow inside her. It felt good to know that they had cracked the case, and it felt even better to have Dean's arms around her.

"As you wish, my lady." Dean put her down.

"Now what do we do?"

"Call Wyman tomorrow and return his laptop to him. Look wide-eyed and innocent and tell him that he left it in the cab, and you did not want to call him that late at night. Chances are that he'll be so embarrassed by the episode, he won't say a word. That is, if he doesn't show up here tonight. The night is still young."

"It's after midnight. I'd say that's unlikely," Janet retorted. "But more importantly, what happens with the investigation now?"

"I'm getting there – hold your horses. I will speak with my boss tomorrow; we now have enough to go on to launch an official investigation. The Feds will probably join us on the case and raid the place for documents and such…"

221

"The way they show it on TV?" Janet gasped, remembering episodes of American Greed.

Dean nodded. "I'm sorry. I know it's hard, but I promise that you and your friend, Lisa, will be kept out of it. The support staff doesn't have much to worry about either. They might be brought in for questioning, but the investigation will not go after them. It's the top brass that they want. It's always the top brass…."

"You mean the Bostoffs: Jon, Hank and Paul, even though Jon is the one who orchestrated the whole thing."

Dean halted, seeing the worry on Janet's face. "I'm sorry, but things aren't always fair in life. And Tom Wyman, definitely Tom Wyman," he added.

"Well, I think I'm going to bed. I'm exhausted. This has been a very eventful night."

Dean nodded, but made no move to leave. "Agreed. I think I should crash here for the night, in case Wyman shows up."

Janet shrugged. "I really think you're overreacting, but you're welcome to the couch." She motioned to the couch where Baxter was napping peacefully. "You might have to share with Baxter, though."

"That's all right; I just want to make sure that you're safe."

More likely you don't feel like dragging your ass all the way to Soho, Janet thought, but she was too tired to argue with Dean now.

"Okay, I'll get you a set of sheets and a pillow." She was about to head for her linen closet when there was a ring on the intercom.

She froze in place, terrified.

"Answer it," Dean's voice was calm. "If it's who I think it is, let him in."

"Okay." Janet picked up the intercom. "Hello?"

"Janet, it's Tom," Wyman's voice had no traces of alcohol in it. "May I come up?"

Janet glanced at Dean, and he nodded back. Without another word, she pressed the intercom button.

"Now what?" she glared at Dean.

"Now, nothing. You give him his laptop and send him on his merry way. I'll be right here." Dean receded into the alcove that housed Janet's bed. "If I hear any trouble, I'll come right out."

"Thanks." Janet had barely enough time to compose herself before the doorbell rang.

Her footsteps measured, she walked toward the door and opened it.

Tom Wyman stood in the doorway. He looked paler than usual, but otherwise he was his usual composed self. His slacks and sports jacket were immaculately pressed, and his hair was slicked back.

"Hi, Janet," Wyman's voice was unnervingly focused. "I'm afraid I've made a bit of a fool of myself tonight. I like to think that I know how to handle my liquor, but there was something about those martinis tonight: they've done me in." His eyes locked on her face.

Janet shrugged. "I was pretty tipsy myself. The bartender sure knew his business."

"I bet." Tom nodded. "You're probably wondering what I'm doing here," he continued, "I don't usually barge into people's apartments at night, but when I got home, I saw that my laptop was missing, and I was wondering if you might have seen it." Again, Wyman's eyes fixed on Janet's face, watching her expression intently.

"Oh, Jeez, I'm such a ditz." Janet slapped her forehead. "I've got it – I was going to call you tomorrow and bring it over to your office." She walked back into the living room, picked up the laptop case from the floor, and handed it over to Wyman."

"Thanks, Janet, that's very perceptive of you." Wyman's gaze lingered on her. "I hope I didn't wake you up." His eyes scanned her clothes. She was still wearing the same dress she had worn to the bar.

Janet blushed. "You did wake me, but, actually, you did me a favor. I fell asleep in my clothes."

"Oh, well, it was a wild night." Wyman gripped his laptop case tightly. "Well, I'll be going now. I've got an early day at the office tomorrow."

"As do I."

"Goodnight, Janet.

"Goodnight." Janet shut the door after Wyman. She looked at her hands and saw that they were shaking. Dean had been right to stay and watch over her.

"Are you all right?" Dean was by her side.

"I'm fine." Janet exhaled. "I'm exhausted, though."

"You go straight to bed; I'll be fine here on the couch."

"I don't think you need to stay now; he's gone."

"Better safe than sorry. I've recruited you to aid me in this investigation, and that means you're my responsibility," Dean's tone made it clear that he was not going to take no for an answer.

"Thanks."

Later that night, Janet lay in her bed, safely wrapped in her comforter. She could hear Dean's even breathing coming from the living room. She was not sure whether he was asleep or not, and she was not going to ask. She fell asleep with the thought of Dean on her couch, only a few feet away from her bed: knowledge that was both unnerving and exhilarating.

 howg

Tom Wyman opened the door of his apartment, staggered into his bedroom, and collapsed onto his bed with exhaustion. What a night this had been! He could not remember the last time he had gotten that hammered. In college perhaps, but even then it was unlikely. He had always known his alcohol limit, but tonight he had been caught off guard. He could have sworn those drinks tasted funny, and then his laptop was missing to boot. He had been meaning to delete scanned copies of Impala Group formation documents from his laptop, but got busy and forgot all about it. The mere thought of the calamities that would ensue should these files fall into the wrong hands made him drenched in cold sweat.

That cock tease, Janet Maple, had made a fool of him. Twice he had been left high and dry. He had never been led on like that by anyone. Women found him irresistible. He began to fear that what she really wanted was not him, but the contents of his laptop, which would explain its disappearance.

By the time he had arrived on the doorstep of Janet's apartment, Tom was fuming, prepared to get the truth out of her by any means necessary. But the moment he saw Janet's face, he knew that he had pegged her wrong. Yes, she was a cock tease, but that was all she was. Janet Maple had no clue as to the importance of the files contained on his laptop. She was not the corporate spy he had imagined her to be in his moment of wild suspicion. Had it not been for the number the alcohol had done on him, he would have had his way with her then and there. It was time the tease was taught a lesson: those who play with fire, get burned. No matter. Tonight he was in no condition, but he would get his due soon enough.

Chapter Twenty-Six

Jon Bostoff stared at the lawsuit summons on his desk. The plaintiff was Date Magic dot com, Inc., and the defendant, Bostoff Securities. The bad news did not end there. Next to the lawsuit summons was a subpoena from the SEC, requesting details on all trading activity in Date Magic dot com, Inc. conducted by Bostoff Securities since the IPO listing. A copy of the New York Post added insult to injury: the article covering the lawsuit against Bostoff Securities was prominently displayed on the front page.

Already Jon's cell phone was overcome with voice messages from newspaper reporters, asking him to comment on the lawsuit. This could not have happened at a worse time. The charity sports tournament Jon had asked Paul to put together to raise Bostoff Securities' corporate profile was to take place next week, but now, the negative publicity would make it look like a sham.

It was twelve o'clock in the afternoon on Friday. Leave it to the lawyers and regulator snoops to ruin the weekend. Jon had received the summons and the subpoena in the morning and left the office immediately. He needed to consider the bad news calmly in the privacy of his home. The reality of the situation was still sinking in. At first, Jon had thought that this was some kind of joke. What reason could a company ridiculously named Date Magic have to sue Bostoff Securities? Slowly, the name began to ring a bell, but he still could not quite place it. Then David Muller's words from Jon's last meeting with Emperial's honcho surfaced in his mind: "An online dating site going public! Their offering price is thirty-five dollars! I'd say the true price level should be somewhere at ten, don't you think? Bulls get rich, bears get rich, but pigs get slaughtered. Well, the dumb hogs who invested in this crackpot of an IPO belong in a slaughterhouse."

Jon Bostoff buried his face in his hands. Now, he felt like he was the one being dragged to a slaughterhouse. David Muller and his hedge fund cronies had orchestrated the trading schemes, but Bostoff Securities was being sued, while Muller continued wreaking havoc on the markets. Granted, Bostoff Securities had received handsome fees for handling Muller's trades. Just yesterday, the hefty revenue stream had been a source of tremendous pride to Jon, but now, it caused him immense worry. The worst part was that this could be only the tip of the iceberg, with more lawsuits waiting in the wings. Date Magic was just one of the many stocks that Muller had manipulated.

Jon lifted the phone receiver. He needed to talk to Wyman. Wyman would find a way to get him out of this mess. Jon cursed under his breath: Wyman's fees were steep. Most likely, Wyman would end up siphoning all of the extra dough Jon had made on Emperial's transactions. Jon frowned. The legal complications were not the only difficulties he was facing. He had already committed most of the funds received from Emperial's trading to a ski chalet in Vail, Colorado: he had put in a deposit and signed the contract last week, with a tentative closing date a month away. The chalet was meant to be a Christmas present for Candace. If he pulled out now, he would forfeit his deposit and be out two hundred grand. Jon clenched his teeth. He felt like a cornered animal.

Whatever happens, Candace must now know, he thought frantically. The possibility of his wife discovering his machinations made Jon red with shame. All he had ever wanted was to give Candace the life she deserved. How did it all go so wrong? Panic prickled his skin; this could be the end of everything he had ever dreamed of. No, he would not let it happen. He would fight until the very end, and most importantly, he would make sure that Candace would be spared his shame.

"Jon, are you there?" Candace's voice rang downstairs. "Jon?"

Damn it, Jon cursed under his breath. Candace had said that she had a school trustee committee meeting. She was not supposed to be home so soon.

Jon took a deep breath in an attempt to regain composure. Candace must not suspect anything.

"Jon?" Candace's footsteps were outside the door of his office. "Are you in there?" The door opened, and Candace stood in the doorway.

For a moment, Jon forgot all of his troubles, pausing to admire his wife. As always, Candace looked radiant: her blond hair was tied in a ponytail, she was dressed in jeans and a knit top, but even clad in this simple attire, she looked spellbindingly beautiful.

"I didn't know you were going to be home early today." Candace smiled. "You should have called me. I wouldn't have gone out." Her eyes fell on the papers on Jon's desk, and her face clouded. "Trouble at the office?"

"Nothing of the kind." Jon smiled confidently, his hand reaching across the legal papers in an attempt to sweep them into the bottom drawer of his desk, but he had been too slow – Candace was already standing by him, her eyes fixed on the lawsuit summons and subpoena.

"What's going on, Jon?" Candace's eyes widened. "You know that you can tell me anything, Jon."

"It's nothing, honey, just some legal nonsense. My lawyer will straighten everything out." Jon felt the firm pressure of

Candace's hand on his hand and almost burst into tears under her knowing gaze. His wife was not only beautiful, she was incredibly intelligent. Did he really think he could fool her?

ഇൻരു

Candace Bostoff knelt by her husband's chair and looked into his face – the face of a man weighted by care and worry. From the moment she had seen Jon's car in the driveway, she had sensed that something was terribly wrong. Jon never left the office early: not for kids' school plays or soccer games or ballet performances; not even when their youngest, Ollie, had fallen off the bike and broken his leg, ending up in the hospital ER. But Jon was home now.

For some time, Candace had intuited that Jon was under a lot of pressure, but despite the many approaches she had tried, she could not seem to find a way to get through to him. Ever since he had taken on more responsibility at the firm, Jon had become increasingly distant and short-tempered. It was as though the husband she knew and loved had been replaced with a career-obsessed automaton. The past few weeks, the tension had escalated, as Jon often seemed to be in the world of his own, snapping at her whenever Candace tried to ask what was on his mind. Everything is fine, he would assure her, patting her arm. Just work stuff; that's all, baby.

"We have to talk, Candy." Jon squeezed her hand. "I've done some things that I'm not proud of."

"Jon, you know that there's nothing you could tell me that would turn me away from you. I'm your wife, and I'll stand by you, no matter what."

"I am afraid you will change your mind once you hear what I've done," Jon muttered. "I am so ashamed." Jon pressed his hand against his eyes.

Candace felt shivers running down her back. For the first time in her life she saw her husband cry.

"You can tell me anything, Jon. I will always stand by you," she repeated firmly. "What is it?"

Over the next hour, Candace listened to the story of her husband's entanglement in the net of his own creation. He had wanted to succeed; he had longed to make her proud. She wanted to scream at his foolishness. He had always been successful, and she had always been proud of him. Nothing would ever change that. Everyone could make a mistake: it was only too easy to stray off the right path. The difficult part was to find one's way back to it. She would never let go of her husband's hand – together, they would overcome their current predicament.

"Jon, you know what we have to do, don't you?" Candace looked into her husband's eyes.

"Yes. I will call Wyman to start the defense proceeding; he'll get those jackals off my back."

Candace laid her hand on Jon's arm. "You have to come clean, Jon. If you cooperate with the investigation, they'll lessen the charges."

"Admit my guilt? Never. Let them prove their accusations first."

"Jon, they could keep digging for years. Muller arranged it so that all the blame would be placed on you: you own Impala group, not Muller. With a lack of evidence, the entire case could be hung on you. But if you come forward and give valuable information to the investigation, the regulators will cut you a deal. They would much rather go after Muller and his friends: an organized string of corrupt hedge funds would make for a juicy case."

"What about Date Magic? The minute they hear that I admitted my involvement, they'll fleece me."

"You can offer them a settlement; besides, once they know about the hedge funds involved, they'll go after them instead."

Jon clasped his head with his hands. "If I admit my guilt, I will have to forfeit all the profits that I've made in the past three years. It will ruin us."

"It will not ruin us. I have my inheritance. You never let me spend a penny of it. I've invested it, and it has grown over the years. It will cover the legal fees."

"Candace," Jon halted. "I will probably be barred from the industry. How will I make a living and provide for you and the kids?"

"We'll figure it out, Jon," Candace paused, determined to be strong enough for Jon to lean on her. "You seemed so preoccupied with your work that I didn't get a chance to tell you that I started my own antiques business. The profits have really started to pick up. It began as a hobby, but now, I think it could grow into something real. It could be a new life for us, Jon. I'd love to have you as my partner."

Jon's eyes brimmed with tears. "You are incredible, Candace. I'm so lucky to have you as my wife. Will you ever forgive me for letting you down like this?"

"There's nothing to forgive, Jon. You got mixed up with unscrupulous people, and you made some bad decisions. Now, everything will depend on what you'll do to remedy your mistakes."

Jon sighed. "Are you sure about this? Is this what you want me to do?"

"Yes."

"All right. I'll call Wyman right now."

"Not that thug." Candace felt a wave of nausea at the memory of Jon's weasel-like attorney. She had met Wyman when he came over to the house for dinner once, and she did not like the man one bit. "We're going to use my family lawyer for this. His firm does litigation. I'm sure he'll be able to help us."

"Your family lawyer?"

"Yes, but don't forget that even family lawyers have to abide by attorney/client confidentiality."

"I have to make sure that my brother and father will not be implicated. They knew nothing about any of this – it was all my own doing. Oh, God, my father – I'm so ashamed…"

"We'll talk to them together, Jon. I'll be right by your side."

"Candace, I've been such an ungrateful fool. I threw away my own happiness."

"No, Jon, you didn't. I would never let you do anything like that."

"I love you."

"I love you too. But there's no time to waste. Every minute counts. We should call the lawyer now."

"First, I have to speak with my father and my brother."

"Of course." Candace nodded. It was going to be a long, tough road, but she would follow her husband every step of the way.

ഐരു

Lisa Foley checked her watch. It was twelve o'clock on a Friday afternoon. She had a manicure appointment at twelve-thirty, and most likely, she would just go home from there. Janet could hold down the fort for her. There were much more important things on Lisa's mind than work. This whole thing was a sham anyway. Tom Wyman handled all the matters of substance, and he never bothered to include Lisa in any of them, which was just as well with her. And once Lisa would finally become Mrs. Paul Bostoff, she would put in her resignation. Being Mrs. Bostoff would be a full-time job. Lisa bit her lip; the wedding was still ten months away, almost a year. If it were up to her, she would elope with Paul tomorrow, but Jon had insisted that they plan a big ceremony, and one could not have a big ceremony on the fly. No doubt Jon wanted to use the wedding as another opportunity for business promotion. He had already given Lisa a list of guests: most of them were corporate executives, with a few low-level politicians rounding off the list. Oh, well, on the bright side, Lisa would have that many more guests to admire her wedding dress, and she would make sure that Jon Bostoff paid for his guests. That reminded her: she still had not heard from Janet about the rest of the wedding party. Lisa hoped that snob Katie would say yes, and she was fairly certain that Joe O'Connor's girlfriend, Daphne, would agree as well. The two should consider themselves lucky to be in her wedding party.

There was a knock on the door of her office. "Yes?" Lisa shifted in her chair with annoyance; she did not want to be disturbed.

"Ms. Foley?" Lisa's paralegal, Meredith Crooner, poked her head through the door.

"Hi, Meredith," Lisa suppressed impatience in her voice. What did her paralegal want now? It was not as if she had very complicated tasks to perform.

"Ms. Foley, I thought you might want to see this." Meredith placed a copy of the New York Post on Lisa's desk.

Lisa resisted the urge to grimace. It was just like Meredith to read the New York Post. She was about to ask what Meredith's point was when the headline hit her: "Company CEO Sues Bostoff Securities for Stock Manipulation." Lisa frowned, her eyes glued to the text:

"Andrew Foley, founder and CEO of Date Magic dot com, Inc., is suing Bostoff Securities for market manipulation of the company stock. Date Magic was initially a private company, but had recently gone public. Subsequent to the IPO, shares of Date Magic experienced a steady decline in price, which Foley attributes to manipulative trading tactics of Bostoff Securities. Date Magic's attorneys filed the lawsuit this morning. Bostoff Securities were served with the summons, but no comment had been made by the defendant."

Lisa looked up at Meredith, who was nervously hovering over her desk. "Thank you, Meredith; I'll get right on it."

Despite Lisa's tone making it clear that Meredith's presence was no longer required, Meredith remained by her desk. "Am I going to lose my job?" Meredith asked, wringing her hands. "I've got two kids going to college next year. I can't afford to be unemployed."

Lisa pursed her lips. If the article's allegations were even remotely true, Bostoff's employees would all be facing much bigger problems than being unemployed. For now, saving face was the name of the game; she must not let the others see her panic.

"Meredith, that's utter nonsense. You are smarter than that. Bostoff Securities is a reputable firm with stellar track record in the financial industry. Its standing will not be affected by baseless accusations and frivolous lawsuits." Lisa's voice sounded so convincing that for a moment, she almost believed her own words.

"Thank you, Ms. Foley. I was really worried there for a while. Well, I'll leave you to it; let me know if you need any help."

Once the door of her office was closed again, Lisa succumbed to her panic, staring at the newspaper in terrified incomprehension. How could a disaster like that have happened? And worst of all, what on earth was she going to do if the article's accusations were indeed true? The fact that the plaintiff was her own cousin did not make matters any easier. Now, she felt like twice the fool: not only did she have no idea about the affairs of Bostoff, she was clueless about her own family members.

Janet had been right. Lisa's cousin, Andrew, was a scumbag. The least he could have done was to warn Lisa that he was going to sue the company she worked for, the company she happened to be the general counsel of, for manipulating his lame stock. The nerve of the guy – just because the price of his pathetic stock could not hold up did not mean that it was being manipulated, but simply meant that it was a good-for-nothing company.

Oh, this was exactly what Lisa needed smack in the middle of her wedding plans. She wanted to be picking out flower arrangements and deciding on catering venues, not refuting a lawsuit summons. Not that she could effectively do the latter even if she tried: Tom Wyman would have to step in. Lisa wondered if Paul and Jon knew about this already. They had to. The article said that Bostoff Securities had been served with the summons, but if this were the case, then why hadn't Lisa heard anything about it? She needed to speak to Paul pronto.

"Lisa?" Paul stood in the doorway of her office.

Her fiancé's timing made Lisa jump in her chair. Normally, Paul avoided seeing her during business hours. On several occasions, she had tried to get him to have sex with her on his desk, but Paul had rejected the idea as inappropriate. He was a stickler for propriety, which was one of the reasons why Lisa thought him to be great husband material – or at least had thought him to be such until a few minutes ago.

"Honey, did you see this nonsense?" Lisa pointed to the newspaper on her desk. "I'm so embarrassed. The company CEO is my cousin. He dropped the bomb on me. I swear I'm going to do everything I can to convince him to abandon this frivolous lawsuit."

"It's all right. I'm afraid it's much bigger than this. Jon just called me. He wants us to come over to his place. There are some things that he needs to explain to us."

❧☙

Dennis Walker studied the expression on Hamilton Kirk's face as he took a seat across from his boss's desk.

"Well, Dennis, it looks like you really screwed the pooch on this one." Ham flung a copy of the New York Post towards Dennis.

Dennis's face remained impassive. Did his boss really think that Dennis did not keep up to date with the newspapers?

"And the SEC has just subpoenaed Bostoff this morning, cutting us off at the onset. Now, all the work we've done is going down the drain, and the SEC will have the lead on the case." Kirk's face was filled with chagrin. "I knew I should have given the job to Laskin," Kirk hissed. "There goes that promotion I've been hoping for. Thanks for delaying my retirement by another five years."

Dennis resisted a smile: he was truly enjoying this.

"Ham, I think you might change your mind after you read this." He handed his boss a manila folder containing the documents he had downloaded from Wyman's laptop yesterday.

"What is it?" Kirk glanced at the folder as though it were a piece of manure. "Could this be the evidence you failed to procure during your time as undercover investigator at Bostoff? Well, I've got news for you: it's a little too late now."

"I'd read it first, sir."

"Fine." Kirk wrung the papers out of the folder. At first, his face was stone cold, but as his eyes read the first few lines, even Hamilton Kirk's famous poker face failed him, his expression alternating between amazement and delight.

For several moments Ham Kirk remained silent, while his eyes burrowed hungrily into the papers before him. Dennis steepled his hands and leaned back in his chair, watching his boss devour the information that was bound to get them both promoted.

"Well, I'll be damned – you son of a gun." Kirk raised the papers in his hand. "You've done it. Now, we'll finally be able to nail those hedge fund vultures good."

"Thank you, sir."

"I always give praise when praise is due, Dennis, you know that. But first, I've got to make a few calls. We've got to make sure that the SEC and the FBI understand that we'll be taking the lead on the case. Without us, they've only got a market manipulation case against a single firm, but our evidence proves an organized manipulation scheme. This is big, real big."

Dennis nodded. At the moment, he knew better than to point out the fact that it was really his evidence, his and Janet's, but he was certainly going to make sure that Janet Maple would get the credit she deserved.

Chapter Twenty-Seven

Janet stood in front of the Treasury building in downtown Manhattan. The strict, somber atmosphere of the financial district suited her much better than the mayhem of midtown. Not that it mattered. After her experience at Bostoff Securities, she did not see herself working for a financial firm in the near future. In fact, she had no idea what she was going to do after the investigation would be completed. Perhaps she would reconsider her career options entirely. There were more things to life than being a lawyer. She could go back to school for a Master of Laws degree and teach, or she could do something completely different: she just did not know exactly what it would be. She had aspired to bring order to Wall Street, but had failed at that when she got let go from the DA's office. She had tried her hand at being a legal counsel, but had failed at that as well. Ironically, in her failure, she had succeeded in fulfilling her initial aspiration by helping Dean Snider unravel Emperial's and Bostoff's manipulative trading scheme. Still, now that her work was done, her association with Treasury and Dean Snider was over.

She had resigned from Bostoff Securities shortly after Treasury had launched an official investigation of Bostoff Securities: an announcement that coincided with Jon Bostoff's reaching out to the SEC and declaring his wish to cooperate with the investigation. Jon Bostoff had admitted to being solely responsible for the manipulative market activities being conducted by Bostoff Securities, stating that his brother, Paul Bostoff, and his father, Hank Bostoff, were completely unaware of the existence of the Impala Group and the relationship that Bostoff Securities had with Emperial, Rigel, Creaton, Sphinx, and Gemini hedge funds. The case promised long and difficult proceedings, but it was already becoming apparent that the investigators' attention was keenly focused on Emperial, Rigel, Creaton, Sphinx, and Gemini, and that Jon Bostoff would receive credit for his cooperation with the investigation.

Janet checked her watch. It was time for her meeting. After a long, deep breath, she opened the heavy door. The security in the building was extremely tight. Janet handed her photo ID to the security guard. Then, she was asked to put her bag through the x-ray machine conveyer and walk through a metal detector. It was like boarding an airplane, only she was not going anywhere.

"Thank you, Miss. Who are you here to meet?" The security guard asked her.

"Hamilton Kirk."

"One moment." The security guard punched a few keystrokes on his keyboard and dialed a phone number. "Someone will be right down to take you upstairs."

Janet stood a few steps away from the security desk, waiting for her escort.

A few minutes later, a trim brunette in her early fifties approached the security desk.

"Janet?" The woman looked at Janet questioningly.

"Yes." Janet nodded.

"I'm Ann Smith – Ham Kirk's secretary."

"Very nice to meet you." Janet shook the woman's hand.

"It's this way." Ann motioned to the elevators.

Janet followed Ann into the elevator and afterwards into the long, official-looking hallway. They walked past the row of offices until they reached the last office in the corner. There, Ann stopped and knocked on the door.

"Janet Maple is here." After motioning for Janet to enter the room, Ann nodded curtly and left.

Janet lingered in the doorway, taking in the surroundings. A lean middle-aged man with gray mustache sat behind a large wooden computer desk. He must be Dean's boss, Janet thought. A moment later, her gaze was on Dean, who sat in the chair opposite the desk. He rose from his seat to greet her, but his boss beat him to it.

"Janet, come in, come in!" the gentleman with the gray mustache stretched out his hand. "It's a pleasure to finally meet you in person – I'm Hamilton Kirk."

"It's a pleasure to meet you, Mr. Kirk, I've heard so much about you."

Dean hurried to greet her, "Hello, Janet."

"Hi." Janet smiled at him. She had not seen much of him since the memorable evening when they had abducted Tom Wyman's laptop—the evening Dean had spent the night at her place. By the time she had woken up, Dean had already left, and they had not talked about that night since.

"Please, have a seat," said Ham.

Janet sat on the edge of her seat, waiting for the meeting agenda to be revealed. She had no idea why Ham Kirk wanted to meet her, but she suspected that it had something to do with the investigation. Perhaps he wanted her to testify, which was something that she had hoped would not come to pass, for she had no idea how she would face Lisa or Paul Bostoff during a hearing.

"Janet, I wanted to thank you personally for your contribution to the investigation," Ham began. "Without you, we would never have gathered the evidence for the case. Dennis spoke very highly of you…"

"Dennis?" Janet cut in.

"Yes, Dennis – the gentleman sitting next to you." Ham's matter-of-fact tone only confused her further.

"Errr, I think there's a need for a slight clarification…" The man Janet knew as Dean Snider turned bright red under Janet's wide-eyed stare. "You see, Janet, while I was working undercover at Bostoff, I couldn't use my real name, so I had to use a pseudonym, Dean Snider. My real name is Dennis Walker."

"And you waited to tell her this until now, Dennis?" Ham shook his head. "Your real name stopped being a secret after your undercover work at Bostoff ended."

Thanks a lot, Ham, Dennis thought, adding, "Somehow it had not come up, sir."

"Well, never mind. I hope you won't hold it against Dennis, Janet – he can be overly diligent when it comes to sensitive matters. But most importantly, I hope that this little misunderstanding will not affect your answer to the question I am about to ask you now." Ham paused. "How do you feel about employment with the Treasury? I could use an investigator like you."

Janet swallowed, too stunned to speak. She had expected a request for her testimony or additional evidence—anything—but an employment offer. This was her first time meeting Hamilton Kirk. Up until now, she had submitted all of the evidence for the investigation to Dean. "Don't you want to interview me first?"

"I just did." Ham grinned. "The materials you submitted to aid the investigation told me all I needed to know about your investigative skills, and meeting you face to face confirmed my opinion. Well, I'm not going to put you on the spot now." Ham picked up a letter-sized brown envelope from his desk. "The details of the offer are inside; I had HR put it together ahead of time. I hope that you will say yes. By the way, Treasury offers excellent health and retirement benefits. These things may not seem important to you now, but they do come in handy as one gets older," he added.

"Thank you, Mr. Kirk. I very much appreciate your offer. It's just that it comes as a bit of a surprise."

"I understand that. I don't expect an answer today, but I wanted to make you an offer in person rather than sending it by mail. I hope to see you again soon, Janet. And please call me Ham."

"Thank you, Ham." Janet rose from her chair. "It was a pleasure to meet you. Now if you'll excuse me, I've got a big decision to make."

"By all means." Ham nodded. "Dennis will walk you out."

Dennis rose from his chair.

"No need; I can find my own way," Janet retorted.

"I know you can, but it's office policy. Visitors must be accompanied at all times – a rule that I hope you won't be subjected to much longer," Ham added.

"Thank you, Ham." Without another glance at Dennis, Janet walked towards the door. Her head was spinning. She needed to get out of there quickly.

She walked brusquely down the hallway, mechanically making a turn for the elevators.

"Janet!"

She kept walking, ignoring Dean / Dennis calling her name. Miraculously, an elevator opened, and she jumped inside, hitting the door close button.

"Janet!" Too late. The doors closed shut, and the man she knew as Dean Snider was left standing in the elevator bank.

When the elevator doors opened, Janet walked out quickly and returned the visitor badge to the security guard. Then she turned for the exit.

A moment later she was outside, leaving the Treasury building behind her.

"Janet! Would you wait a second! You can't just run away from me!" A male hand touched her shoulder.

She turned around. "What do you want, Dean? Oh, wait, it's Dennis, isn't it?"

"I'm sorry. I meant to tell you, but somehow I never got around to it."

"Or maybe you thought you didn't have to since you already had gotten everything you needed out of me."

"That's not true, and you know it."

"Do I?"

"Look, aside from my occupation and my name, I am the same man I was when I was working at Bostoff."

"And who is that man? I for one have no idea who he is."

"He is the man who would like to take you out to dinner. How does tonight at eight o'clock sound?"

"I have plans." This, of course, was a lie, but she was not about to let him know that she had no social life to speak of.

"Break them."

"Why should I? To hear more of your lies?"

"To hear the truth," he paused, the blue-gray of his eyes locking in on her face. "Janet, I messed up. People make mistakes. That's what makes us human. Please, give me another chance. Even Jon Bostoff got a concession from the investigators for his cooperation, and surely, my transgressions are not nearly as bad."

Janet smirked. The man was funny. It was one of the first things that drew her to him: his wit and his blue-gray eyes. "All right, eight o'clock tonight. Where are we going?"

"It's a surprise." Dennis grinned.

"Then how will I know where to meet you?"

"You won't. I'll pick you up at eight."

"Oh, right, you already know the address."

"That's right. See you tonight. And Janet?"

"Yes?"

"I hope you'll accept Ham's offer. I think you'll be great at the job."

"I need some time to think about it. It's a big step."

Dennis nodded. "Big steps can lead to really great things."

"You sound like an expert."

"Something like that. We can discuss it in more detail over dinner tonight."

"See you then." As she turned to walk away from Dennis, Janet could no longer suppress a smile spreading over her lips. Dating a coworker could get complicated, but after everything she had been through, she was certain that she could handle a little complexity in her life.

The end

Don't want to miss out on other books by Marie?

Go to www.MarieAstor.com and add your email address to the mailing list.

Printed in Great Britain
by Amazon

49843180R00149